ᎠᏆᏕᎦ

Ghosts
and
Goosebumps

ᎠᏆᏕᎦᏫᎤᏁᏆᏃᎠᏆᏍ

ᏫᎩ♁☉ᏜᎷᏇᏋᎮᏆᏫᎩᏫᏪ☉ᏐᎩᏫᏪ☉ᏜᎷᏇᏋᎮᏆᏫᎩᏫᏪ☉ᏐᎩᏫ

Ghosts and Goosebumps

Ghost Stories, Tall Tales, and Superstitions from Alabama

COMPILED BY Jack Solomon and Olivia Solomon

Illustrations by Mark Brewton

BROWN THRASHER BOOKS

The University of Georgia Press

ATHENS AND LONDON

Published in 1994 as a Brown Thrasher Book by
The University of Georgia Press, Athens, Georgia 30602
© 1981 by Jack Solomon and Olivia Solomon

Printed digitally in the United States of America

Library of Congress Cataloging-in-Publication Data

Ghosts and goosebumps : ghost stories, tall tales, and
superstitions from Alabama / compiled by Jack Solomon
and Olivia Solomon ; illustrations by Mark Brewton.
xiii, 202 p. : ill. ; 23 cm.
Originally published: University, Ala. : University of
Alabama Press, 1981.
"Brown thrasher books."
Includes bibliographical references (p. [187]–198).
"Alabama folk tales in the Library of
Congress": p. [199]–202.
ISBN 0-8203-1634-2 (pbk. : alk. paper)
1. Folklore—Alabama. 2. Tall tales—Alabama.
3. Superstition—Alabama. 4. African Americans—
Alabama—Folklore. I. Solomon, Jack, 1927– .
II. Solomon, Olivia, 1937– .
GR110.A2 G46 1994
398.2'09761—dc20   93-40015

ISBN-13: 978-0-8203-1634-5

British Library Cataloging-in-Publication Data available

Frontispiece by William Lower

www.ugapress.org

Contents

Acknowledgments

The compiling of this collection of folk tales and superstitions was greatly aided by the assistance of many people. We owe our heartfelt thanks to the student collectors at Troy State University and Alexander City State Junior College, who pursued their field work faithfully and enthusiastically; the Alabama field workers who collected folklore for the WPA; the informants who generously offered their tales and superstitions; our illustrator Mark Brewton; the librarians at Alexander City State Junior College, Frances Tapley, Peggy Causey, Bob Schremser, Carolyn Ingram, Joyce Robinson, and Eula Hardaway, who secured necessary bibliographical aids, out-of-print volumes, and publications not available in the library at Alexander City State Junior College; our typists over a period of five years, Janice Riley, Sandra Florine, Sharon Atkins, Phyllis Hornsby, Cindy Lowery Branch, Brenda Coley, and Elna Wolsoncroft, who worked cheerfully, no matter how illegible the handwriting; Sarah Ann Warren of the Alabama State Department of Archives and History, who assisted our research in the Alabama WPA folklore collections and supervised a microfilmed reproduction of the Alabama WPA Slave Narratives; United States Senator John Sparkman of Alabama, who, over the past eighteen years, has most freely and graciously given us assistance in many academic and community endeavors and who answered our initial inquiry about the status of the Alabama WPA folklore collections; Rick Sellers and Eddie Sokol, former aides to Senator Sparkman, who secured for us the manuscripts of the Alabama WPA folk tales in the Library of Congress; our kind friends and neighbors, who have given constant encouragement; our families, who have stood by us in all weathers; our children, whose love has given us a forceful motive for discipline when all else failed; and the folk of Alabama who gave us this collection of folk tales and superstitions, treasures we now return to them.

Foreword

Ghosts and Goosebumps is a collection of folk tales and superstitions from central and southeastern Alabama. The bulk of the material was gathered in the course of field investigations made between 1958 and 1962 by Troy State University students enrolled in an introductory folklore course. The volume also includes folk tales and selections from the Alabama Slave Narratives gathered in Alabama by field workers in the National Writers' Project, Folklore Division, of the Works Progress Administration (WPA), as well as some findings reported by students in folklore classes at Alexander City State Junior College, 1972–1977. Since findings reported by Alexander City State Junior College students are relatively scant, these are included with those gathered by Troy State University students; "Troy tales" and "Troy collection" refer to both field investigations. Material was gathered in the following counties: Escambia, Butler, Wilcox, Conecuh, Barbour, Lowndes, Geneva, Dale, Coffee, Covington, Crenshaw, Pike, Bullock, Elmore, Montgomery, Tallapoosa, Coosa, Lee, Macon, and Sumter. Excerpts from the Alabama Slave Narratives were made from the original manuscripts deposited in the Alabama State Department of Archives and History at Montgomery; the WPA folk tale selections were chosen from manuscripts housed in the Library of Congress.

This volume, like its predecessors *Cracklin Bread and Asfidity* and *Zickary Zan*, is aimed at the general reader who is interested in folklore. We also hope that this anthology will be useful as a supplementary text in introductory folklore courses, especially in high schools and community or junior colleges. Thus we offer some general introductory comments at the beginning of each section as an aid to enjoyment and understanding and bibliographical information for those who wish to pursue the subject further. By "Ghosts and Goosebumps" is meant all the supernatural and humorous lore in Alabama folk tradition, primarily the narrative, from ghost tales to anecdotes to short statements or superstitions. The book is meant to provide a pleasant dip into a folk miscellany, pleasurable reading without the intrusion of scholarly debate. For this reason we have not included an index of folk tale motif or type. Over the last fifty years European and American folklorists have made valuable contributions to the study of world folk tale analogues and universal motifs, but these indexes best serve the scholar and teacher. Ultimately, every folk tale stands on its own tongue, and there is no convenient, definitive classification, no magic formula to which it can be reduced. Folk tales belong to everybody, nobody, and somebody; in actual performance a tale belongs to a specific teller and audience. It may resemble hundreds of other tales in different folk communities, but it is its own self, at once an expression of timeless human attributes and of a somebody, or a few somebodies, in a particular time and place. The folk somebody has a name, the folk somewhere is a real place, and behind every tale and superstition in *Ghosts and Goosebumps* is a real and worthy person.

Not every reader will find every tale to his liking or every superstition exactly as he remembers or knows it. The range and variety in both style and subject are wide; not all the tales are first-rate. Folk humor is often dismissed as the lowest kind of comedy—witless, simple-minded, even moronic—and it contains scatalogical, burlesque, vulgar, and shaggy-dog elements. Similarly, the folk supernatural is sometimes morbid, grotesque, obscenely necrological. To fail to admit these qualities would be a decided error. Value judgments about the folk mind and its expressions in song, dance, art, and literature, however, are condescending and pointless. The folk mind is what it is, in any folk culture, and those with more sophisticated tastes should look elsewhere. Participating in a tale-telling session under natural circumstances, without tape recorder or pencil, is the best way to experience a folk tale and to acquire affection and respect for the folk. If the tales in *Ghosts and Goosebumps* are read aloud, they regain much of their original power. Oral recreations will allow the reader to grasp more acutely subtle differences in syntax, diction, vocabulary, and narrative and dramatic structure and to feel the rhythms and timbre of Alabama folk speech, which is not a single entity, but a wonderfully differentiated language, displaying peculiarities from one geographical section to another, even from one county to another.

These differences are observable throughout *Ghosts and Goosebumps*. The Troy tales are outstanding in a genre that may be called folk conversations: a bold, simple vocabulary, direct, commonplace English sentence structure, uncluttered syntax, the whole an easy, running commentary in the style of natural conversation with familiars and friends. The Troy collection also includes fully developed folk fairy tales, anecdotes, brief recollections of pranks, practical jokes, and customs, and monologues. The Mama Berch tale and the lying contest clearly derive from oral tradition, not from the nineteenth-century almanacs that featured tall tales embellished by literary hacks. The WPA tales and the Tallapoosa River Valley ghost legend present a telling contrast: in the latter, the retelling reflects the highly romanticized style of the original documents, diaries, and letters; in the former, the oral folk quality is filtered through the WPA interviewer and/or editor, a process that sometimes faded or otherwise altered the original tale, but was also sometimes highly successful. The selections from the Alabama WPA Slave Narratives are, for many reasons, more difficult to assess, but, in general, though the transcriptions of dialect may seem forbidding, most of them are interesting and valuable as records of antebellum, black folk supernatural beliefs and humor. Here, again, an oral performance will remove most impediments and give the reader a feel for the folk language and conversational or tale-telling style.

A very few tales may be awkward, clumsy, or crabbed, but most vibrate with the energy of Alabama folk, and all are worthy of attention, for, although a community usually produces only one or two naturally gifted storytellers, every man, woman, and child has some tale to tell. It is those ordinary folk, not the stunning yarn-spinner or revisionist folklorist, who speak the tales in *Ghosts and Goosebumps*. And if their voices crack, tremble, mutter, trail off with uncertainty, shyness, reluctance, fear, or shame, if they miss the point, lose the way, search vainly for the right word or phrase, if they rail, exaggerate, show off, meander, or forget, then, so much the better. These frailties bespeak their humanness—and which of us can crack a joke or dramatically summon up the terror of a midnight visitation with a folklore researcher, a college student, standing at our elbows? The marvel is that the young collector and the informant shared a genuine folk experience; they crossed the line between young and old, educated and uneducated, and the resulting accounts are honest efforts to record and faithfully reflect our heritage in the folk supernatural and humorous.

With one exception (the alteration of dialect to ordinary spelling in Sonja Taylor's reporting of the tale of General Jackson's ghost), the editors have made no corrections in grammar, spelling, or sentence structure; the tales and superstitions are printed exactly as they were submitted by student researchers and informants or as they were found in WPA manuscripts. To regularize grammar or spelling in folklore anthologies is a contradiction in terms; to alter another's manuscript is dishonest. Student researchers were warned against making grotesque transcriptions, and they successfully conveyed the informants' tone, style, and rhythm without imposing their own view or caricaturing folk speech. We have, in some instances, supplied titles for tales. Because our aim was to present a profile of oral folk literature and folk beliefs occurring widely over rural and small-town Alabama, we have included only a few contemporary tales, "The Ghost Nun," "The Girl and the Yellow Ribbon," the story of the Halloween ghost of Mobile, and "The Lavender Party Dress." Because so many superstitions were reported from so many people, we do not list the names of informants in that section. In view of recent court rulings and statutes regarding the right of individual privacy, we have, as in previous volumes, omitted personal addresses of informants.

We grew up in a time and a place where folklore scarcely existed as a subject of scholarly investigation. For us, it was life and truth, and like the rest of the folk we assimilated our folklore heritage gradually and naturally, daily, yearly, from our elders and peers, parents, uncles, aunts, cousins, grandparents, neighbors, schoolfellows, and playmates, all of whom cast, like the golden apples of Atalanta, riddles, songs, tales, jokes, pranks, proverbs, remedies, superstitions, beliefs, and customs in all the paths of our small journeys to school, church, store, and back home. Vile poultices, bitter potions, and scalding teas healed our measles, mumps, sprains, bruises, colds, and fevers. We read earth and sky for prophecies of rain and frost, wind and drought, and we knew when the devil was beating his wife with a frying pan; we played jacks and marbles, hide-and-seek and fox-and-hounds, stalked about on Tom Walkers, wished on the first star, and went to sleep with the mockingbird lullaby or poor, foolish Chicken Little, Henny Penny, Goosey Loosey, and Turkey Lurkey on their way to a fatal rendezvous with Foxy Loxy, who sometimes woke us with more adventures in the henhouse; and on Sundays we heard hymns with that strange wondrous quaver, an intimation of Glory. Just within earshot were tales of murder, illicit passions, and suicide. Ghosts, witches, portents, and all sorts of mysterious creatures and unearthly visitants took up residence in our heads. Although neither of us ever encountered a single spirit, it never occurred to us not to believe in them. Rationally, we may believe they do not exist, but in our heart of hearts those bloodcurdling tales of terror possessed the unquestioned reality of things handed down over centuries as sworn truth. We are lovers of folklore and the folk, not investigators of supernatural phenomena. As such, we cannot vouch for even one of the supernatural experiences in *Ghosts and Goosebumps*; that study we leave to others. We do vouch for these tales as folk experiences. They are a delight to hear and read, they show us much of rural, small-town Alabama folk life, and they bring us close to the symbolic truth and the poetry of the folk mind. Putting together this book has been for us a pleasurable labor, a remembrance and memorial of home and times gone by, and, most of all, an act of friendship for and with the folk, reaching from the present to the past and into the future.

Altogether, *Ghosts and Goosebumps* displays a splendid Alabama tradition in folk tales, the lore of the supernatural, and folk humor. By happenstance the voices in the Troy collection and the WPA folk tales are mostly white; in the Slave Narratives the voices are those of black people. Here we may observe balance and complement, and though each of these folk has imparted its own identity, our heritage is uncommonly similar. The sum is marvelously revelatory of Alabama folk life and lore over the last century and a half, our works, loves, fears, hopes, and laughter from sunup to sundown, with the moon and stars and night for rest and dreaming.

ᏊᏯ₿ᏋᏏᏜᏁᏰᏟᎧᏋᏯᏰ

Ghosts
and
Goosebumps

ᏊᏯ₿ᏋᏏᏜᏁᏰᏟᎧᏋᏯᏰ

ᎤᏍᏗᎦᎹᏍᎭᏅᏂᎤᎤᏍᏗᎦᎤᏍᏗᎦᎹᏍᎭᏅᏂᎤᎤᏍᏗᎦ

Introduction

ALABAMA FOLK TALES:
THE SUPERNATURAL AND THE HUMOROUS

Like the folk themselves, folk tales are marvelously diverse, by turns fearsome, fantastical, earthy, witty, salty, charmingly innocent, sly, wicked, chaste, merry, ribald, serene, rambunctious, showing people in all weathers and many coats, our endless vices and occasional sterling virtues, our faith, hope, fears, and loves. Folk tales come from everywhere, from here to there and back again, from any time and every place, and Everyman is their creator. Out of our common humanity arises their universality; out of our separateness, each person a being who lives and dies in his own time, space, and personal dimensions, issue their splendid differences. Everyman is one, and every man speaks with his own voice.

Some folk tales derive from myths or narratives about primordial events of cosmic significance: the coming of the gods, the creation of the world and man, the mysteries of life and death, poetized explanations of universal natural occurrences that give rise to religious, social, and political systems of thought, wherein customs, beliefs, rituals, and rites are codified and sanctioned. To this category belong nearly all folk tales of the supernatural. Other tales arise out of history and focus on heroic quasi-historical figures who overcome both mortal and superhuman foes. Such legendary creations may be kings, saints, outlaws, or eccentrics, and they are worldwide, national, or local in occurrence and transmission—Robin Hood, King Arthur and the Knights of the Round Table, Jesse James, Johnny Appleseed, John Henry, the village miser, the town cuckold. Still other folk narratives combine elements of both myth and legend, showing mortals in close association with the supernatural, their incidents and characters often romantically or comically embellished. Among such are fairy tales beloved by young and old, Rapunzel, Coat-of-Rushes, Red Riding Hood, Cinderella, and Hansel and Gretel, a folk potpourri where witches, goblins, elves, leprechauns, and dragons consort with human heroines and heroes and mysterious guardian forces effect magical transformations.

Whatever its type, the folk tale in its purest state is orally transmitted, and we must be careful to distinguish it from artistic retellings, dramatizations, and literary usages of folk tale motifs. In the broadest sense, however, a narrative may be termed folk if it is fully representative of the culture of the folk from whom it springs, if it reflects the ethnic, racial, social, and national characteristics generally accepted as belonging to a particular folk. Folk antecedents, for example, lie just beyond Homer, Chaucer, Boccaccio, and Shakespeare. Originating with and circulated orally by the folk for generations, taken up by minstrels, scops, and wandering storytellers, these tales finally coalesce in the writings of a single mind. Thus, proportion, language, and treatment distinguish a literary folk narrative from the oral folk tale, for both embody the consciousness and character of the folk. Regarded in this light, Achilles, Odysseus, Beowulf, Siegfried, and Gilgamesh are folk heroes, and their adventures are readily entered into by a folk audience. Ichabod Crane and Rip Van Winkle, although the creations of a single mind, are certainly American folk figures; Hawthorne's dark romances and Poe's tales of terror are set in the mode of the folk supernatural; Melville's Ahab and the great white whale are overwhelming mythic creations engaged in an archetypal struggle played against a mythic background; William Faulkner brought hundreds of folk tales and characters from the American South into his fictional kingdom.

American folk culture exhibits four well-defined centers that disseminate, transform, perpetuate, and transmit folklore—the home, the school, the church, and the store. Although these centers were especially significant in rural and small-town folk life of the nineteenth and early twentieth centuries, they retain their functions even in the present. The store has its counterpart in any modern gathering place—the subway, sidewalk, juke joint, truck stop, pool room, coffee shop, bowling alley, and bar; the school, from kindergarten to college, still serves as a clearing house for jokes, riddles, pranks, customs, and celebrations; the church continuously revitalizes rites as old as man; and the home preserves seasonal festivals, holds to its own personal folk life and lore within the family, and ultimately receives all the other kinds of lore from the other centers.

Certain kinds of folklore can be readily associated with each center—the church, for example, with folk architecture, memorial sculpture, gravestone carvings and inscriptions, religious folk song, rites, and customs. But the folk tale cannot be said to belong exclusively to any one center; there are legions of tale-tellers all across the country, and any one of them will speak at the drop of a hat. Let the wind shift, and there they go—makes-no-never-mind where we are when the storytelling notion strikes us. Not so long ago a kinsman and a friend wandered into our house around suppertime. At midnight they were still talking, tale topped tale richly, inexhaustibly, a panorama of central Alabama folk life unfolding in the sardonically witty, ever so slightly malicious lies and legends of a historian and in the anecdotes and convoluted narratives of a country lawyer seasoned by fifty years of courthouse rhetoric and spit. At Little League practice somebody invariably remembers the time the local baseball team was trailing four runs: bases loaded, two outs, 3–2 count, the batter hits a hard grounder way beyond second; while the center fielder scurries after it, the ticket-taker, a gigantic fellow, opens the double gates of the stockade fence, the ball rolls all the way down the hill to Five Points, four runs come home, the game is tied up, and in the ensuing fray half the players go to jail. The same ticket-taker is said to have once been called on to umpire; reluctantly he complies and does very well until the third inning when the opposing pitcher gives up the fourth walk. The batter starts toward first, the umpire turns from base to base counting runners, then suddenly hollers, "Hey these bases is all took, you go over yonder and sit on that bench until I can find somewhere to put you." At the kitchen table, on the front porch, in the church and school yard, at the store, American folk tales go on and on, the same tales over and over, freshened and strengthened by new tellers in every generation.

A printed folk tale cannot possibly convey the total effect and meaning of the entire folk storytelling experience. Recordings, motion pictures, and television remedy many of the defects of published folk tales, but even these media do not fully capture all the subtleties of the actual performance. There, language, subject, and action are all enhanced by the personality of the teller, his gestures, facial expressions, and pantomime, by the real life setting and those indefinable cultural and personal factors that unite the folk audience. All these elements are, of course, absent in *Ghosts and Goosebumps*. Yet, despite these deficiencies, Troy State University students, handicapped by a lack of time and a dearth of finances and equipment, succeeded far more often than not in taking down the tale in the language of the teller, in evoking the diction, syntax, rhythm, and timbre of authentic Alabama folk speech. And in most cases the informants, most of whom were white, middle class, and rural or small town, though a few accounts are rendered in Negro speech, clearly had a knack for tale-telling. The accounts are brief to moderate in length, forceful and direct in structure and speech, and because they are told either in the first person or from the point of view of the folk community, invested with all the immediacy and authority of first-hand knowledge or personal experience.

Two broad types of folk tales are fully represented in this Alabama collection: the supernatural and the humorous. On the surface there appears to be little connection between them, but in many respects they are fraternal twins. Both serve to entertain, both depend on exaggeration, distortion, or some unusual or magnified quality in folk life and character; the former is recounted as truth or fact, the latter creates an illusion of truthfulness or veracity, and in both there is a temporary, willing suspension of disbelief. The ghost tale is a tall tale designed to arouse or dispel fear; the tall tale uses the same techniques to provoke laughter; and both provide a catharsis through the recognition of certain experiences common to all folk. This folk catharsis is always plainly evident when the tale is actually told: "My Daddy used to tell that old tale," "I been knowing that all my life," "That same thing happened to my cousin" or aunt or neighbor. A thread of comedy may appear in the most terrifying tale of terror, and the existence of a great body of jokes, anecdotes, and folk pranks about the supernatural confirms the common root of humorous and supernatural folk tales.

But there are significant differences: nobody ever really believes a tall tale—rather, we recognize in it some truth about ourselves—but a tale of the supernatural always leaves some room for belief. The particulars of any given tale may be doubted, but few of the folk entirely exclude the possibility of supernatural occurrences. Indeed, we cannot lay our fascination with the supernatural to rest: our grandfathers saw balls of fire, angels, and headless apparitions; we see strange lights in the heavens, glittering disks, and marvelous ships that sail through nebulas, quasars, black holes, and endless galaxies. In the last decade the contemporary cinema and the popular novel have feasted on the demonic and created a whole new space mythology, but apprehension of the otherworld has always been a folk instinct. Whether or not we believe in the existence of ghosts is irrelevant—there is a great subterranean world of supernatural lore in American popular culture and folk tradition, inhabited by witches, ghouls, vampires, werewolves, monsters, demons, and ghosts, apparitions sometimes gray, wavering, insubstantial, and sometimes shockingly three-dimensional. The folk tales of the supernatural in *Ghosts and Goosebumps* are of that world. Eerie and strange the landscape may be, colored in the red of blood and the black of night and death; horrifying and troubling the apparitions and portents, yet all is familiar, a genuine Alabama folk landscape filled with plain, simple ghosts of plain, simple Alabama folk, trailing their gowns across the headstones of small, homely cemeteries, clattering in barns and splashing in wells, howling under white frame churches, flailing wooden shutters and descending sooty chimneys, hitching a ride on the tailgate of a wagon, snatching off quilts and pinching big toes, fiddling in the attic and dancing the night away in deserted houses—revenants and visitants going back home to Elba, Clio, Louisville, Wetumpka, Goodwater, Samson, and Eufaula.

The supernatural is expressed multitudinously in the traditional songs, tales, customs, beliefs, and verbal lore of the folk. Though its substance exists beyond and outside the natural, the occurrence is invariably linked with natural phenomena that are perceived and interpreted by some means other than rationally derived evidence, whether inductive, deductive, or analogical. These happenings are attested to repeatedly, passing from one generation to the next, and witnesses may swear to the truth of a tale of the supernatural as old as recorded history, assigning to it real persons, definite places, and a specific historical time. Anglo-European supernatural lore of the folk represents the survival of archetypal myth, and although a folk tale acquires new spatial and temporal dimensions and transformations in setting, character, and language as it is orally transmitted over the centuries, the mythic core is ageless and universal. Motifs of the supernatural in *Ghosts and Goosebumps* are directly traceable to the great Teutonic and Classical mythologies of Europe, and Christian influences are also widely present.

The relationship of a local folklore to a larger mythology may be demonstrated by this short, gruesome Alabama tale:

> Franklin Mc Duffie shot himself with a shot gun and when he did it blew his head up into the top of the tree. When it rains the blood of Franklin comes up out of the ground where the death occurred. This happened in Geneva County.—Maybelle Schlich

As an emblem of life and death, blood figures prominently in the primitive rite of human sacrifice of a scapegoat, in the cults of Osiris and Dionysus, and in the Eleusinian mysteries; in the New Testament blood is a central symbol of the Lord's Supper, a commemorative ritual of the Crucifixion. Blood is always present in the magical rites of European witchcraft; the Anglo-Germanic folk hero Faust signs his pact with Satan in blood, and, in Marlowe's tragedy, as the devils drag him off to Hell, he sees the blood of Christ as it "streams in the firmament." Although the scapegoat in this Alabama tale is a pitiful suicide, the recurrence of his blood is both a rite of remembrance and, in its association with rain, a symbol of fertility and resurrection.

Folk tales of the supernatural always contain two distinct elements: the apparition and the portent. The apparition is the figure of the otherworld, whether ghost, demon, witch, spirit, or some other creature; the portent is a natural phenomenon apprehended in some new and mysterious way, which heralds the approach of the visitant and may symbolize his claim on this earth. The portent as animal is rooted ultimately in primitive religion: the animal worshiped as god, the god appearing as animal. Sacrifice requires an animal both as appeasement of the god and as divination of the will of the god; hence a diviner or sorcerer is akin to the prophet and to the priest who guards and serves the god. Every sort of animal has served in rites of sacrifice and divination—cats, dogs, fowl, rams, cows—and the European witch, high priestess of the black arts presided over by Satan, the devil or "little god," always has a familiar, usually a cat, in whom supernatural powers are invested, and she is capable of transforming herself or migrating into her familiar. Numerous tales mention the animal portent—rabbits, dogs, cats, horses, snakes, and squirrels. Among the other common portents reported by Troy State University students are the door that mysteriously opens and closes, the inexplicable light, a ball of fire, unusual disturbances in nature, and unexpected, frightening noises, cries, and strange sounds. These auguries often foretell death, but not always the violent sort. Sometimes the death is ordinary, like the passing away of the fiddler in the following account:

> In the year of 1910 a man by the name of Jeb Jackson, he was a fiddle player, he would play very often for old timey square dancing. So Jeb was taken sick and died one night about 10 o'clock. About two hours before Mr. Jackson died a fiddle cut loose and started playing up in the loft of the house. It played off and on all night.—Charles Grimes

Omens are also the instruments of justice:

> A man killed another man. The murderer went away. Some people took the bones of the man and made handles for their knives and forks. Later the murderer visited these people. When they began to eat, the blood began to run out of the handles of the knives and forks that the man was using. People knew he was guilty.—Mrs. C. E. Kirkland

Or they serve to remind us of murder, suicide, and other violent acts, for example, the bloodstain that cannot be removed:

> One time two women were fighting and one of them killed the other. The blood is still on the door at the house where they were fighting. Later on some people moved in and saw the blood and tried to wash it off. They washed it off, but when they got up the next morning it was back on the door.—Olene Staggers

The apparitions in these Alabama tales are as plentiful, various, and different as those who "see" them or experience their presence. They may appear suddenly at a place familiar to them in life, perhaps going about an accustomed task, as does this old broom maker:

> Grandpa knew an old Negro woman who used to always make brush brooms in her spare time. He would always speak to her as he passed

for she'd be sitting on an old log working with her brooms with a little dog beside her. One day he saw her just as she was in life and started to speak, but then as he thought about it, he remembered she had just died a few weeks back. As he opened his mouth, she disappeared.—Mrs. J. T. Langford

In general, however, ghosts are Shakespeare's "restless spirits' reenacting the pain of their deaths, as in this oddly poetic account:

At Water Grinders Mill a woman was drowned. At midnight she comes up from the waters and hollers. Grave and loud she screams. Families living near the site have heard her holler.—Mrs. Winston Cole

They may be dressed in ordinary attire, but usually they appear in the white or gray of grave cerements, their physical characteristics often unrealized. Their identities may be unknown, or they may be instantly recognizable, especially the troubled ghost who piteously seeks out his family or loved ones. Often they are macabre:

In Eastman, Georgia, a woman got her head cut off by a train. Every night after then around midnight you can see a woman walking up and down the streets without a head.—Jeryl Fordham

Some otherworld beings are merely disembodied voices that speak directly to the living, urging remembrance or the discharge of some obligation to the dead:

I was sitting in my kitchen one night by the big open fireplace in the kitchen when we lived over on Mr. Claude's place. My sister ain't been died and left her little children there long, helpless, and somebody had to take and raise 'em, so us took them. Anyhow that night, it was kinda done getting to be cool and we had a big oak fire on. I was sitting in the kitchen rocking and thinking, the children all in bed, the old man was studying, and I sees this big ball of fire with hot coals glowing from it, dropping slowly down to my floor. I reckon I didn't move, I just don't remember I was so scared. Anyway this ball of fire touches down to the floor about as far from me as you, and a big black smoke rises up and my sister's voice, the mother of them children that was in the bed and done asleep, says, "Angels know I am here; my children better be took care of or worser things will be sure to follow." By the time I heard them words I kinda shook my head like I had been dreaming or something and everything done gone, just like nothing had ever been, hadn't even scorched my floor.

I never did say a word to nobody about that until the next day. My old man didn't much want to believe what I done seen, but something happened later that changed his mind. I can't tell you about that. If you ever sees a haint or spirit and you wants to get rid of it quick, just ask it what its doing there and it will go away.—Mrs. George Matthews

Rarely are they benevolent. A wondrous exception is the kind ghost of this touchingly personal record:

> Grandpa said that after Grandma died, she still came and tucked the cover around him and then vanished.—Mrs. Gus Cheatham

If apparitions call any place home, it is the immemorial haunted house of our childhood dreams, complete with creaking doors, moans and screams, clanking chains, flapping shutters and torn curtains, dark stairways, black cats, ravens, bats, frogs, lizards, caldrons, coffins, and trap doors—all the paraphernalia of vengeful, unhappy spirits. There is not a single community in Alabama that cannot lay claim to such a house and its patron ghost. Nearly always the haunted house is associated with violence and tragedy, but sometimes it is inhabited by a playful, fairly harmless, amusing but irritating spirit known as the poltergeist, a prankster who delights in performing sleight-of-hand tricks and practical jokes—suspending furniture in midair, turning over chairs and tables, breaking dishes, and hurling cutlery. Inconvenient and embarrassing to have about, he is not so sinister as demons and devils. His very name distinguishes him from other ghosts: it derives from *poltern*, to knock. Hence he is easily recognized; his presence is always indicated by noises variously described as raps, taps, pops, or knocks. Is this a peculiar sort of otherworld Morse Code he taps out to communicate with the living? A description of such a charming mischief-maker appears in John G. Parks's "The Samson Homestead." The family grow so familiar with their poltergeist that they name him "Old Pop," and twice he manifests himself: "His body was like that of an alligator, his head and claws like that of a panther, and his speed was like lightning." Mr. Parks had more than Old Pop to talk about—his narrative includes two other major tales. That's the way of the folk—often they interrupt themselves, one tale reminds them of another, and they are likely to stop short of the climax or punch line and start in on something new—or comment on the weather or explain who's kin to who, meandering back to the first anecdote when they get good and ready. The telling and the listening are all the better for those peregrinations. Mrs. B. M. Jarvis tells a tale of a poltergeist who tapped on the windows, turned over barrels of water, made clothes fall down in the closet, and caused so much general havoc that "They decided to move and burn the house down. Well, they moved, but it took them a long time to burn that house down." With just such subtle, masterly strokes do the folk reveal their often humorous attitudes toward ghosts. Another special ghost who wanders about these haunted houses is the guardian of treasure, kinsman of dragon treasure-keepers, who, despite money needles, shovels, spades, and the most carefully laid plans, is always victorious over the greedy, cunning could-be robbers. Treasure-keepers, poltergeists, murderers and the murdered, suicides, atheists, wicked men and good-men-and-true— the ghosts of all these float through the pages of *Ghosts and Goosebumps.*

Many of the accounts of the supernatural in this collection are folk conversations or monologues about personal experiences with apparitions, portents, and other inexplicable occurrences, reminiscences in which the informant sounds as if he's sitting right next to us. Such conversations are stamped with the personality of the speaker. Their authentic tone is striking: Mrs. Maggie King's encounter with the angel of the run-a-bout, Sue Peacock's testimony of seeing her dead brother as she walked home from picking cotton, E. C. Nevin's version of the mysterious light in the swamp. Other tales belong to the folk community, and the informant simply does his part in passing them on: the lady in white who rides the doctor's buckboard through an Elba gully, the well at Mt. Olive where a murdered husband splashes, the Celie ghost of White Water Creek in Coffee County brutally killed for a silver plate in her head, the headless woman of Sweet Gum Bottom, the drowned spirit at Tippin's Eddy, the beast of Patsalega, the piteous creature of Panther Creek. These communities often produce renegades and criminals, and ghosts or some portent keep the memory of their crimes green: the grave of an atheist struck by lightning, the devil's head image that appears on the tombstone of a wicked woman, the uncaring mother grieving "in the east and southeast" for children she ignored in life, the too-soon-buried or unhappy dead scratching on his coffin. Still other tales are known throughout American folklore: Ella Kate Allen's Halloween ghost and Maybelle Schlich's yellow ribbon Gothic tale, both current in contemporary college lore, Dixie Martin's "Lavender Party Dress," fictionalized by the folklorist Carl Carmer (*Dark Trees to the Wind* [William Sloane Associates, 1949], reprinted in Flanagen and Hudson's *Folklore in Literature* [Row, Peterson, 1958]) and given musical treatment in a popular song of the 1950s, "The Sweater," and Mrs. A. Jack Griffin's tale of the ghost nun, World War II folk tale. Sonja Taylor's "Always a Hole" is a localization of an international motif, the trench or hole, dug by an unjustly executed man, that can never be filled. Troy State students submitted five other variants of the trench tale, two about the legendary Bill Skeeto. Whether personal reminiscences or voices from the chorus of a folk community, in their use of worldwide motifs these accounts from central Alabama are part of the traditional Anglo-European folklore of the supernatural.

The folk exorcise the demonic with laughter, and the humorous ghost lore in this collection, like the other tales, has been reported from every state and region in America: the luckless drunk who falls in an open grave, the corpse that suddenly rises from the coffin, the race with the talking cat, another bewildered drunk who takes two fishermen (or nut gatherers) in a cemetery for God and the devil, and Viola Liddell's cantankerous Nanny Burson and Olene Williams's Martha, both of whom derive from the well-known comic figure of Anglo-American folksong and tale, "The Farmer's Curst Wife." In these anecdotes about the supernatural, the joke is never at the expence of the ghost but at the hapless victim who tries to escape:

> One night two drunks had gathered a bunch of hickory nuts and were deciding where they could go to divide them. It just happened that they would go inside the cemetery and divide them up. They both sat down in the middle of the cemetery and began to divide their hickory nuts, saying "one for you and one for me." A few minutes later, another drunk came staggering through the cemetery. He, however, was drunker than the other two. When he saw these men saying "one for you and one for me," he turned ghostly white and ran all the way to town. He told the townspeople that they had better get to the graveyard quick, because the Lord and the Devil were sitting in the middle of the graveyard dividing up the people.—W. O. Screws

Henry C. Scott's "When the Devil Got After Me" succeeds through its vivid details and authentic folk speech in creating both an atmosphere of terror and a delightfully comic ending: the devil gives up at the foot of the hill, Henry runs on to the house, and hollers, "Open the door, Ida, open the door while I make another round! The Devil's after me!" In Tallassee, Alabama, folks tell the same tale on a local character terrified by a huge dog: round and round the house he runs, the dog nipping at the seat of his breeches, his wife running inside the house from window to window to keep up; finally, he waves and hollers, "Be ready, Marthy, I'm a'comin' in on the next round!"

The relationship between humorous and supernatural folk tales is nowhere better illustrated than in the Bloody Bones species. Told by an adult to frighten a child, it is a mock ritual of terror that depends largely on oral devices for its effect. As Bloody Bones comes for his prey, the teller's voice takes on sepulchral tones and his face a fierce aspect, the bodiless voice of the specter comes closer and closer, Bloody Bones comes through the gate, to the first step, the second step, the porch, the front door, the foot of the bed, and the teller, who has also come closer and closer to the listener, suddenly reaches out and grabs the child, hollering, "I got you!" Just before the climactic moment, full recognition dawns: the child himself is the victim marked for revenge and there is absolutely no way out of it! No matter how many times you tell it, the child begs to hear it again, and that says something important about the nature of human fear: if the terror is half playlike we can enjoy it. Folklorists call Bloody Bones a "jump" tale because the teller "jumps" at or grabs the listener who, naturally, jumps away. Several variants appear in this collection, and in all of them, mortals are punished for some trespass committed against the otherworld: the girl in "Raw Head and Bloody Bones" keeps her word not to tell but the ogre comes for her anyway because she has seen too much; the boy in "Big Toe" and in the liver–bubble gum story and the husband in "Golden Arm" pay for thoughtless mutilation or desecration of a corpse; but the old woman escapes either because she is ignorant of the source of her bone or willing to give it up. "The Boy and the Knife" variant exhibits two additional motifs: the subterranean descent and the seeker confronted by many doors or passageways. Here the suspense-building device of the approaching voice is almost lost, and the evil force is clearly identified as the devil, the red man behind each of the ten doors. The storyteller affirms the moral, "That learned the mother to never buy another red knife," but clearly the boy also commits a transgression by telling what he saw. Notable, too, is the mother's failure to protect her son—the ten quilts, corresponding to the ten doors, are his pitiful, futile defense against certain destruction.

Witches are not so common in Alabama as ghosts, yet most small towns and rural communities claim a local practitioner of the ancient black arts, and the tales of witchcraft collected by Troy State University students also exhibit worldwide motifs and types: the witch of Fairfield, Alabama, is the ancient Greek Circe whose magical potion transforms men into animals; the motif of the severed hand/ cat's paw as emblem of the transmigrating witch is found in the tales of Mrs. Maggie King and Mrs. Espie Eldridge; Adeline Campbell reports the motif of the mysterious night-riding witch; and Mary Glenn Merritt's tale of the magician tree-planter echoes the folk belief that a tree planted for a child dies at the same time its human counterpart dies. The tale of a witch's unrequited love for a mortal presents both the concept of transmigration and the power of silver to injure or kill an inhuman adversary, and in J. D. Fowler's tale, a squirrel hunter turns back the curse of a vindictive witch by a countercharm that involves imagistic magic. The folk conversation reported by Roy Adams offers interesting comment about the sudden materialization of spirits, especially those newly dead, and the passage of the soul into animals—the three hound dogs atop gravestones and the widow who tries to run off bewitched rabbits with her broom. The ambivalence of the folk attitude toward the supernatural is evident in the tale of the witch burned at the stake: though the unnamed teller clearly discredits belief in witches, the witch-burner is punished by supernatural means.

The witch has found her most enduring expression in fairy tales, a kind of tale now almost exclusively associated with children but once the delight of all the folk. Brought to Europe in the Middle Ages by Arabian merchants, some scholars suggest, they enchant us with all sorts of marvels, not the least of which is their emphasis on the cunning and outright wickedness of sorcerers and witches who murder humans out of sheer malevolence. For children, the witch is the sum and substance of evil, the distillation of all nightmares, and while they may quite matter-of-factly accept ogres, trolls, giants, and other monsters, they feel real fear of her, perhaps because of the aspect of cannibalism. Like its prototype "Hansel and Gretel," the Alabama tale "One Little Pear" is about innocent children who suffer under a wicked stepmother. In the European analogue the stepmother becomes the witch of the gingerbread house who devours human flesh, but our variant introduces both a moral note and a stern psychological truth—the child murder is a direct result of the stepmother's greed and abhorrence of all charitable instincts, giving food to a hungry beggar. The motif of human hair growing through a plant or tree, common in world mythology, is nicely accommodated to southern folk life, green onions for supper, and, as in other folk tales of the supernatural, a murdered victim's cry from the grave functions as an instrument of justice, identifying both victim and murderer. In another Alabama folk tale of cannibalism from the Troy collection, a big fat man consumes four members of the same family but the family bird effects their miraculous escape: "Then all of a sudden the man burst open and everyone got out and lived happily after that."

Among the tellers of tales about portents and apparitions we are bound to find some disbelievers. A narrow but definite stream of skepticism runs in the folk mind, and this collection contains several reports of experiences informants believed at the time to be of supernatural origins but which later proved to be rationally explicable— Lee Lat Wilson's devil in the cemetery turns out to be a cow, chains rattling near New Tabernacle Church in Coffee County belong not to specters but to ordinary hogs, a Pike County angel is a goose, and one ghost is nothing more than a dog fennel bush. Skeptics among the folk call these the "real" ghosts. A psychologist could tell us much about our complex reactions to the supernatural in these tales, but the folklorist sees the endless perpetuation and transformation of myth and symbol against the background of a well-realized folk landscape. Here are glimpses of a lost day, a horse and buggy time when folks sat up all night with the dead and dying, hoed and picked cotton, pulled corn, quilted, made brush brooms, cleaned clothes with battling sticks, drew water from wells, and met the devil rather regularly. And here and there is another kind of "realness," the bonds created by human sorrow: the ghost of poor Audrey Nell who dies begging for peas and coffee, the spirits of two little tubercular girls swishing by forever in the stiffly starched dresses they always wore in life, the mother and child burned to death in the same terrible accident. These accounts cannot fail to link us to our past, to humble us, to remind us that all flesh is mortal.

Such reality lies at the heart of folk comedy. Perhaps the best definition of a folk tale is that it comes near the folk, as a mirror of one's own life within a folk community. Thousands of folk tales derive not from myth, legend, or the romance of fairyland, but from the character of the folk. The hero of these tales, whether animal or human, is one of their own, admired, pitied, scorned, ridiculed, hated, loved, respected; his adventures, familiar to the folk audience either through oral tradition or by direct contact, occur within an easily identified folk setting; and character and events are described and narrated in the folk speech of both tellers and listeners. Such are the tall tales of America.

Long before the settlement of the New World the tall tale was well established in Anglo-European literature and folklore. Comic exaggeration and absurdity appear in fairy tales like "The Three Sillies" and "Puss-in-Boots"; many of the fabliaux of Chaucer and Boccaccio are tall tales that hinge on practical jokes; Shakespeare's Falstaff is the apex of a long, unbroken stage tradition of liars and con men; Voltaire's *Candide* is one tall tale after another; and the incredible adventures of Jonathan Swift's Gulliver occur in a setting of skillfully contrived authenticity. The American fondness for wild extravagance and distortion is evident in colonial accounts of witchcraft, and within the first half of the nineteenth century we could boast a fully developed folk and literary tradition of tall tales. A major stream of American tall tale literature flows all the way from Washington Irving's Rip Van Winkle and Ichabod Crane through Mark Twain's Huck Finn, Tom Sawyer, and Connecticut Yankee, to Faulkner's *The Reivers* and John Barth's creations. Alabama has its own literary folk con man in Simon Suggs, the outlandish hero of James Johnson Hooper's *Some Adventures of Captain Simon Suggs, Late of the Talla-poosa Volunteers*. The very air men breathed in America seemed to nurture the robust, uproarious spirit of folk heroes who could outdrink, outwork, outlie, outfight, outwit, and outshoot anybody in the territory—Buffalo Bill, Jesse James, Billy the Kid, Paul Bunyan, Davy Crockett, John Henry, Casey Jones, and Mike Fink.

Sagas and ballads about such figures multiplied all across the country, and their transformation into mass popular heroes was inevitable. Davy Crockett quickly found his way into almanacs, newspapers, and dime novels; the motion picture industry erected a celluloid world for the outlaw and the cowboy; Walt Disney gave us a cartoon Paul Bunyan and Johnny Appleseed, old folk heroes under new guises, and Mickey Mouse, Donald Duck, and Bugs Bunny, the inheritor of the trickster Brer Rabbit. Pogo's crew succeeded the other beasts of the Uncle Remus cycle, and the Charlie Brown gang and the Sesame Street Muppets are our latest national mass media folk figures.

There are still thousands upon thousands of unnamed tall tale tellers and jokesters all over America who memorialize local folk heroes and their adventures, comic and heroic, and pull the same pranks their great-grandfathers delighted in. Although the tall tales and folk pranks in this collection may lack the clever, bright style of television and cartoon folk heroes, they faithfully reflect Alabama folk life and humor. Here are coon dogs of extraordinary intelligence, serpents of miraculous powers, a hermit who walks through a river, champion liars and lying contests, Uncle Bert Keaton, the peace-loving schoolmaster turned reluctant hunter, and the marvelous Hunt, an outrageous spoof of every man's hunting and fishing lies.

The practical joke literally brings the spirit of the tall tale to life. Some psychologists aver that pranksters are infantile, hostile, and masochistic. Maybe so, but most of the Troy pranks are lighthearted and harmless, humorous rites of passage, traditional folk experiences passed on to the uninitiated, who, in their turn, pull the joke on the next generation. Dumb bull, snipe hunting, smut, palm reading, rosin strings, seeing stars, thimble, chasing purse, and buger at the spring—in all these, decency sets the boundaries of play, prankster and victim share in the fun, and nobody gets hurt. Little is required for these jokes—a piece of string, a board, an old bedsheet, a thimble, a crocker sack—a reminder that the folk make do nicely with whatever is at hand. High spirits and good nature take up the slack.

If there is any one single quality that stamps a tale as folk, it is language. The Troy tales exhibit numerous grammatical, idiomatic, and syntactical constructions peculiar to the speech of Alabama yeomanry, and these strike the ear pleasantly, familiarly, as they do in our actual social discourse. They are constructions natural to us, and even a silent reading echoes with the very inflections and tone of our speech, the many subtle variations in pitch, volume, timbre, and rhythm. Common among them are the addition of the *uh* or *a* sound that precedes the present participle, as in *ahollering, acoming, abumping;* the use of *real* as adverbial modifier of degree, as in *real sick, real pretty* (meaning sicker than sick, prettier than pretty); a fondness for the double negative, as in "didn't pay no attention" and "couldn't hardly" (a usage denoting intensity or emphasis); the exchange of past tense for the present, as in "it come in sight" or "it come a big rain"; the exchange of objective and nominative, as in "Mama, sister, and me been over to Nancy's"; the preference for weak, regular verb endings, as in "he knowed"; frequent word coinages, as in *ambering* for *ambling*; the preference for *they* over *there* as expletive, as in "They was a boy"; the use of *pure* or *purely* in the sense of *absolutely*, as in "I purely felt the sprangs of that buggy give"; idiomatic expressions that convey time and distance: "pretty good little bit," "a little piece down the road"; and traditional folk idioms that convey strong feeling or signal an abrupt transition or a conclusion: "I vow and declare," "I swear and declare," "Many a time" (or night or day), "She's living today to tell it," "all at once." The intent and origins of other idioms is less easily discerned: a fiddler or a dancer "cuts loose," but an angry man may also "cut loose" with a string of curses; one who experiences difficulties and frustrations in accomplishing a given chore "had a time cooking supper," "had a time trying to milk that cow"; and any habituated action, whether good or bad, may call forth "bad about," whether bad about lying, or bad about waking up at the same hour every night or, as in one of the tales here, "bad to wear" stiff-starched dresses.

In motif, theme, subject, attitude, figurative devices, and language the Troy folk conversations and tales exemplify the perpetuation of traditional Anglo-European lore and its translation into the Alabama folk mind and landscape. Readers will have their own ghosts, specters, haunted houses, witches, Homer Powells, Will Foleys, dumb bulls, thimbles, and snipe hunts, and we hope they will set them down on paper or share their folk recollections with each other and their children and grandchildren. Tales such as these in *Ghosts and Goosebumps* put us in touch with ourselves, our neighbors, and families. More than anything else, they point back, down the road we came by, and forth, up the road we are traveling, toward understanding and friendship.

ᎠᎥᏣᏍᎶᏡᎻᎾᏞᎾᏲᏃ

The Tales

Chimney Corner Tale

Mr. Joiner's grandfather said his grandfather said that his great-great grandfather experienced a supernatural appearance.

One night, great-great grandfather Joiner and his family were in bed. It was around 1840 and people in those days lived in the daytime instead of night. Anyway, the Joiners were frightened away by a noise like a hissing sound.

A great ball of fire came down the chimney and circled the room two or three times then went back up the chimney. There was no explanation for the appearance.

Olene Williams

Cemetery Haunt

There is a cemetery near Coffee Springs, Alabama, where a ball of fire haunts or guards the graves. People passing on horseback late at night have seen it sitting on a grave or tombstone. It has followed many people all the way to their homes. If they rode faster, it went faster, if they went slower it also slowed down. One night it followed a Mr. Thompson to his home, he went to the barn to stable his horse and when he came back it was on his front porch in front of the door. When he went up on the porch it disappeared and was seen going back to the road to the cemetery. Even though it was resting on the porch, it was not burned. There was no sign that the fire had been there.

Jim Shields

One Stormy Night

One stormy night a man in the neighborhood was coming home with a sack of corn. He had a time trying to keep the horse he was riding calm. An old lady living nearby heard someone holler and at the same time saw a coffin slide down her rail fence. She sent her boys out to see what had happened. The old man and the horse were both dead in the woods, so he must have died the moment the casket was seen.

J. T. Langford

Buried Alive

A certain woman died. She asked not to be buried in an oaken casket, but they buried her in one anyway. One night there was a great storm. Lightning struck only one grave—the grave of this particular woman. It struck in such a way that it split the grave open. The story is told that the woman's hair, which was red, had grown real long and her fingernails were long and jagged. There were also scratches on the inside of the coffin as if she'd been trying to get out.

Lana Silverthorn

Ghost Wagons

One night several people were staying at the home of a person who was dead. Different people would come in and others left until they heard the sound of a wagon approaching. No one came in. The sound continued but no one came in. This happened all night until one of the men decided to look. He opened the door quickly and saw a ball of fire was making the sound that sounded as if moving at a great pace. The ball of fire was making the sound that sounded as if wagons were approaching.

Mrs. George Holliday

Oak Tree Murder

There is a big oak tree overhanging the narrow road that runs from Darlington to the Camden highway. It is just a big ordinary oak and would deserve no comment were it not for one strange fact about its existence.

The story is that many years ago there was a killing under this tree and the red blood of the murdered man colored the white sandy road. The traces of blood vanished in the normal manner and they were seen no more until one day after a rain. The blood stain had returned and it remained as long as the ground was wet. This route was continued through all the years since the murder and it is said that if you pass under the big oak at any time when the ground is wet the blood stain can be seen.

Mrs. R. E. Lamberth, Sr.

Tallassee Bell Ringer

Many years ago a huge bell in the bell tower on the old mill in Tallassee was rung every hour to let employees know what time it was and awake them to come to work. If it was one o'clock the bell would ring one time, at two o'clock it would ring twice, at 3 o'clock three times and so on according to what time it was. Mr. Thomas Moore, the bell ringer for years and years, came in to work one night and became very sick and went home; later he was found dead about 1 o'clock but employees swore the bell rang all night long every hour on the hour.

Wilson Patterson

Floating Casket

Miss Maggie Folmar heard this when she was a child and says it really happened.

The family told that a young sister saw a vision and told them she would die. She saw a casket floating across the room and it went over her bed and her brother's bed. Her brother was a year younger than she. She said after it passed her brother's bed, it burst into a white powder in the middle of the room. A few weeks later she and her brother got sick. One died one day with pneumonia and the other the next day with scarlet fever.

Jimmie Sue Phillips

Haunted Church

When Mr. Strickland was a boy he had to walk past a Negro church. Behind the church was a pond. One night as he was going home he heard a baby crying down near the pond, he went to the pond and the crying grew louder but he could not find the baby.

Mr. Strickland also says that at this same church at night there would be lights on but when you would go look in the windows the lights would go out.

Webbie Strickland

Funeral Light

We had just moved into a new neighborhood and lived right across from a church. The day before, a funeral had just been held at the church, and that night we were preparing for bed, I just happened to look out my front window. There, shining through the windows of the church was a purple light. It was still burning when I pulled down my shade. There were no electric lights in those days, and we could never explain of the light.

Mrs. George Matthews, Jr.

Omen of the Cat

Mrs. House states that when she was a young girl, her baby sister got real sick. A group of neighbors came to sit up. All the young people were in the kitchen. All at once a big white cat just appeared in the room. No one saw it when it came in. They hollered "scat," but the cat didn't pay any attention to them. In a few minutes the mother of the sick child came in. The cat followed her around in the kitchen making a peculiar sound like "Lordy, Lordy, Lordy."

They tried to scare the cat away, even trying sicing the dogs on it, but it wouldn't scare. About midnight the cat left. No one saw it when it disappeared.

The next day the sick child died. After the funeral the family moved to another place. In about a month another child got sick just like the first child.

One night while they were sitting up with this child, the same cat appeared again. No one saw where he came in at. He appeared three nights in a row, no one could scare him away. On the third night the cat disappeared and they saw something like a white sheet going up the elements.

The second child to get sick died that night. They never saw the cat again.

Peggy Ham

A Warning

One night my husband saw somebody standing over me. It was three o'clock in the morning. We got outside, went around the house and looked under the house, but couldn't find nobody. I told him he was just dreaming and he said no, he was as wide awake as he had ever been in his life. Two weeks later my son got sick and died. I sure do believe this was a warning to us.

Mrs. George Holliday

A Sign of Death

Mrs. Wooton said her husband's first wife died in childbirth. Then when she and Mr. Wooton married she wanted to take the baby but Mr. Wooton's parents wanted to keep it. One night the image of the baby came into the bedroom where Mr. and Mrs. Wooton were. A week later the baby fell out of a wagon and died. Mrs. Wooton said the image she saw was a sign of death.

Nora Wooton

Atheist's Grave

There was a man who lived in this town who was an atheist. When he died his family put a slate marker on his grave. Three weeks later lightning struck it and broke it into three pieces. The family bought another marker and the same thing happened again. For a long time they just let it stay the way it was but the city decided to erect another marker. Three weeks later lightning struck it again and broke it into three pieces.

Mary Glenn Merritt

Omens

When the Wootons lived in Blountstown there was a lumber stack, with a stream behind it, in back of the house. Agnes's best friend lived in a house down near the stream with her sick uncle. One night Agnes was outside and she saw this white figure ambering along toward her friend's house. That night her friend's uncle died. Mrs. Wooton said this was a sign of death.

In this same house there was a quilting wire in one room. One day Mrs. Wooton called Agnes to come to the quilting room in a hurry. When Agnes got there she saw that one of the wires was curling and uncurling. This went on for about an hour before it stopped.

Agnes Wooton

Mother-in-Law's Ghost

When Mother was seventeen she was making plans for her wedding with my father. She spent a lot of thought on this big step and was weighing the pros and cons of the situation, wanting, like all girls, to be happy. One night she had a dream that helped her make up her mind to a large degree. In the dream that helped her make up her mind, a woman talked to her and told her that she was going to be happy. That marrying my father would not be a bed of roses for he had never had a mother and it would take a little patience to help get him over this. She told her that he would be good to her and that she would be wonderful for him. With this motherly talk, the dream ended.

Later, Mother told Daddy about it and together they told Grandaddy. When Mother described the woman (her hair style, features, dress, and a pin) it was a shock to Grandaddy. He then got some old photos of his wife that had died when Daddy was a baby. It was the same woman that Mother had seen in the dream and she never had seen the picture nor had the slightest idea what Daddy's mother looked like.

Dutchie Sellers

Grandaddy's Ghost

Late one afternoon my uncle and Grandaddy Bedsole were coming into the house for supper. As they were ready to enter the house my uncle saw a huge ball of fire hovering over the house. He said it seemed to float around just above the roof. Uncle tried to get Grandaddy to look at it, but he said Uncle was seeing things and dismissed it.

The tale upset my grandmother, who said it was a sign that there would be a death in the family soon. That night my grandaddy died.

After his death Grandaddy was heard walking through the house and going to his room. When the step was followed it stopped. No one could find anything to cause the noise.

No logical explanation was ever offered other than it was the ghost of Grandaddy.

Mrs. Mattie Bedsole

A True Story

This is a true story told to me by my mother. My brother was desperately ill with measles. This happened when we lived on a Turpentine Still or place where my father was in the turpentine business. Doctor Spears from Baker, was our family physician, and came every day to see my brother while he was so sick. This particular day, there was a severe thunderstorm and lightning struck two little girls which prevented Dr. Spears from coming, as he was working with these children. When he finished with these little girls 4:30 A.M. the following day he came to see my brother.

There were no telephones, and my mother did not know why he hadn't come, so she kept coming to the front door all during the night looking for the doctor.

My mother was aware of the Negroes (who lived on the Turpentine Place) telling her about the lights appearing where someone was going to die, or where someone had already died. The Negroes said they had seen lights on the place on many occasions.

Between nine and ten o'clock that night mother went again to the door, still looking for the doctor. She noticed two lights coming from around the Commissary, which was located about one hundred yards from the house. One of the lights went out, but the largest one came on up the front gate. It went up and down twice, just the height of the gate, then back to the Commissary and went out. My mother called my father who witnessed the lights and they were never able to figure them out.

My parents sat up all night with my brother every night, while he was sick. As I stated above, Dr. Spears came about 4:30 A.M. the following day and after carefully examining my brother, told my parents that my brother was out of danger and had passed the crisis.

Marie G. Weed

Haunted House

In the house—

The doors could be left closed but when they returned the doors would be open.

What happened one night—

Mr. Shields was almost asleep, in bed. The door was closed. After awhile the bolt clicked, door opened. He listened, got up, closed the door, pulled on it and went back to bed. Again the door clicked and opened. This happened three times.

Mr. Shields got up one morning to build a fire, looked out the window at the side of the room and saw a horse. It passed the front window and turned up a row in the field and disappeared. Later, he went out to find out which way it went. There were no tracks even though the ground had been freshly plowed. He never did understand what this was.

Jim Shields

Haint Horses

When we lived up on the other side of Mama's house, out in that little house in the field, the man who owned it previously had died.

There has been many a night I couldn't sleep because of hearing horses galloping continuously around the house. They were haint horses; never saw a track the next day.

Mrs. George Matthews, Jr.

The Door That Wouldn't Stay Shut

I, Fannie, use to go spend the night with Annie. We would sleep in a side room. When we went to bed we fastened the door. I know it was closed good because I did it. The door came open. Annie got up and closed it again because it came open. When we got back in bed and got quiet the door came open again and I told Annie I was going to shut it. She told me it was coming open again, but I got up and closed the door anyway. I locked and bolted it, and made sure it was closed. When I got back in bed, Annie said, "Fannie, it is going to come open one more time. When it is closed that time it won't come open anymore." So sure enough it came open again. I closed it and it stayed closed the rest of the night. Annie said it came open every night three times before it would stay closed.

Fannie Kelley

God and the Hailstones

One Sunday as a very religious family was returning from church in their wagon, a hail storm set upon them. They whipped their mules into a run, and when they reached home, the back of their wagon was filled with hailstones. Some of the hailstones were so large they did not melt for over a week. The way they were able to stay a few feet ahead of the storm is looked upon as a miracle that could only have been brought about by God. He gave them this special protection because they always had been so faithful to Him.

George May

Big, Huge Ball of Fire

Once upon a time Mrs. Wells and her Lloyd went to Luverne shopping. They sent on the wagon and it took them a long time to go and come. When they came back it was night. They had to pass by a friend's house. The friend was sick. Just before they got to his house they saw a big, huge ball of fire on top of the house. They couldn't imagine what it was. They stopped to see their friend. He died that night. They vow and declare that this is true.

Mrs. Pearl Clark

The Lavender Party Dress

One time two boys were going to a dance. It was after dark and they were going along a dark road in a wooded area, when they saw a girl in a lavender dress walking along the road. They stopped and asked her if she would like to go to the dance with them and she said yes and got in the wagon with them.

They went on to the dance and each of the boys enjoyed several dances with the girl. About 11:00 o'clock they went back home. When they got to the place where they had picked her up they offered to take her home, but she told them she would walk from the road as it was not far. After she had gone and the boys had gone down the road, one of them remembered that he had loaned her his jacket. They decided to go down the road and overtake her and get his jacket. They went down the road hoping to see her but didn't. At the end of the road they came to a house and knocked on the door. An old woman answered the door and told them that her daughter had been dead for fourteen years and if they would go the graveyard up the road they would see her grave so they went to the graveyard and there on the girl's grave they found the boy's jacket.

Mrs. Dixie Martin

The Omen of the White Dog

Daniel was driving his wagon down a dirt road one day when a little white dog started following him. He watched the dog because he acted kind of strange. The dog started chasing after the horses so Dan just popped his whip at him. Every time he would hit at the white dog, it would disappear and show up on the other side of the wagon. The man was very intelligent. He was the doctor for a community in North Alabama. When he got home that night he told his family about it. They did not believe him. He said he kept hitting at the dog and it would disappear and reappear on the other side of the road.

Two weeks later Daniel was killed at this same spot in the road where the dog had been following him. No one ever saw the dog again. He was murdered and no one caught the murderer.

Mrs. Lloyd Jonson

The Devil's Lightwood Knots

Once a boy was hunting and saw a big image that looked like the devil. He was piling lightwood knots around a tree. The boy decided to shoot him, but the shot didn't even faze the image. He then decided it was the devil piling up lightwood knots to burn him. This frightened him so he ran home. He took his mother down there to see it. When she got there, she could not see the figure, but found the lightwood knots piled around the tree.

Mrs. Mola Cotter

Company Coming

Grandpa and Grandma Mills were sitting on the front porch to their old log house on the Troy Highway one night when they saw a light bobbing down the road toward the house. Thinking there was company coming, Granny told Grandpa Mills to go inside and fetch some chairs for the company that was coming. They watched the light as it came nearer and nearer the old gate. Just as it reached the gate it dropped to the ground and went out. The folks on the porch waited but nobody ever came up the path to the house. Grandpa went out to the gate with a light of his own and found nothing there and no footsteps.

Mr. William F. Mahone

Ten Things to Know About the Ghosts

1. Never laugh at ghosts.
2. Ghosts never speak unless spoken to.
3. Ghosts hardly ever appear in the daytime, usually at midnight.
4. If you're walking at night and you walk through a warm spot, you're walking through a ghost.
5. People born at midnight can see ghosts.
6. All dogs can see ghosts. If you want to see one, get behind a dog at midnight and look between his ears.
7. If you wish to speak to a certain ghost, go to its grave and walk around it backward twelve times.
8. If you want an easier way, go at midnight and call them by their first name.
9. If you meet a ghost walk around it nine times and it will disappear.
10. If you're running from a ghost, if you have the chance, run over a bridge; ghosts can't travel over running water.

Rita Shaw

The Doctor in Elba

Legend has it that a certain gully near Elba is haunted. The story is told of a certain doctor who, making a call about two o'clock in the morning, was riding his buckboard through the gully when he saw a lady in a white dress walking along the road. The doctor stopped and asked her if she would like to ride. She neither looked up nor answered his question. The doctor got a little nervous at that, so he speeded his horse up a bit. The lady did the same with her walking. She kept an even pace with him for several miles. Finally he looked around and she was seated on the back of his buckboard. He was going pretty fast by this time and he looked around and she was seated on the seat by him; however, she got off the buckboard just as he got out of the woods. The doctor went on and made his call, and it is said that to this day when someone rides through that gully at night the lady in white rides with them.

Bonnie Dean

The Ghost Nun

Two soldiers were going back to base after being home a few days on leave. Somewhere on the road they were stopped by a nun who asked for a ride. As they traveled along, the soldiers talked of war. The nun, who was riding on the back seat, spoke and told them that the war was going to end before the year was out (1942).

When they came near a small town, the nun asked to be taken to the cemetery and left there. The soldiers supposed that she was going to visit a grave, and they asked her if she wanted them to wait for her. She told them no, but she added that they might give the priest at the next town a post card which she handed them.

When the priest read the card, he asked the soldiers if they would recognize a picture of the nun if they saw it; they said they would. The priest brought out a large book in which were many pictures of nuns. He turned the pages until the soldiers stopped him. They told the priest that that was the nun. It was the picture of a nun who had been dead several years.

Mrs. A. Jack Griffin

Ghost Party

Many years ago there was a young man who would ride the Sunday afternoon train from Ariton, Alabama, to Tennille, Alabama, a few miles to see his girlfriend. He would have about two miles to walk from the railroad tracks to the girl's house. While walking back to the tracks one Sunday night about ten o'clock, he passed this old vacant house. There was a light inside and the sound of music and dancing was coming out of the house. So, he decided to stop by and see who was having a party, but when he came close to the house the light went off and the sound of music and dancing stopped. No sooner had he walked back to the road, the light came on and the sounds would be heard again. He tried approaching the house several other times and each time the same thing would happen. No one else has ever seen the light or heard the music, but this young man of many years ago will swear that he is telling the truth.

Bill Barefoot

Splashing in the Well

About four miles from Tallassee there is a little community known as Mt. Olive. The community derives its name from the church and the church derives its name from the name of mountain on which Jesus went to pray when he realized that the end of his life was drawing near. Perhaps this is symbolic and perhaps not.

Anyhow, that is not my tale. My tale concerns a happening in this little community which has many folklore elements.

Back of the oldest store in the community there is a Negro shack. This shack has been empty for some time and will probably stay empty for time to come. You see, the house is haunted by the spirit in the well.

Back many years ago there lived a Negro and his wife. The wife of the Negro was dissatisfied with her better half and wished to live with another of the hands there on the place. 'Tis said that he fell in the well as he was getting a drink of water, but that sounds odd in that she married again before all of his relatives got home from the funeral. Be that as it may, his ghost is still splashing around in the well. Nobody with good sense is going to live in a house where there is a mysterious splashing in the well. The splashing is just heard at night and it is worst of all on nights when the moon shines into the well. If you don't believe this tale, just go to the house and you will hear the splashing in the well also.

Sonja Taylor

Pladding Clothes

Alpha Tatum was hauling a load of cotton on a wagon from Monticello to Montgomery in the year 1866. After selling his cotton he and the Negro man with him decided to spend the night at an old vacant house en route back home. They slept on the porch. About midnight the Negro heard a noise, he awoke my great, great, grand-father. Tatum listened and later said the noise sounded like a woman pladding clothes with a pladding stick. The noise was coming from the direction of the well, but when he went near the well the noise would stop. After they walked away from the well the noise would start again. Having an uneasy feeling Tatum decided it best to move on for the night. A few miles down the road, they came to a farm house with a light on. They stopped and the man living there told them how a white woman had killed a Negro woman at the pladding block with a pladding stick near the well when they asked about the noise at the old house a few miles up the road.

A. M. C. Tatum

Scratch, Scratch, Scratch

Back in 1888, each man in the county had to work on county roads for ten days out of every year. T. M. Stroud from Elba, Alabama, was working his ten days with two other men. They were camped for the night at Woodland Grove Church in Coffee County.

There was a man buried in the cemetery of Woodland Grove with an unusual story about him. It seems that before he died he ordered his casket and had it made where you could take off the top and slide back a panel and view him. He requested that he be put in a vault above the ground, and every ten years his family must slide back the panel and look at him. The family obeyed him four times and finally decided to bury him under ground.

This particular night T. M. Stroud and the other two men had eaten their supper and prepared beds in the back of the church in front of the altar. As they turned out the light, they heard a scratching sound, similar to that of a dog. They lit their lanterns and went outside and searched under the church where the scratching sound had come from. There was no dog. They retired again but the scratching continued louder than ever. It sounded as if it came from the front door this time. They got up again and searched the church again but heard the scratching once more in the top of the church. They checked the church once more and checked the grounds outside the church to see if someone was trying to scare them. They found nothing at all. They retired again and were almost asleep with the scratching still going on, when they heard a window suddenly rise. They jumped up and no one was around. They don't know why it went up.

Finally they tried to ignore it and go to sleep. In the middle of the night they heard a tree fall right near the church. The next morning, they searched for the tree for two hours and never found one. The three men think it was this old man trying to rise out of his grave.

T. M. Stroud

Silver Dollar

This is a legend that happened in Coffee County near Jackson's Bridge on Whitewater Creek. It is in North Central Coffee County. It happened right after the Civil War.

There was a Negro woman named Celie. Before she was freed she was working one day and a mule kicked her in the head. They took her to the doctor and he put a silver dollar in her head as a plate. Later on a man named Green Fowler and two other men killed her and got the silver dollar out of her head. They covered her up with leaves and left her there. Someone found her in the morning. They say she haunts that place even now. Some people have seen her in a long white dress with seven buttons down the middle. She supposedly has followed people behind their wagons. There are a few people in Coffee County that will not go across Jackson's bridge to this day.

Mrs. Low Hussey

Dancing Skulls

About three miles north of the crossroads known as Rosebud, in the south-central section of Wilcox County, there sits on top of a small grass covered hill the remains of what was once a large frame house. The house does not differ from any of the other tumble-down, weather beaten frame houses around the country, that is, in the way it looks. There is a great difference, however, in the history of this house and those of its kind that are so common to us here in the South.

This house, which now consists of one large room that has held up in the fight with nature through the years, was once a hospital. The exact dates of its service in this capacity are not known but many people say that it dates back before the War of the Confederacy. It is known that the hospital had been abandoned before the turn of the century.

In the front yard of this structure, that is today occupied by an old Negro woman, her daughter, and an afflicted boy of about twenty, there is scattered about an assortment of grave markers in the form of headstones and slabs. There are not many of these, but the small number there suffice to give the place a weird appearance.

The attic of this structure is filled with human skulls and the occupants of the house and the Negroes of the section say that within these skulls lie the spirits of their former owners. The belief is that these spirits are very sensitive and are easily excitable, and when they become upset they dance about in the attic and frequently about the walls and the ceiling. In times of great excitement, especially during storms, these "ha'nts" even venture out into the yard and hover around the tombs that hold their companions.

Henry Bonner

Spirits Calling

A woman tells of going to Selma, Alabama, and of stopping on the way to pick up an aunt. When she stopped at the aunt's house, she heard a voice calling to her. Thinking it was her aunt, she turned around to answer her, but saw no one. She says that the voice sounded exactly like the voice of her great-aunt who had lived in the house many years before, but was then dead and she was sure that "Aunty" was just wanting to know where she was going.

Evelyn B. Dean

Grandmother's Ghost at the Foot of the Bed

My mother told me that she and her sister were in bed one night when they thought they heard something at the foot of their bed. They looked up and there was a figure in white. They were both scared to death but they didn't make a move or say anything for a pretty good little bit. Then my mother started to scream and the figure disappeared. They said it looked just like the picture of their grandmother. Both girls saw the figure.

Sarah Stewart

Ghost of the Bridge

In Bayview, Alabama, near Birmingham there is the story told of an old man murdered his wife late one night and threw the body in a lake near his home. The house, still standing, is only about a hundred feet from the lake. There is a bridge across the lake which is still in use. It has been reported that the man's wife has been seen walking across the bridge at midnight with her head in her hand. There also can be seen a light constantly burning under the bridge at night. As of now no one knows the source of the burning light.

Sandra Reynolds

Girl in a White Dress

One Halloween night a boy and girl were coming back from a party. As they drove by the Mobile docks, they saw a girl in white walking. They stopped and she asked them to take her to a certain address. When they got to the address, the girl had completely vanished. The boy and girl decided to go ahead and find who had been at the address. A woman came to the door and stated that she had been expecting them; that they had come to bring her daughter home. She explained that her daughter had been killed on Halloween night at the docks five years before and every Halloween night since then she tried to come back home.

Ella Kate Allen

Brother's Spirit

Late one year in August mama, sister, and me been over to Nancy's picking cotton. When we came out of the field Nancy asked us to stay and eat supper so we did. When we got ready to go home it was already dark. Way on down the road we saw a man coming toward us. Mama told us to get over on the other side of the road. When we got to the man he just disappeared before our eyes. Mama said that was our brother who had died from pneumonia.

Sue Peacock

Uncle Charlie

Long ago before a bridge was ever built across the Tallapoosa River a ferry boat ran back and forth across the river at Tallassee to carry employees who lived on the east side of the river to the old cotton mill on the west side of the river. For years and years an old colored man ran the ferry from dusk to dawn. The only way to communicate was to holler back and forth across the river to get this man, "Uncle Charlie," to carry them across the river. After he died it is said that one could hear him calling his master, Mr. John Wilson Patterson, who fought in the Civil War, at night, "Is that you over there Master John?"

Wilson Patterson

Floating Mary

During the operating days of the old mill on the west bank of the Tallapoosa River in Tallassee, a woman, Mrs. Mary Steward, was blown from the top floor of the mill as she stepped out the door during a cyclone. However, she mysteriously opened her umbrella and floated to the ground unharmed.

Wilson Patterson

Stone Creek Ghost

About a half mile behind the East Tallassee Baptist Church on the road to Oak Heights an old bridge crosses Stone Creek. Several years ago a man trying to avoid running over a child in the road crashed through the bridge and was instantly killed. It is said that if one drives to the bridge at midnight when there is a full moon he can cut off his lights and motor, roll down the windows and sound the horn 3 times, a ghost will come up on one side and go across the bridge. If you start the car and try to take off, the ghost will hold the car back and the car will just spin in the road until the ghost is across the bridge.

Todd Pierce

Switch Broom Ghost

An old lady was on the verge of death and two women were sitting up with her and dozed off to sleep to be awakened by the sound of an old switch broom sweeping the floor and something saying wake up, wake up, wake up three times. When the two women awoke, they found her dead.

Todd Pierce

Ghost Tree

About eight or nine miles outside Tallassee between Redland and Wetumpka is a wood frame house with a huge oak tree on the right side of the house. Several years ago a boy about 16 years old complained to his parents about hearing something in the tree and seeing something pass by his door at night. His parents thought he was just seeing and hearing things and did nothing about it. Later the boy fell from the tree while trying to get a cat down and was killed. After this his parents began seeing the ghost that he had talked about. It is said they tried to cut the tree down but it could not be cut down. They got several people to cut it down but no one could. The family then left and offered anyone the house free if they would live there.

Todd Pierce

Three Bridges

On the Meriweather Trail, a country road near Pine Level, Alabama, are three wooden bridges. The old story is told of what happens to a person who crosses these bridges at night during the dark of the moon. When you cross the first bridge you will hear chains rattling. When you cross the second bridge you will see a headless horseman playing a guitar, and when you cross the third bridge the headless man will jump on your car and go with you for about a half mile. If you are walking he will walk with you.

Kathryn Moore

Mushroom Toes

Every time my grandmother passed this old house on the Nota-sulga road she'd tell this story: The man who lived there was real mean to his wife and made her go barefoot all the time. She'd beg and beg for a pair of shoes but he wouldn't buy her any. Well, she took sick and died, and he buried her out in the yard, and he didn't buy any shoes to put on her feet. The next morning he came out there and there were ten mushrooms growing up just like toes where he'd buried her. He chopped them down. Next morning he went out in the yard and the mushrooms had grown back, ten, just like toes. He chopped them down again, but the next morning he went out to see and there they were, back again. He never could get rid of the mushroom toes, no matter what he tried. And if you'll go out there in that yard, you'll see ten mushrooms growing, just like toes.

Charles E. (Buddy) Moncrief

Little Audrey Nell

One day Audrey Nell got real sick with pneumonia. She died begging for some peas and coffee. They were afraid to give her these things because she had such high fever.

The next night her sister, who always slept with Audrey Nell, heard and felt the other side of the bed shaking. She called her mother and she came with a light but they couldn't see or hear anything.

When the mother got back to bed it started again. The mother told the sister it was only Audrey Nell trying to wake her up to get her some peas and coffee.

After awhile they heard a noise in the kitchen. They went in there and found a broken cup and plate on the floor. The mother assured the daughter that it was only Audrey Nell trying to get some peas and coffee.

Peggy Ham

Stiff Starched Dresses

This family lived in a five-room house where two girls had died with tuberculosis. The girls were bad to wear dresses that were starched real stiff. At night it seemed as if you could hear the girls walking through the house and could hear the dresses rattle.

L. P. Helms

Spirit of a Suicide

About thirty years ago an awful mean man shot himself in the house my grandfather lives in. The house is setting on a hill and just below the house is the cemetery he was buried in. After you pass the cemetery there is another house on a hill in which his mother and father lived. When he shot himself, he was leaning against a door leading into a hall. At night that door opens by itself and squeaks and people say it is the man's ghost returning. On a rainy night they say there is a light that comes out the chimney from the room he killed himself in and goes down into the cemetery to his grave and then up the other hill to the house where his mother lived. People believe the light has something to do with his death.

Dorothy Greathouse

Cat Haint

There was a nice house in the community but no one could live in it because it was haunted. No one knew what haunted the house. One day two Irishmen came through the community and wanted some place to spend the night. They were told of the house that was haunted and they said they would spend the night there. That night they spread their supper on the floor and a cat walked in. The cat walked up to the supper and laid its paw on some food and said, "This is my piece." One of the men took out his knife and cut the cat's paw. The cat left the room screaming like a woman. Then another cat came in and the same thing happened. When the men left the next morning, they told the people of the community that the house was haunted by the women who had once lived there.

Lurlean McCullough

Sweet Gum Bottom

There is a place west of my home that is known as Sweet Gum Bottom. There is dense woods on each side of the road. And the story goes, that a headless woman has been seen in this bottom a number of times.

The last report of her being seen was by a friend of ours, by the name of Ollie Frank McVay. He was going home from Andalusia one night a few years back, and night overtook him in this bottom. He said he looked back and this headless woman was holding to the back gate of his wagon. Trying to get in. He rushed his mule to a fast trot. She let go of his wagon and went into the woods.

Exa Jones

Angel on the Buggy

I can tell you something I seen one time. We had a single seated buggy and called it "run-a-bout."

Me and my sister was playing on it. I just laid down on the seat. While Buddy was gone to the house, I pure felt the sprangs of that buggy give when the angel stepped on the back of the buggy. He looked over the back of the buggy at us and smiled and was gone right then. I can remember and I'll never forget that.

Mrs. Maggie King

The Haunted Fountain Place

There was a place over in Walton County owned by a Mr. Fountain. Mr. Fountain was murdered unjustly, and afterwards ghosts began to appear. Some evenings about dusk a huge white object could be seen coming down the road. It would get near the house, then disappear. At night various noises could be heard, such as a very large stream of water pouring in a barrel, an awful lick on the house that would cause the dishes to rattle and could be felt, a noise like a man hitting his pants with a switch and stamping the ground at the same time. Also a man could be seen near dark some evenings without a head. A noise like someone tearing boards off the house could also be heard.

A brave man didn't believe there was ghosts. He went to spend the night with folks who lived there, but as soon as the noises started, he left, and wouldn't go back anymore.

Sidney Taylor

Flaming Lady

Just outside the city limits of Dothan there is a place where a man used to live who had a beautiful wife. She had been unfaithful to him, so he took her and chained her to the bridge. The chains can still be heard rattling when you drive a car over the bridge. After she died he burned her. If you drive up in the driveway you can see it still burning on a post. No one can go up to the burning head and put it out because he will shoot anyone who tries to come within range. So, anyone can see where he has his "Flaming Lady."

Judy Jones

Tippin's Eddy

Near Brewton is a creek named Tippin's Eddy. Folks say that a girl once was lost in the woods around the creek and believed to have drowned in the creek. When her body was found it was mauled and covered with moss. To this day on some nights a green light can be seen moving around in the woods. Some believe it is the girl coming back. Some have even heard footsteps on the bridge. Some have even tried to shoot the light out but the light is still there.

Mary L. Parker

Wash Pot Ghost

This old woman said that before her little girl died she had a vision the night before telling her about it. Afterwards the little girl died— (she burned to death at an old wash pot while the woman was washing). She said that after the death at a certain time every night chains would rattle out at the wash pot.

Mrs. Mary Coleman

Rising Spirit

Mrs. Bessie Watts said her father told her he was sitting up with a friend who had died. He went into the kitchen for coffee and looked into the room where the body was and the sheet lifted off the body. There was no breeze or other cause for the sheet lifting.

Mrs. Bessie Watts

Halloween Ghost Tale

It all happened many years ago, but even to this day it is not a dream; it was a nightmare. Teenage boys usually run in groups, or gangs, and ours was no exception. It was customary to gather from time to time at one of the gang's homes and the activities were varied. On this particular night we had gathered at one of the boy's homes and, since it was Halloween, we engaged in the ever spine-tingling activity of telling ghost tales. There was a very old, near toothless, granny who led this particular session and by the time she had finished we—all of us that had to go any distance home—dreaded those moments ahead.

I had about a mile to go down through a swamp to a branch and up a gentle incline to my own home. The first part of the journey was pleasant enough, but when I arrived at the edge of the swamp I began to feel queer sensations up the back of my neck and into my hair. I was comforted somewhat, shortly, when I saw a light coming toward me bobbing as a lantern does when someone carries it when he walks. But when I came up even with the light and was about to speak, to my utter amazement there was no one to speak to! The light was an errie green color—something of a supernatural glow. I shall never forget that I froze with fright and yet somehow I did not run. The bobbing light continued on its merry way and I continued on mine—with frequent glances over the shoulder. I had been scared before and have been scared since but have never felt that paralyzing effect of a lantern at night moving along without a sign or a carrier. And to this day I don't really know what it was I saw. Perhaps it was a pocket of marsh gas, maybe not.

E. C. Nevin

General Jackson's Ghost

Student Collector's Note: An elderly Negro and his wife live in a little cottage beside the Coosa River which flows right by Fort Toulouse where Andrew Jackson defeated the Creek Indians in August, 1824. The fellow swears that Jackson's ghost returns to the fort on a certain night in August.

Some folks say General Jackson's dead and buried, but I knows better. General Jackson's ghost still rides about on a lonesome night in August. Some folks say it's on the night he defeated them 'air Creek Injuns here long about 1824. I don't know myself. I don't know 'dat much history. But I do know that a certain night in August I sees a ghost on a white horse come rushing in from down about the river-bank.

He ain't never spoke to me, and I sure ain't never spoke to him. My dog always begins to moan and carry on, and then I commences to hear the sound of horse hoofs pounding. It used to scare me something terrible, but I'm sort of 'customed to it now.

I don't know but I've heard it told that the only way to stop this ghost is to put a silver bullet on old Jackson's grave. Trouble is, nobody that knows of the ghost knows where the grave is and them that know where the grave is don't know that the body and the ghost ain't both in it.

Appears to me that I can count on seein' de Gen'l around fer several years to come. Now that I'm used to it, I sort of looks forward to seeing him. It's like homecoming.

Sonja Taylor

Haunted Road

One time there was a woman and a girl burning trash and the little girl caught on fire and the mother tried to put her out. Both of their clothes were burned off. The man that lived near them rode his horse up the road in a gallop to get the doctor. They both died.

You can be walking up that road on a dark drizzling night now and you can hear the horse's feet galloping up the road behind you, if you stop and step aside the road and let it get by, it will hush.

Mrs. M. M. Chestnutt

The Weeping Woman

A long time ago there was a woman who had two children. She did not love them; so she mistreated and neglected them. The children were always hungry and thirsty even cold because their mother was too busy going to parties and dances to take care of them.

Finally one of the children died and later the other died too. The woman felt no remorse. She continued to lead a very gay life. When she died, she had not confessed her sins or repented her ill-treatment of the children. Now she appears in the east and southeast grieving for her children. Her soul is doing penance for her sins.

Mrs. Tommie Gorrie

Falling Ashes and a Voice

A new family had just moved into a house where the mother of the family living there previously had just died. At night and sometimes in the daylight hours, ashes would fall from the ceiling and they could see the form of a woman.

The man living in the house was told to ask her this: "What in the Name of the Lord do you want?" and he did this. She told him to see that her children were cared for, and with that she left. It is true that after he asked her what in the name of the Lord did she want, she never came again.

Mrs. Lee Stanford

Baby Ghost

One night Mrs. Lee's father was coming home from town, when he got to the graveyard a little baby crawled across the road. He stopped the wagon and looked all over the woods and the cemetery but he couldn't find the baby.

Mrs. Biddie Lee

A Lad of Seven

I was a lad of seven when I experienced something that has lived with me through the years.

I dressed for bed one night about 8 o'clock and went up the hall to the front of the house to my bedroom.

When I got in the bed I looked out in the hall; I saw a ghostly figure. I screamed and ran to my mother.

I had never seen the man that had died in this room several years ago. When I described the man to my mother she told me this man's name.

James J. Kilpatrick

Ghostly Duel

Near Luverne at the Otton Place people said that you could see two men fighting. One had a head, but the other did not have a head. When people passed by the house they reported a sound like that of wood falling from the top of the house. My source said that she lived in the house for a year and that someone would knock on the door all the time but when you went to the door no one was there.

Mrs. Minnie Leverette

Clothes Wire Ghost

One day a man was taking the clothes wire down from his sister-in-law's yard. The woman's husband had been dead for about three days when this happened, nothing strange had taken place up until then. As the man was in the process of getting the wire down, helping the woman get ready to move, a voice was heard. The man was told to leave the clothes line, not to take it. With this the man stopped.

The man always believed this was the spirit of the dead brother-in-law. Later he did go back and get the line.

Mrs. Gus Cheatham

Women In White

Years ago two brothers were coming in late one night from a date. Both went horseback. There was a cemetery about a half mile from their house, and one brother just happened to get there before the other. His horse began to tramp around and around and wouldn't obey. Then he saw two ladies dressed in white parading back and forth across the road. They were beautiful women at that. Their robes swept the ground as they danced.

Soon the other brother rode up, and they both witnessed the scene.

Mrs. J. T. Langford

Ghost of the Pretty Girl

When John B. Smith was young they once moved to an old log house with an old wagon wheel hanging on a nail on the front porch. After they went to bed at night which was about 8:30 they could hear the front yard gate squeak and then someone would come up on the porch and rattle and beat on the old wagon wheel. Then into the front room would come a pretty girl with long black hair that looked just like John B. Smith's dead sister. Then she would go into the back room where John slept and pull all of the cover off him, wrap it around her and then go back into the front room. There she would laugh and dance for about five minutes. Then she would disappear and the cover would fall to the floor.

John B. Smith

The Tramp's Good Fortune

Once a farmer died leaving his house to his sons, but the house was haunted and when they tried to spend the night at the house they would hear voices. One day a tramp came by and wanted a place to sleep, so one of the sons said that if he could spend the night in the haunted house he could have it. So the tramp went to the house, but when he started to bed he heard voices. He asked the voices what in the name of the Lord did they want and the voices told him that the old farmer had hidden his money in the fourth brick up the chimney. So the tramp got the house and the sons got the money.

M. S. Formby

Ghost Car and Driver

My mother says that there is a story of a man on a car that appears and disappears on a lonely stretch of road around Purdue Hill. Last December my mother and father were driving to my grandmother's. As they started across a small bridge, they saw this man sitting on the railing and a few yards farther his car. As they came even with the place, the man and his car were gone.

They told my grandmother about it and she said that a number of people have seen the man and car. She said it was the ghost of a man who had killed himself in a car wreck on the bridge. They swear this is the truth.

Curtis Guy

Old Tom and the Devil

Tom thought he would have to go into the valley-like place in order to get religion. It was here that he had to pray. One day while he was there, he placed his hat on a log and began to pray. Old Tom had been told that when he prayed he would encounter the devil in the form of a dog with a chain on him. As he prayed he saw a dog coming toward him with a chain on. Tom said he knowed it was the devil so he got him a stick and hit the dog and he fled. Never again was he bothered by the devil after this.

Hattie Jordan

Tombstone Devil's Head

A little above Clio on the Louisville highway is located the Pea River Baptist Church. A woman was buried in the cemetery there. She was extremely mean and of unusually low morals. She met an unnatural death, though no one seems to know exactly what the circumstances were. Some time after her death an image of the devil appeared on her tombstone. The mysterious appearance of this image was apparently the work of some supernatural force.

One man, about sixty years of age, who was born and raised in Clio but now lives in Ariton, told me he has heard this story all his life. He has actually seen this, and describes it as the image of the devil's head which can be seen because it has turned darker than the rest of the stone.

George May

A Fair, Pretty Night

A fair, pretty night Mr. and Mrs. Buck Eldridge were riding home in their buggy, returning home from a revival held each year the second week in July at the Mt. Enon Baptist Church. Since they had to go about ten miles it was 9:30 at night when they reached the bend of the road just before you get to their home. Just as they reached the bend a huge black something came out in front of the horses. The horses stopped and immediately became so frightened they tried to turn around in the road, but since the road was so narrow they couldn't, they started running as fast as they could forward. The black animal seemed to rise and go over the trees. It wasn't a dog or skunk or any animal as large as a horse and yet it had four legs. This animal was never seen again.

Ollie Johnson

Bear Ghost

A man was going through the woods on a wagon when a bear, a huge black one, got on with him. When he got home he heard that the old man in the nearby house had just died. The man believed that the bear was really the dead man who had ridden with him.

Anyway, the man driving the wagon was nearly dead when he got home. His horses, too, acted wild. It took some time for the man to recover from shock.

Mrs. Gus Cheatham

My Home

The house my mother and I live in is old. Throughout time there has been many deaths as well as corpses in my home. One night after Mama and I had gone to bed, the lights were all out, there was a ray of light as bright as sunlight that shone through the window.

This light did not light up the entire room, nor did the light face into the darkness; but it was bright as day where it shone. It just happened to be on Mother's entire face and shone on my pillow and a small part of my face. We both got up and there was a ball of light about two hundred yards away in the barn yard. It was about the same size as the sun, as it appears to us. That night we went to sleep with that ray of light shining on us with the darkness as black as pitch.

That incident happened twice. The second time it was seen from the next bedroom from approximately the same location but from a different angle. It's hard to believe, and I am slow to believe on the grounds of one person. Mother and I both were witnesses to this happening. We have no idea what it was.

As I've already stated, my house is old and has ten large rooms. I think about the people who lived there who are now dead as my grandparents, aunts, and Father. One night Mother and I, after having gone to bed, saw two green lights shining in the fireplace. Mother said they were probably marbles which my nephews had let roll onto the hearth and into the fireplace.

J. C.

Spirit of a Crazy Woman

My mother has told me several times of a haunted house that her family lived in. As I remembered it there were two girls and two boys and my grandmother, the remainder of the eight children were already married and had homes of their own and my grandfather was dead. I have been shown the house several times and it appears quite neat and ordinary. The story was told something like this:

When we moved to Montgomery for a while we lived in Highland Gardens. We had not lived here too long before we began to notice strange things. At night we could hear footsteps, but when the boys went to see who it was, there was no one there. Sometimes when I would go into bed the cover would be turned down and the pillows fluffed. When we checked on this no one knew who did it. We could all be in another room or we could hear noises, but none of us could have done it because we were all together.

We decided to move and then we found out that a crazy woman had owned that house before us. She swore she would come back and haunt it before she committed suicide.

Dutchie Sellers

Patsalega Booger

Many years ago there was some type of animal, everybody thought it was an animal, in the swamp of the Patsalega that killed the people's hogs, cows, and other animals.

Every once in a while, they could hear this thing hollering. Crowds of men would take guns and dogs in the swamp to kill the thing. Well, every time the dogs would come out hollering with their tails tucked under. They would run a while, then turn back to their masters. It either died or left, folks never knew.

Laura Turner

The Story of Panther Creek

One day a woman had gone on horseback for a visit to the neighbor's house. On her way home at sundown, she heard a sound which she thought was her uneasy husband calling for her. She rushed to the spot from which the sounds originated. The sounds were made by a giant death's head.

Today when you pass Panther Creek, it is said that you can hear the voice-like sound of the panther and the screams of the lady on horseback.

Mrs. Phil Williams

The Girl and the Yellow Ribbon

There is a story of a little girl named Mary and a little boy named Bill. Mary and Bill were friends all their lives. They played together before they started to school, and there was one thing about Mary that Bill was curious about. She always wore a yellow ribbon around her neck. Bill asked Mary why she wore this ribbon, she told him she would tell him later on. So when they finished the first grade, Bill asked Mary if she would tell him then. She told him to wait about five more years and she would tell him. Bill continued to be interested in why she wore the yellow ribbon and after five years he asked her again why she wore the yellow ribbon around her neck. She told him to wait until they finished school and she would tell him because it wasn't really too important. Bill and Mary started going steady during their high school years and after they graduated Bill asked her again why she wore the yellow ribbon around her neck. She told him she would tell him on their wedding night, but on their wedding night she again put off telling him. So on their fifteenth wedding anniversary he asked her again. She told him it was really nothing and she would tell him later.

Bill continued to wonder about the yellow ribbon and when Mary was on her deathbed, he asked her to please tell him about it before she died. She told him that it really wasn't important but she would show him why. She slowly untied the ribbon and took it off, when she did her head fell off.

Maybelle Schlich

The Samson Homestead

I lived in a haunted house. My grandfather bought the farm and renamed it "Buzzard Roost." The known happenings and those told to me by my parents are here related.

It seems that "Old Pop" (the spook) would turn up in the most unusual places and at the most embarrassing times. I have been trying to go to sleep when it would pop right under my pillow. The sound was like that of a closed bucket and lid expanding and popping. Any closed container made of metal pops with the changing temperature. Removing all lids from containers did not alter this popping since we did this, so we learned to live with the racket which became known as "Old Pop." It sounded off every thirty minutes day and night by the clock and could be heard all over the house. It moved into the smokehouse, barn, garden, and elsewhere.

One day Dad and a neighbor man were squatting beside the smokehouse wall talking. Old Pop sounded off behind the man. He jumped, surprised, and exclaimed, "What was that?" Dad replied, "Old Pop," so an explanation had to be made. The man vowed he would not be caught there after dark and soon left, still disturbed.

Old Pop used to keep Grandfather company while he tried to sleep at night. He would pop at the foot of his bed, under his pillow, over at the dresser, and so on during the night. Grandfather never became alarmed as he was a religious man. He also believed in the supernatural too. He witched for water, used a dip-needle for finding precious metals, and tried to find oil.

One day my grandfather, Dad, and three neighbors hitched up the team to the wagon, loaded in shovels and picks, and set out to dig up a buried treasure with the aid of a newly acquired dip-needle. They were gone all day and into the night. My mother, sister, and I heard the wagon coming far off and went out on the front porch carrying the kerosene lamp to welcome them home. As they approached the front gate a strange thing happened. From the big spring out in the pasture came a grinding, rumbling racket. Then the sound of running horses and the grunting of straining animals was loud. Hundreds of hooves were pounding around the spring. Strange, for there were no horses or cattle in that pasture. Scared? You bet I was and so were all of us, Dad and Grandfather included. The sounds ended and we went on to bed. The next day no tracks of animals could be found around the spring. A small oil slick which was on the large spring possibly explains the noises.

Old Pop got to be a nuisance. He embarrassed us before company and ran people away. Grandfather went to live in Little Rock, Arkansas, and Dad moved near El Passo, Arkansas, to a new farm after the mortgage fell due and we could not pay it. A new farmer moved in with Old Pop. A few weeks later, the man met my dad in El Passo and asked what that popping racket was out at the farm. Dad explained and the man's hair stood up on the back of his neck. He moved out immediately and no one has lived there since. The house fell to decay, and the land grew up in bushes and then into trees. One crop of saw-logs has been cut from the land and another is ready for cutting since that time.

Once Grandfather attempted to describe Old Pop to me. He said he would come up and knock the tubs off the washbench and knock down the rubboard; so he saw him twice. His body was like that of an alligator, his head and claws like that of a panther, and his speed was like lightning. Grandfather was not afraid of Old Pop, since he was his friend. I shook, but he said he would not hurt me either as I belonged to him (Granddad).

Three miles up the valley was another haunted house. It has an iron fence around the yard. The story goes that a beggar came through the yard gate and asked for food at the back door. The wealthy wife turned him away empty-handed. He walked out, closed the gate behind him, and died of starvation out by the barn. Now, each year at this time footsteps can be heard coming up the path, the iron gate unlatches and swings open, and the steps stop at that back door. Later, retreating steps can be heard, the gate closes and latches, and the steps end where the man died. This house, too, remains empty.

John G. Parks

The Uncles and the Headless Woman

My grandaddy's old home is about 200 yards east of my home, and it has always been known to be haunted.

During my grandaddy's and grandmother's lifetime, there were several noises to be heard, such as large barrels filled with trace chains, tin pans, and old plows. Rolling under the ground, the noise would start from a building out front across the road known as the buggy house and it would continue toward the back of the house, until it went out of hearing.

Sometimes at night you could see an object the shape and size of an old round bread sifter go dancing through the yard. It was bright and glittering like the stars.

One time a headless woman went through a window in a small bedroom on the front porch of this same old house where two of my uncles were sleeping. They said she pulled their toes, and stroked their foreheads, then tucked the covers around them, and disappeared through the same window she came in. It was a window with a wooden shutter. The uncles are John and Willie Harrelson. This happened when they were small boys, and they are in their seventies now. They centered this is as true as the sun rising in the east each morning.

Exa Jones

Ghost in the House

When I was a little girl my grandmother used to tell me the story about a haunted house that she used to live in. When grandmother was about twenty she lived in a house that no other family would live in: it was haunted by unseen people or ghosts.

Grandmother said that at night she could hear someone walking around the house, then they would tap on every window that they passed. Great-grandmother would go outside and look around, only to find a dark empty night.

After several nights of this, they would hear someone in their attic walking around and it sounded like—turning over barrels of water. Her daddy would go into the attic and take the whole family along with him. There would be one or two barrels of water turned over and no one upstairs. Grandmother told me why they kept water in the attic but I don't remember.

While they were in the attic they would hear a horrible sound downstairs. So the whole family would dash down the stairs and find no one there, except all of their clothes hanging in the closets had fallen down.

They decided to move and burn the house down. Well, they moved, but it took them a long time to burn that house down.

Mrs. B. M. Jarvis

The Witch of Fairfield

There was a woman that lived in Fairfield community that was believed to have been a witch. She would put an ad in the paper wanting people to work for her. Men would come to work for her and when they would get tired of working for her they would tell her they couldn't work any more. She would tell them that was all right, just to have one last drink with her. This drink had magic power in it, so that everyone who drank it turned into a beautiful pig. She soon filled her pig pen with beautiful pigs. And one day she decided she better take them to market, and as each pig was sold she would call the name of the man and say how she hated to see John or Jack or Jim go.

Peggy Ham

The Cat's Paw

Everyone knew old Mrs. Kirland of Route One, Midland City, because she lived by herself during the 1800's. She liked to sew and kept her sewing machine by the window. There were no screens on the window. There were no people who had screens on their doors. Mrs. Kirland had a shutter type window of wood which she would open at night in the summer time and get the cool breeze if there was any stirring. She sould set her lamp on a table so the breeze would not blow it out but she could see to sew.

Now every night a black cat would come to the open window and meow and annoy Mrs. Kirkland as he stood with paws in window as she tried to sew. She, being a widow, asked some friends to come over one night and see if they could do anything about the cat that annoyed her by staring at her through the open window with his paws on the window sill. So, Mr. and Mrs. Samuel Beverett came over. Mr. Beverett was ready for the cat when the cat appeared and put his paws on the sill. Mr. Beverett had an ax ready to kill the cat but when he went to kill the cat the only thing he hit was the cat's paws which fell off inside the window. Mr. Beverett picked up the bloody paws and apologized to Mrs. Kirkland for not being able to kill the cat.

Exactly a week after Mr. Beverett tried to kill the cat at the exact time, his hands were cut off mysteriously as if by a witch. He didn't even have to see a doctor. They just seemed to begin shrinking and were gone.

There is no explanation except folk say that a witch did both cuttings and you can't fight the power of witches.

Mrs. Espie Eldridge

Man Witch

Man was spending the night at a haunted house. Nobody would stay in it and after supper he was reading his newspaper and a cat walked in and said, "There is two of us here tonight." He reached in his pocket and got his knife and cut off his right fore foot and the cat left.

Next morning he heard of a man in the neighborhood being sick. He went to see him and he wanted to shake hands with him. This man handed him his left hand and he asked for the right hand. The man told him he had it in his pocket and he was the witch.

Mrs. Maggie King

Burned at the Stake

Years ago there was a woman, she was poor, but liked by mostly everybody until she became so poor that she had to move from town, into an old two-story house in a clearing deep in the woods.

Her hair was long, and with having to work very hard, she soon began to look like a "witch." Nobody went to see her anymore.

There were people who didn't like her. There was one person in particular who did not like her. But of course these people were superstitious and began to spread rumors of her being a witch. Soon almost everybody in town thought of her as "the witch."

One night the person who started these rumors about the witch went to her house and brought her to the town square. There they tied her to a stake, built a fire around her and there she burned.

It is said that the person who had her burned was walking down the street where the witch was burned and he heard a voice, a soft voice like that of a woman's. He looked around but didn't see anybody. Then he heard screams, just like the night before when he had the witch burned, she was screaming and she died. The next morning the man was found dead in the same place where the witch was burned. He had a cross in his hand.

Witch Riders

There was an old oak tree with low hanging limbs. Around this tree a path was beat out like one that was beat out around an old syrup mill. This trail was directly under these low hanging limbs. At night time someone with a horse would ride around this trail with each hoof in the same track each time. The limbs or leaves were never broken and no trail or tracks leading to or from this tree. It was thought in olden days that witches rode this horse. People would go and take turns watching, trying to see who was riding the horse, but no one ever found out. As soon as the people would leave whoever was riding would ride again.

This tree and place was near Mrs. Adeline Campbell's home in Chilton County. She is living today to tell it.

Adeline Campbell

Ghost Wind

One night this man and his sons went to town. The moon had come up and was shining pretty when they started home. It was a pretty spring night. All of a sudden the wind began to blow around a tree. It looked as if it would blow the tree over. That was the only place the wind was blowing.

L. P. Helms

Enchanted Trees

There was a man who had the power to put a spell on trees. He had several children and every time one was born, he would plant a fruit tree. Because of this spell he put on the fruit trees, every time one of the children would die the tree planted for that child would die too. He had one son who had gone to join the services. A few months later, the tree planted for the son began to die so they knew their son was dead. Sure enough, two days later they received word that he had been killed.

Mary Glenn Merritt

Magic Ball of Cloth

Mrs. Nellie Burks was living with her second husband when her daughter Nell and Mr. Ace Henly had planned to get married. Mrs. Burks would not give Nell up. Ace Henly bewitched her by putting a spell upon her. She became so weak she could not walk. One day her husband helped Miss Nellie to the front porch to sit in a chair and watch him move the door steps and put new ones up. When he moved the bottom step, he found a ball of cloth with something in it. He put it into the fire and burned it. The spell was broken and Miss Nellie gained 20 pounds in four weeks.

Mrs. Nellie Burks

The Old Maids' Spell

Once upon a time there were two old maids who were thought to be witches. People were afraid of them because the women could put curses on anyone they chose. One day the old maids became mad at a woman who lived near them. They put a spell on the woman and she broke out in big bumps. The bumps burst and something like sweet gum balls came out of them.

E. Z. White

The Bewitched Hunter

Once a man was out hunting squirrels. He had killed two when he walked up on an old woman washing clothes at a water hole. She asked him for one of the squirrels but he wouldn't give her a squirrel. He promised to kill her another one and bring it to her but she told him that he would never be able to kill another squirrel.

The man walked away into the woods and squirrel after squirrel he shot at but not one could he hit. Days and even weeks went by and he wasn't able to hit a single thing he shot at. He was worried. A friend told him that if he would carve an outline of a woman on a green tree and drive a twenty-penny spoke into her heart and for nine days drive the nail a little deeper each day that on the ninth day the witch that had put the spell on him would be dead and the spell broken. He followed his friend's advice and on the ninth day when he had hammered the nail into the tree it seemed as if a great burden he had been carrying drifted off his shoulders. After that he could shoot and hit his targets as good as he ever could.

J. D. Fowler

Mr. Adams Recollects on Spirits

"We was walking home one day when I seen something walking across the front yard of our house. We was about 300 foot from the house and I said to her, 'Do you see that woman?' she said, 'Yeah, I see 'er.' We watched the woman and she walked across our front yard and set down on the fur corner of the doorstep and then she was gone. She just disappeared. I knew who she wuz to start with but I told her it was a woman but she seen it too. 'What was it?' I asked. 'It was that woman's spirit, that's what it was.'

"There was a old widder woman who lived there afore we did and she said she had seen rabbits run across the yard and she'd try to hit 'em with a broom but she couldn't hit 'em. They'd be right there in front of her but she couldn't hit 'em with that broom. They'd be her spirit in shape of a rabbit.

"I've had people look me right in the face and tell me they didn't believe it, but I know better. They wuz some preachers at the house one day and I asked them about it. They said it was my imagination and I said, 'What if we both seen it at the same time?' 'Well that's different,' they said. I don't know about that. Even if she hadn't seen it, I knew twern't my imagination, my eyes don't lie to me."

His wife verified the story while he went on—"Didn't you know

your spirit could take the shape of a dog, or cat, or horse, or anything
it wants to?" I answered no. "Well it sure can."

His wife said hers sure was not. She didn't believe in any superstitions but she sure seen that woman's spirit.

He went on—"One day my brothers was walking in front of them.
He told the others 'Look at that woman, there's a woman boys, see
'er' but they couldn't see 'er. Well, they walked up the road to where
they was an old woman's house and that old woman had died a few
minutes before. It was that woman's spirit coming to meet them. My
brother told this fer the truth and he wouldn't lie about nothing. He
also said the other brothers never seen the woman."

Mr. Adams then told about his father, while opossum hunting one
night with friends, came upon three graves out in the woods: "There
was three of the skinniest hound dogs ever seen on them graves. One
on each grave. One feller was gonna run 'em off but they didn't pay no
attention to them, they just set there. They wasn't dogs at all, they
wuz them dead peoples' spirits," related Mr. Adams.

Roy Adams

Silver Bullet

There was a girl very much in love with a boy that was her neighbor but he didn't care anything about her. She kept running after him
but he would not pay any attention to her. Finally, everywhere the
boy would go a little white rabbit would appear. The boy hunted a lot
and the rabbit would always follow him. One day he went hunting
and prepared a silver bullet to shoot the white rabbit because witches
could not be killed with anything but silver. When the rabbit

appeared, he shot it in its shoulder and it limped off. The next day he
went over to the girl's house and asked how the family was getting
along. The father said everyone was fine except the daughter. While
she was out gathering wood, on the day before, she broke her
shoulder.

Lurlean McCullough

Buried Money

The old Powell homestead in the Harmony Community north of
Troy, Alabama, has been haunted for years. Restless spirits can be
seen most any night about the premises. The Powell family buried
their money before banks were common, and they had plenty of it.
The ghosts came with the death of Mr. Powell. His family knew that
not nearly all of the money was found. Mrs. Howard told me that
when I go out there and the ghost appears, for me to fall on my knees,
look up to the Lord, and say, "Jesus command these spirits to be
still," and then the ghost will tell me what it wants of me. Usually it
tells where buried wealth is hidden. When the wealth is recovered,
the ghost will no longer stay at the house.

When the Montgomery Highway was being plowed through the
Powell farm, Mrs. Mattie Powell seated herself in a chair under a
shade tree and watched for buried containers possibly filled with
money. Sure enough, they turned up a jar filled to the top. The road
crew turned it over to the old lady who waited many days for a
possible find. She was badly stove-up with rhematism and could
hardly walk. She said that she knew they never found all of her
husband's money. Much more is rumored to be buried there still.

Mrs. J. C. Howard

Money Needle

Mr. Riley said a man came to him one Sunday morning and wanted
him to go hunt money. The man had a money needle that he said
would not fail. Mr. Riley and the man went to a place and the needle
began to work. It led them for a distance, stopped at an old house
place way back in the country. The man left Mr. Riley until he could
go get something to work with. After he left, a woman, nicely dressed,
came out of the corn patch, crawled over a rail fence and knocked off
one of the rails and disappeared into a deep swamp. When the man
returned, Mr. Riley told him of the strange woman and said, "You
can dig if you want to, but I'm going home."

Jim Shields

Never Contrary a Ghost

One time a friend told George Faulk that there was money buried near a certain grave at Beulah cemetery. He went there with a money needle and found the spot. He dug a spot full of money and a woman appeared and said that's my money, but you can have it if you will give my sister ten dollars of it. He took the money home, and the next morning the money was gone. He went back to the spot and it didn't look like the dirt had ever been bothered. So he dug again and found the pot of money in the same place. The woman appeared again and said he could have it if he could give her sister ten dollars. Mr. Faulk did this and he got to keep the money that time.

Jimmie Sue Phillips

Missing Money Pot

Money had been dug up on Guy Jones' land near Oak Grove about 30 years ago. There was a light that would rise up about as high as the head and travel around, sometimes under people's feet, and then disappear. Also a headless woman would appear in the same vicinity, then disappear.

Later, a treasure hunter dug a hole in an old cotton house, which was floorless, about five feet deep. There was a mulberry tree there too and he cut a big root from it. A print of a round bottomed money pot was left there in the bottom of the hole, and that's all, except some loose change in the dirt around the hole. No one has even known who dug up the money.

Jim Shields

The Old Cowart Place

As the legend goes, there is a certain house on the Luverne Highway, called the Old Cowart Place, which is supposedly "hainted." Many years ago, says Griffin Donalson, a Negro family lived there. "They was supposed to have throwed some money in the well out back of the place 'cause they didn't trust the banks. One night I spent the night with my uncle Shelton Griffin and I seen some lights shining from a distant and when I got up to go see, they disappeared. One night me and a gang of boys was goin' up to the place to look for the money. And from a distant we could see the light shine. We got us a fork-ed stick and put a silver dollar between the fork-ed and we tried to find the money, but never did. They say when you do this you can find money that's buried. My step-grandmother said when she lived there you could hear footsteps. My uncle Shelton said you could see the lights in the house sometimes from a distant and it'd shine clear through the windows and you would see the wood part through 'em for a mile down the road, and you know that's a pretty for piece to see a light. There's no way to explain 'em cause they disappear when you git there. And that's about all there is to it except it sure scared me."

Griffin Donalson

Raw Head and Bloody Bones

Once a little girl left her lunch pail at school after her mother had told her over and over again to bring it home. Late that evening her mother told her to go get her lunch pail or she would not fix her a lunch to carry to school the next day.

The little girl was afraid because several people had heard the screams of little boys as "Old Raw Head and Bloody Bones" carried them away through the dark woods. It was getting darker but the little girl's steps got slower and slower. Finally she was coming out of the door when she heard a bloodcurdling scream. She quickly looked up and there on the roof was old Raw Head and Bloody Bones eating a little boy for his supper. The little girl was too frightened to run. She just stood there and looked. Old Raw Head spied her.

"Little girl, just as shore as you tell what you seen this evening I'll come and eat you. I don't like little girls much but if you even think of telling I'll git you fer shore."

"Oh, please don't eat me. I'll never say a word." The little girl seemed to fly home.

That night she wanted to tell her mother so badly but she was so afraid of what Old Raw Head had said. She could just see his raw head with those terrible bloodshot eyes and the blood oozing out of his bones. She couldn't sleep and around midnight she heard a voice way off.

"I'm coming to git you! I'm coming up the road! I'm coming through the gate! I'm coming in the yard! I'm on the first step! I'm on the second step! I'm on the porch! I'm in the front room! I'm in the bedroom! I'm by your bed! I GOT YOU!!!"

Jerry Terry

The Big Toe

One time this little boy, he was 6 or 8 years old or so, was out in the garden with his Mama and Papa and they was hoeing out weeds. The

Mama she picked her apron full of young turnips and directly she went on in the house to put them on for supper, and the boy and his Papa went on hoeing. By and by the greens got to cooking, and they commenced to smelling them. The Papa said, "I sure wisht we had some meat to go in them greens." They'd done eat up all the sidemeat, you see. And that little boy he was getting hungrier and hungrier. And he said he wisht they had some meat to cook in them greens too. They kept on hoeing, but the little boy got slower and slower, he was just going on in his mind about how good some meat in the greens would be. Directly something run past him, left a crack in the dirt like a mole will, and he heard it, but he didn't see nothing but that crack, and he kept hoeing and he come down on something. He bent over to see what it was struck his hoe and he scrabbled around and seen it was a big toe. He never said a word, just put that big toe in his pocket and went on hoeing. After awhile the Papa said, "Let's us go on to the house, it's near about suppertime"; so they did. The Papa he drawed some water and washed up in the basin and the little boy he did too, and when his Papa wasn't looking he reached down in his pocket and took out that toe and washed off the grit. So the little boy he went on in the kitchen and come over to the stove and smelled the greens. His Mama was putting down bread and she wasn't no ways looking at him, so he lifted the lid off the pot and slipped in that big toe. Then he went on out in the yard and started chopping stove wood. He was so hungry he thought he'd die and that toe got to smelling so good he couldn't stand it. But finally his Mama come to the back porch and called supper. Well, they all set down and eat up the pot of greens with some bread and milk. Now the Mama knowed she hadn't put no meat in them greens and Papa knowed it wasn't no sidemeat at all left, but neither one of them never said a word about it. And the little boy he never said a word neither. After supper the Mama washed up the dishes and the little boy and his Papa went on out on the front porch. And the Mama she come on out there after awhile. They was all full of greens and wore out and sleepy, and the Papa he said, "I'm going on to bed and lay down"; and in a few minutes the Mama said she was going and lay down, but the little boy he said he was going sit on the porch awhile longer. So she went on and left him out there. Directly the little boy heard something way off down the road and he run hopped in the bed and pulled the cover over his head. But it kept coming, closer and closer, and he commenced to make out what it was saying:

Where's my big toe? Where's my big toe?

I want my big toe. I want my big toe.

It come on and come on till it sounded like it was just even with the house.

Where's my big toe? Where's my big toe?

I want my big toe. I want my big toe.

It come on up the steps and went crost the porch and through the front door and down the hall:

Where's my big toe? Where's my big toe?

I want my big toe. I want my big toe.

That little boy was so scared he stuck the pillow over his head. And it come on in the room and come on to the foot of the bed:

Where's my big toe? Where's my big toe?

I want my big toe. I want my big toe.

I got it!

(Grabs your big toe.)

Olivia Solomon
(as recollected from the many
tellings of Olive Louise DuPriest
Pienezza)

Who's Got My Liver?

One time a woman sent her little boy to the store to get some liver for supper. She gave him just enough money to buy the liver, but when he got to the store he saw bubble gum of a new kind and he wanted some so bad he could taste it. His mother had told him not to come home without the liver so he didn't know what to do. Finally he decided to get the bubble gum and worry about the liver later. On the way home he got worried about not doing as his mother told him, so he stopped at a graveyard and dug up a body and cut out the liver and wrapped it in a piece of paper he found and took it home to his mother. She cooked it for supper and all the family said it was such good liver.

That night when he went to bed he heard a voice in the distance calling "Who's got my liver?"—"Who's got my liver?" It got closer and closer until it was at the foot of his bed. Just when he thought it had gone he heard the voice at the head of his bed say "It's you!"

Bonnie Dean

The Old Woman and Her Bone

There was an old woman who was very poor. She lived alone out in the country. She ate wild vegetables and took bones which she got from the country store and boiled it to make soup. It was a long way to the store and it took her a long time to go after it and get back. She usually was late in the afternoon getting home, not long before dark came.

One afternoon as she got home, she just put the bone in the safe so she could make her soup the next morning because she was tired. She lay down across the bed to rest for awhile and she fell asleep. As she was laying there sleeping she heard a voice say to her, "Give me my bone." This voice seemed to be getting closer and closer, so she crawls under the sheet. Soon the voice was right at her bed and she was scared to death, so she eased the sheet back a little way and said, "Take it." The next morning the bone was gone and she was never bothered again.

Martha Metcalf

The Golden Arm

Once upon a time there lived an old man and woman. The woman had a golden arm and when she died, the old man took the golden arm and exchanged it for money. This infuriated the old woman and she came back to haunt her husband. At night when the old man was sleeping she would come and say:

> I'm on the first step, I want my golden arm.
> I'm on the second step, I want my golden arm.
> I'm on the porch, I want my golden arm.
> I'm at the door, I want my golden arm.
> I'm in the living room, I want my golden arm.
> I'm in the hall, I want my golden arm.
> I'm in your bedroom, I want my golden arm.
> I'm at your bed, I want my golden arm.

At this point the teller jumps at the listener and say, "I got you!"
[The name of the informant has, unfortunately, been lost.]

The Boy and the Knife

Once there was a boy and his mother who lived on a hill. His mother went to town one day. She brought home the boy a real knife. She told the boy not to go near the well but he did. As he was playing pitch it went down the well. The well didn't have any water in it. So he went and told his mother that the knife was down in the well. She told him to get it or she would beat him. So he went down to get the knife. There were 10 doors so he went to the first door and knocked. A little red man came to answer the door. The boy asked have you got my knife. The man said go to the next door so he went to the next door and knocked; another red man came to the door, the boy asked have you got my knife; the red man said go to the next door. So he went to the next door. It kept on till he came to the last door. The boy knocked, a big red man came, the boy asked have you got my knife. He said yes. The boy asked him for it, he said I will give it to you but if you tell who gave it to you I will get you tonight. So the boy promised not to tell. He got out of the well. His mother asked him who gave it to him. He told his mother that he promised not to tell. His mother said I will beat you if you don't tell me. So he told her that the devil gave it to him. That night he asked his mother if he could sleep with her. She said no. So he got 10 quilts. That night he heard something outside; it went like this

> "I going to get you
> I going to get you."

It came on in the house, got the little boy, and left a note that said, "I have your little boy." That learned the mother to never buy another red knife.

Martha Metcalf

The Big Fat Man

Once there was huge fat man who lived out in the country. There was also a few other families scattered in the country not a long distance from him. The mystery was what he ate to get so fat.

One day there was a family of four who needed some meat for dinner so the mother sent her daughter across the way to get the meat so she could cook it for dinner. Her daughter was gone for a long time. The mother did not know that she had met up with the fat man. So the mother sent her son after his sister. The little boy saw this man so he asked him what he ate that made him so fat.

The fat man told him that he ate a loaf of bread, drank a glass of water, drank a barrel of milk, and ate a little girl. The man said I will eat you too if I can catch you. So the old fat man caught the little boy and ate him too.

The mother, being worried about the children, sent her husband after them and he ran up on the same man, and the fat man told him the same tale and added he had ate a little boy also. The fat man ate the father also.

When the children and their father did not return mother started out looking for them. But she told the bird if she wasn't back in a certain time to come see about them. As the family didn't come back the bird went out to hunt for them. He met the same man who had ate all his friends and the large man tried to get the bird but the bird flew into a tree and then all of a sudden the man burst open and everyone got out and lived happily after that.

Mattie Metcalf

One Little Pear

One time there was a man and his wife, and they had three children, a boy, Bill, and two girls, Susan and Mary. And the man's wife died and he married again. He didn't know it but he married a wicked woman. Well, one day the stepmother told the children that she was going to town. Now on the farm were lots of pear trees and the stepmother said, "If any of you pull a pear I'm going to take you out to the chop-block and cut off your head." Shortly after the stepmother left, a poor hungry man came by and said, "I'm so hungry, please give me a pear to eat." Mary said, "No, my mother will chop off my head." Bill said, "No, my mother will chop off my head." But Susan slipped around and gave the poor man a pear thinking that with so many that one would never be missed. But the wicked old stepmother was hiding so she could watch the pear trees. When she saw Susan pull the pear she ran and caught her and chopped off her head before the other children could miss her. She buried Susan's body under the doorstep and her head in the garden.

That night Father asked, "Where is Susan," and the stepmother said, "She has gone to spend the night with her grandmother." Later Father sent Mary out to the garden to get some onions for supper. As Mary started to pull up the onions a voice cried:

"Oh Sister, Oh Sister, don't pull my hair,
For Mother has killed me for pulling a little pear."

Mary rushed back into the house and told her father that she couldn't get the onions. So Father said, "Bill run out into the garden and get some onions." Bill ran to get some onions but when he started to pull up the onions a voice said:

"Oh Brother, Oh Brother, don't pull my hair,
For Mother has killed me for pulling a little pear."

Bill ran back into the house crying and told his father he could not pull up the onions. Father replied, "I will go and get the onions. As he started to pull the onions a voice said:

"Oh Father, Oh Father, don't pull my hair,
For Mother has killed me for pulling a little pear."

Angrily Father rushed back to the house and told the stepmother to go get the onions. As the stepmother started to gather the onions a voice cried:

"Old Devil, Old Devil don't pull my hair,
For you have killed me for pulling a little pear."

As the wicked stepmother ran back into the house something jumped from under the doorstep and knocked her down dead.

Joe Bates

Goose Ghost

My husband told me this story about an experience he had when he was a young man. He lived in the Center Ridge Church community in Pike County.

The roads were mostly deep sand beds at the time. One night, as he walked home from a party, he had to pass the cemetery. Naturally, he had an eerie feeling, and had to sum up lots of courage. He quickened his steps, but before he got past, he heard a flapping sound coming from the cemetery. Instinctively, he glanced that way, and there was enough moonlight for him to see something white rise above the ground and quickly disappear. They looked like the wings of an angel! The sand was deep, but his feet almost had wings, because it didn't take him long to reach home, and in bed.

The next morning he told his experience to his father, and they went to the cemetery. In a sunken grave they found a large goose, worn out from trying to fly out of the hole.

Mrs. Nina Swain

Woman in White

Grandpa Cotton used to tell about a man coming by the church on a stormy night. He looked into the church and saw a woman in white with her arms stretched out and standing in the pulpit. The man went in and saw that it was a woman who was mentally disturbed and who lived in the community. The man in the church took the woman home.

Ruth Tye

Railroad Light

People living on the old railroad saw a light down there near the trussel every night at about the same time. This scared some of the people because every time they went down there with their light, the other light would go out.

So, one night before time for the light to appear, several people got together and hid down there with their light. They found out that it was a crazy man and that every time he would hear something, he would put his light out.

Louzina Rhodes

Rattling Chains

About 65 years ago people passing the Tabernacle Cemetery in Coffee County would hear a noise which sounded like chains rattling. One night a group of men had been hunting and were passing the cemetery. The group became afraid and all ran except one elderly man who was not able to run. He decided he would see what it was making the noise. When he got to the church he found a hog with side chains sleeping under the church. It was a custom for people to put side chains on the hogs to keep them from crossing fences, so this hog had found a dry, warm place to sleep, under the church.

Brave Enough

About 69 years ago people would be passing the Ebenezer Cemetery from night to night and would see a ghost going from the church to the cemetery and back to the church. One night a man started by there, going after a doctor and got brave enough to get close to the form. He found it was a billy goat.

Mrs. Erie Harnsby

Guess What It Was

Once upon a time a man was going home on his horse. He had to pass a church and cemetery. He came to the cemetery and the horse stopped. He would not budge an inch. The man looked and he saw something gray-looking waving back and forth. It scared him. He turned the horse around and went home another way. The next day he went back to see what he could see in the cemetery. Guess what it was. It was a big dog fennel bush blowing in the breeze.

Mrs. M. M. Chestnutt

Riding Double

One night a man was riding his horse home after having gone to see his girl friend. Before he got home the rain began to fall rapidly. The nearest stop was a church so the man thought he would wait there until the rain ceased. As the horses paused to come to a halt something jumped on his horse with him and the horse took off in a hurry.

After a little distance this thing hopped off, and this man ran the rest of the way home, falling in the doorway nearly dead.

Later it was discovered that a crazy woman had gone to that same church that very night. This man never outlived this tale, nor did he ever believe that it was the crazy woman who had ridden with him.

Mrs. Everett Russell

Scared to Death

One night about eighty or ninety years ago, a big crowd was gathered at a certain house. One woman there said that she wasn't afraid of anything. There was a cemetery near and someone bet this woman that she wouldn't go there alone. The woman took the bet. To prove that she had been there the woman took a fork to stick in a grave and leave there for the others to see the next morning. When she didn't come back for quite a while some of the people at the house got worried and went to get her. When they got to the cemetery, they saw the woman bending to stick the fork through her apron when she stuck it in the grave, and when she tried to get up she couldn't move. Thinking that the ghost had her, she died of fright.

Mrs. Dalton Thomley

Thump, Thump, Thump

There is a haunted house located in Goodhope, Alabama. If one would go inside at night, he would hear a thump, thump, thump. They would hear pistol shots. There would be a storm and blood would drop from the ceiling.

The house at one time was a barroom and many people were killed in this barroom. There was one funny thing about this; they were all killed with pistols.

One night Mr. Screws decided that he would solve the mystery, because he did not believe in anything being haunted. When the night fell, Mr. Screws and a friend of his entered the house. Immediately they heard the thump, thump, thump. They heard pistol sounds. And blood started dripping from the ceiling covering their feet. They then began their search for the mystery of this haunted house. They discovered that the thump, thump, thump was caused by a rat in the attic dragging a bone across the floor. The blood was the blood of all the people that had been killed there. It had dried in the floor boards of the upstairs, where the people were killed. And when it rained, it would wet the boards and the blood would drip down into the next floor. They did not find an answer for the pistol shots, but they are still heard till this day.

W. O. Screws

Crying Baby

There is a house about 7½ miles from Dozier, Alabama, close to Goodhope. This house is said to be haunted. It was said that a woman that lived there killed her baby and you could hear it crying. The baby would cry like it was in terrible pain. Three families had already moved out of this house because of hearing this baby crying. So when Mr. W. O. Screws and his family moved in, and they heard the baby cry, they were ready to move out also. But one night Mr. Screws decided to be brave. When the baby started crying, he started looking for it. He took a candle in the dark gloomy house and searched for the baby, he searched and searched and could not find anything. He would not give up though. The next day, the baby began to cry again and Mr. Screws started hunting again. This time he found the baby. It was not in the house. It was not even a baby. It was a northwest wind blowing a piece of tin. His reply was that he killed the baby.

W. O. Screws

Noises in the Loft

There had been several families that lived in this particular house and each family had heard noises in the loft. They were too scared to go up there to see what it was. This happened to each one of the families. They would just move out. They thought someone was haunting them.

After the last family left, Mama and Papa moved in after other folks had warned them about the noises there. Sure enough, that very first night, they heard the most awful noises in the loft. Well, Papa wasn't as scared as the other families were, so the next morning, he went up in the loft to see what the noises were. Well, he found out. He only found a chain with some leather tied to it. And this leather had been chewed, he figured by rats. After he took the chain down, they never heard any more noises.

Louzina Widow

Devil in the Graveyard

At Shady Grove, Lee Lat Wilson passed the cemetery on the way to the store. She saw something coming out of the earth with horns. When she got to the store she told the man that the devil was out in the graveyard.

Jake knew she was honest and must have seen something. On investigation he found a cow sunk in a grave with her head sticking out and horns showing.

Mrs. Pat Kilpatrick

Nanny Burson

There was once a cantankerous woman who fussed at her husband all the time. Her name is believed to have been Nanny Burson. She made her husband promise her that if she died first he would never marry again. She told him that if he did and ever built a new house that she had wanted, then she would "ha'nt" him sure. In due time Nanny died and her husband did marry again and built a new house for his pretty young wife. Not long afterward a cyclone came and one outhouse after the other went tumbling away, until finally the house was lifted off its foundations and set down again undamaged except for a lack of pillars. When the man viewed his destruction he remarked, "Now ain't that just like Nanny!"

Viola G. Liddell

Aunt Martha's Ring

Aunt Martha died and they carried her to her grave. At least they thought she was dead. Her heart had stopped beating and she was cold and still.

Aunt Martha had a ring which was very valuable. They buried her with the ring still on her finger.

Two crooks were at the funeral to watch with care to see where she was buried. That night they paid Aunt Martha a visit.

The two crooks opened the grave. They found the hand with the ring on it. The finger was swollen and the ring would not come off. They took a knife and began to cut Aunt Martha's finger. Aunt Martha awakened.

That night Uncle Henry and the kids were sitting by the fire. They heard a noise out by the front gate. A voice was calling, "Henry, Henry."

Henry said, "That's Martha!"

Olene Williams

A Pretty Good Race

One time a man was walking by a cemetery and a haint came up to him. When he saw it, he started running. When he had run about a mile he sat down on a log because he thought that he had gotten away from the haint. About that time the haint came up to him and said, "We had a pretty good race didn't we?" The man looked at him and said, "Hell, we just started," and took off.

Carl Chavers

Ain't it a Quiet Time?

People went to this house and couldn't stay. Nobody would live there. They said it was haunted. A black cat would come up and do 'em bad. A man went one time and got a newspaper and sat down to read. Next thing he knew a black cat was there by him and had on his glasses.

Cat said, "Ain't it a quiet time" and the man said, "Not as quiet as it's gonna be." The man started running and the cat did too. Man sat down to rest and the cat did too. Cat said, "We had a tight race," and the man said, "Not half as tight as the next one's gonna be."

Mrs. A. S. Nash

How to Make a Mans

A little boy asked his mother one day how to make mans. She told him out of mud. He goes down to the branch and starts one. Got him all done but one arm when night come. That night it come a big rain and washed it away.

It wasn't long before he went to town and he saw a one-armed man. He just gazed at him. The man says, "Son, what are you looking at me so straight for?" He said, "What did you run away from me for before I got you done?"

Mrs. Maggie King

The Settin' Up

A Negro died and they tried to lay him in his coffin but to no avail. Each time he would rise back up. They finally found that a muscle in his back was taut. They tied the Negro in his coffin with a rope.

They were sitting up with the corpse one night prior to his burial. All the Negroes began to get sleepy. Each one would get sleepy and say, "If you'se gonna sit up, den I'se going to bed," until the last one was left in the room. He was sitting there dozing when the rope on the corpse came loose and the dead man suddenly sat up.

The lone Negro turned to the corpse and quavered, "If you'se gonna sit up, I knowse I'se leaving!"

Olene Williams

Peg-Legged Man and the Drunk

A grave was dug one afternoon in the cemetery and was not going to be used until the next morning. An old man who had a peg leg came along that night and fell in, and he could not get out. A few minutes later a drunk man came along and fell in. It was so dark that he did not see the peg-legged man. He said, "I'm going to climb out of here," the peg-legged man said, "No, you won't because I've already tried and I couldn't get out." The drunk, thinking he was hearing a ghost, said, "Well, by God, I sure as hell can," and he did.

Mr. Hulon Nolin

One for You and One for Me

Two boys went nut hunting. On their way back they stopped at the cemetery to divide the nuts between them. They were inside the gate of the cemetery sitting on the ground. One would say, "I'll take this one and you take that one." A man was walking by the cemetery and heard the voices which he thought was God and the devil choosing people to go with them. When the man heard this he ran up to an old man's house who hadn't walked in twenty years, and told him what was happening in the cemetery. He brought the old cripple down to the cemetery and sat him on a fence post. The boys kept on counting and finally they said well there are two on the outside which they had dropped before coming in, so, they said, "You take one and I'll take the other." When the old crippled man heard this he started running and beat the other man back to his house.

Willie Dora Cauley

This One's Mine: That One's Yours

Two people went fishing and caught a sack full. They were coming back and had to walk past a graveyard. They were tired so they decided to divide the fish at the graveyard. They went in and poured the fish out on the ground and started to divide the fish into two piles, saying, "This un's mine and this un's yours." Now they had dropped two fish at the gate when they went in, so they said they would just get them when they came back. Two men came along and heard something in the graveyard and eased up to the gate to see what it was, and they could hear the two fishermen mumbling, but couldn't tell what was being said. They eased on up a little closer and they could hear "This un's mine and that un's yours." The two men decided that it was the devil and God dividing the dead. When the fisherman got ready to go they said to each other, "Come on and we'll get those two at the gate." The two at the gate said, "Be damned if that's so, you'll have to catch us first."

Jimmie Sue Phillips

Sheep Stealers

There were two men who always passed the graveyard at about the same time every week. One was carrying the other one on his back because he couldn't walk. They had to pass too by this graveyard to get to the fellow's farm where they stole some sheep.

The owner found out what they had been doing and he decided to stop it. The very night that they were supposed to come by the graveyard, this fellow was hiding behind a tombstone waiting for them to show up. He hears them coming along and they are bragging about how many sheep they had stolen and so forth. About that time, the owner said, "If you can get 'em, you can have 'em." Both men took off like a streak of lightning and the one that couldn't walk was outrunning the other.

Louzina Rhodes

When the Devil Got After Me

I was right along in the road a little piece from Mr. Frank Scarborough's house, I heard a wagon. It went like a mule and wagon and new gear, and mules running way over in Mr. Frank Walker's field a mile away.

I thinks to myself what are they doing out there at night with a wagon? It was dark but the moon was shining.

I come on down and it kept acoming on down towards the branch. This branch was thick, you couldn't hardly go through it. It come on into that branch and when it hit that deadening in there, them logs begin to brake, you could hear it plum into Choctawhatchee, went just like a gunshot. It kept on acoming towards me but I was in the road and it was in the woods after it left the field.

I come on and as it got nearer, I broke to run until I got to the top of the hill where I could see it, and I stood there a little. It come in sight and I could see the tree tops go down. I went close to where it was. It went like a pair of mules, I could hear the bresh chains and the body abumping. I could see the bush tops and the tree tops—trees two or three inches through, just bending down on the ground. When I got there ready for it to come in the road, I walked backward five or six feet. I stopped there and the bushes hit me on the hat as it went by.

Then the bushes straighted up, the racket stopped. I couldn't hear a thing in the world.

Then I heard something singing over my head. It went kinda like a freeze coming on, you know. I moved a little further up the road, it stayed over my head. I couldn't hear nothing but that singing. I crossed the branch, and run to the foot of the hill. When I turned to stop there, a hundred horses wouldn't amade no more racket. Their feet was apopping like on brick. They was asnorting. It sounded like a plum drove of them.

I turned to run but I couldn't get a foothold on the ground. I reached up and got my old hat. I went up the road and they was right behind me—looked like they was gonna catch me. If I could just have got a foothold, I woulda went on and left them. When I got to the foot of the hill, they stopped, but I didn't stop. It was bout 200 yards to the house.

I run in and just dived asprawlin in the porch.

Now I'll add a little bit to it. This ain't the truth. I begin to run round and round the house, ahollering, "Open the door, Ida, open the door while I make another round! The Devil's after me!" I sprawled in the floor. She says, "What's the matter, Henry?" I said, "The Devil's after me."

I got up the next morning and went back down there. The bushes had all straightened up and there weren't no mud on them. There wasn't a bit of sign. I come back and looked at my tracks. They were 8 ft. apart. I was a running, but I didn't know it.

That happened just exactly like I told it except that part about the running around the house.

Henry C. Scott

Student Collector's Note: Other tellers of this tale add that when Mr. Henry started to run, he had on a big straw hat with a tiny hole in the top. When he finally got home he had pulled on the hat so hard that the hole had enlarged until the hat was hanging around his neck.

Mrs. Priscilla Mahone Tracy

Ghost of Parker's Island

In 1927 my husband had a portion of Parker's Island leased for farming and timber rights. He was offered the lease of the Rucker-Cowling Plantation south of Elmore, Alabama.

The family was thrilled over the house which was considered a beautiful landmark then. It was set in a two-acre grove of oaks, with a white picket fence around the inner yard. There was a breezeway connecting the dining room and kitchen to the main house. My oldest daughter still compares many rooms to her early memories of this home.

As we were looking over the house the former occupant was busy storing many of her things in a back room that she had kept for storage when leasing the house to us. She kept muttering to herself, "I wouldn't live another day in this house if it were the last one on earth." I thought she meant it was so large and hard to keep, therefore didn't give it another thought until later.

In the spring of 1928 strange things began to happen. In the middle of the night we were awakened to the sound of crashing glass. Huey, my husband, and I would grab flashlights and rush to the kitchen but everything would be just as we had left it when we had gone to bed.

In the afternoons when the children would be outside playing, I would sew for the forthcoming baby. Often I would know that I wasn't alone. The door knob would turn, the door open, then shut, and the knob turn back. Once we were on the breezeway letting the little ones play in a tub of water and heard footsteps coming from the main part of the house. We waited, the door opened, shut, and still no one entered, but the rocking chair rocked.

Each time the former occupant came by I would tell her of these things and have her open the storage room, but never was anything out of place or broken.

When we decided we could not take the strange events any longer and were planning to move I was waken by chains being dragged around the house. We looked, but again everything was in perfect order.

That night I dreamed that four men had a disagreement over a card game and one of the men was shot, dragged from the house in chains and put in a creek nearby. I asked the former occupant about my dream the next day. She turned white and said, "that's close." We stayed on longer than we had thought to but never heard anything or saw doors opening, chairs rocking or other objects moving again.

as recalled by Mrs. Huey C. (Thelma Esco) Womble
and told to Emma McDade

A Tale and Five Variations:
Always a Hole

According to a tale which is commonly told in Elmore County there is a hole that no amount of cement or anything will fill.

Once there was a man who was falsely accused of a crime. The judge was not very interested in finding the actual criminal and the people were not very interested in giving the man time to prove his innocence. Well, the mob decided that hanging would be the best way to rid the town of the man and the expense of trying his case, so they were going to hang him.

The whole community gathered under a stately oak and the hanging proceedings were well under way. The man's horse was slapped and the horse ran. Unfortunately, the rope was too long, so instead of breaking the man's neck, he was only standing on one toe. Determined not to let anything get the best of him, the judge reached out with his cane and dug the dirt from under the man's toe. Since his entire weight was now supported by his neck, the man was soon dead.

They say that to this day there is a hole under the oak over in East Tallassee which no amount of cement can keep filled. You see, less than a month after the hanging the man was found to be innocent and the hole must stay there to remind the people of the wrong they committed.

Sonja Taylor

This man came home from the war to see his wife in Newton. This made three other men mad because they could not come home. These men said he ran away from the Civil War and had him hung for this. All of these men died or got killed within the next three months, because they had an innocent man hung. Two were thrown off their horses and one just died. When I was going to the Baptist Institute three of us girls went out there. Somebody told us that if the hole under the man's foot was filled with sand at night, then the next day it would not have the sand in it. We filled the hole and next morning the sand was really gone. This proved that the man was innocent.

Mrs. Willis Wilson

No one will ever live in the old Sketo place because of the noise of horses running around every night at 12:00. Mr. Sketo lived in the early eighteen hundreds. He was a fine hard working man but his son, Jim, was a sorry good-for-nothing. Now Jim was always getting into trouble, so the final blow came when he stole a fine horse at Newton and rode all the way to Echo on the horse. Jim's father had to report the theft. Jim was hanged by the neck until dead. So every night horses run around the old Sketo place to remind the father that he had his son killed. Until this day no one will stay in the old Sketo place house.

Mrs. Epsie Eldridge

It seems that during the Civil War one Bill Sketo, who lived in Newton, either got a leave or deserted the Confederate Army long enough to come home to his sick wife. Several of the townspeople who had sons or husbands in the Army were very angry that Bill Sketo was able to come home while their kin were not able to do so. In this fit of anger, they decided to hang Bill. When they did this, to their dismay, they found that his feet reached the ground. They hastily dug a hole under his feet and left him there to die. The five men who were most responsible for his death all died an unnatural or violent death themselves. One of them was struck by lightning, another was found dead in a ditch along the side of a road, a third was killed when a limb from a tree fell on his head, and the other two met a similar violent fate.

George May

December 3, 1864, a good man, Bill Skeeto was hanged from the

limb of a post oak near the foot of a bridge on the west side of the
Choctawhatchee river at Newton by Captain Brear's Home Guard.
When the buggy was pulled from under his feet so that they would
not support him his feet caught on the ground. As he struggled there
George Echols took his crutch and dug a hole under his feet so as to
clear them. From that day until now that hole in the ground has been
cleaned out by some strange hand, seen or unseen, and thousands
have noted the phenomenon.

Tatum Bedsole

Once there was this Negro accused of murder in Ozark. He said he
wasn't guilty, but they were going to hang him. They took him out to
this tree with the best limb they could find. He was so tall, they
couldn't find one high enough. They decided this one was high
enough that it would give him a good fall. He still was pleading not
guilty after they put the rope around his neck. They went ahead with
it anyway and his big toes drug the ground as he swung. It made a
little trench. Later, they found out that he wasn't guilty after all. That
trench is still there to remind people of him. They can go and fill it up
and the next day it will be open again. They say his ghost comes and
digs it out.

Wayne Purvis

Tallapoosa River Valley Ghosts

In late summer of 1979 we were invited to a house haunted by
many ghosts. We examined the architecture and visited all the haunting sites and though no spirits accosted us on that lovely day, the
present owners gave us access to a written history of the house and its
various occupants, both mortal and supernatural, together with
ghost phenomena attested to for well over a century by numerous
people, including the family that now resides there. The following
account is extracted, paraphrased, and condensed from that history.
Because the owners requested anonymity, no exact locations or historical personages are mentioned.

The reader will observe stylistic differences between this extended
tale and the briefer folk conversations and monologues collected by
Troy State University students. The contrast between written and
spoken folk tales of the supernatural is instructive. The primarily oral
tradition does not pause for much reflection or analysis, nor is the
folk tongue partial to lengthy description and character portrayal;
rather, landscape, circumstances, personalities, and setting are all
identified or designated briefly and vigorously so as to get "the good

part." This is not to say that the folk can't and don't tell a long tale; to the contrary, a good tale-teller can go on for hours. The differences lie in focus and intent. "Tallapoosa River Valley Ghosts" approaches the domain of romance and legend where real historical time but dimly suffuses inexplicable happenings, and its writer evidently intended to bring together several tales emanating from one special house that accumulated spirits, apparitions, and supernatural occurrences even as various owners altered its physical structure over a period of 140 years.

Legends and romances are at the peripheries and outermost boundaries of history, and, like history, they are, after a time of seasoning and oral circulation, often written down. The pen brings certain shifts and transformations, imparts texture, atmosphere, delineation, and though the folk instinct and substance still undergirds the whole, the resulting account is far different from the original. The idea that a house may be inhabited by generations of apparitions is, of course, common in Anglo-European folklore of the supernatural. This one belongs with all the other haunted, romantic houses of the legendary Old South.

In the rich Tallapoosa River Valley of 1840, a young man cleared new ground and built a log house, two large rooms separated by a dog trot. Forty years went by: the log house served as residence, trading post, church, and schoolhouse in that wilderness community. In 1880, oxen pulled it to a nearby town; the first round-log house was merged with a second similar square-log house, and the new owner made various improvements, including a latticed walkway leading to a separate kitchen, keeping room, servants quarters, laundry room, smokehouse, and woodshed. In 1910 a third owner used lumber from another demolished old house to add an attic bedroom and a new dining room. We, the present owners, have made the house quite comfortable—we have also made ourselves comfortable with several unidentified graves on the front lawn and with all the ghosts who have lived with many generations of different families.

The "footsteps" ghost or "invisible walker" is a "seasonal visitor who arrives twice a year, spring and fall. He enters the same door, the sound of the door opens, then closes; then the steps, always the same path, down a porch, into a hallway, into another hallway, where they stop. We do not hear them leave."

The footsteps are those of the first owner, a plantation owner violently jealous of his beautiful wife. Often he returned from his work to determine if she were entertaining any guests; on one of these unexpected returns, he found his wife kneeling at her prayers. Guilt stricken and remorseful, he suffered a stroke, and on his deathbed vowed that he would always come back to look after her. And he does, "always the same walk, the same path." The beautiful wife became ill not many years later, and those tending her felt just before she died "a cold breath." When they complained of it, she answered that it was her husband keeping watch at her deathbed. "He keeps his vigil yet," and to this day, on the south side of the bed, in that room, those who sleep there will feel the "cold breath," no matter the season of the year.

Another "cold spot" may be experienced in "the little hall" at a spot where was formerly located the outside door of the original round-log house. Here, in the dead of night, long ago a half white, half Indian brave came to inquire of his Creek mother, nurse to the white children of the owner. "As was the custom in those days, when a night caller came, someone covered the door with a gun." The brave was informed that his mother had died and was buried on the premises; the brother of the owner, who held a gun behind the door, interpreting the brave's grief and shock as a threatening gesture, shot and killed him. "The cold spot marks the young man's death place to this day, even though it is now inside the house."

In those days when the small round-log house stood near the river, a quiet stranger came seeking employment. A hard worker, he was given a cot. "His only possession was a home-made wooden box which he kept under his cot." One day while clearing new ground, his leg was almost severed. While the mules and wagon were being readied to take him to the nearest doctor, he begged to be carried to his "box." Knowing it was probably his dying wish, they acceded. Over and over he shuffled papers in his box, then fainted from loss of blood. In the wagon, as the mules pulled harder and harder, the dying man regained consciousness long enough to plead, "Please take me to my box for my gunny sack." When they finally reached the doctor, the stranger was dead. Returning home, they opened his box in an effort to find the names of his kinsmen. Within the gunny sack was a small bag of gold and a locket which held the picture of a lovely young girl. "No name, address nor any link to his family was found, so they used his gold to bury him, marked his grave with a slab that read 'Stranger Bill.' Stranger Bill returned to shuffle the paper, seeking his gunny sack, and many people refused to use the cabin for that reason. He still returns, he does no harm, he just shuffles the paper in his box; never finds what he's looking for, so he keeps looking."

Another questing ghost of this house visited by many unseen spirits we call "the searcher," who may be heard opening and closing drawers of a chest, trunk lids, and wardrobes. Again and again come the sounds of searching for something lost. There once lived a young couple in the house, and their first child brought much joy. The mother painstakingly fashioned for her child an exquisite christening garment. On the day of the christening, the mother attended the funeral of a relative and rushed home to lay out her child's clothes. Inexplicably, the christening robe had vanished, and the young mother looked everywhere for it. Finally, she gave the baby to her parents and asked that they go ahead to the church while she made one last search. At last, though, she gave up. Her husband had taken the carriage for his kinspeople, and she, hard pressed and late, had no choice except to ride horseback. In her haste she took a shortcut; from deep within a roadside thicket something frightened the horse, and he threw his rider to instant death. Ever since that day, the young mother returns to the house, opening and closing drawers, chests, wardrobes, and trunks in a futile search for her child's christening robe.

The ghost of the wrecking bar followed his house when it was demolished and the timbers used to build an attic bedroom for the two log houses. During the War Between the States, a plantation owner was harvesting his crops far from his town house. Alerted that Yankee soldiers were approaching, he sent a faithful slave into town with instructions to carry his wife and family to the safety of a church and to hide valuables in corn sacks, loosen some boards in the loft of the house, and store the corn sacks there. When the plantation owner returned home, he found his house empty of slaves and family. He crossed the yard to the tool-shed, picked up the wrecking bar, and started towards the house when suddenly a Yankee soldier cried, "Halt!" Ignoring the pointed gun, the plantation owner came on, inviting the soldier to come inside for a drink of cider. Again the soldier cried, "Halt!" but he walked on. The soldier fired and the plantation owner lay dead, the wrecking bar beside him. The family returned. Night after night they heard the sounds of boards being pried loose in the loft. Years went by, the family members all died or moved away. Nobody would live in a house where a ghost came nightly to pry up boards. The last heir finally sold the house for demolition, but the wrecking-bar ghost made his way to the attic bedroom. And there he still loosens boards to find his valuables, hidden a hundred years ago.

In the square-log house is a room that served many families of this haunted house as a parlor. One day, after the War Between the States, the father of a lovely eighteen-year-old girl brought home a young man to speak of certain business interests. There in the parlor his daughter rocked as they talked. He came often, and soon the stranger and the girl were exchanging "shy, loving glances." Shortly before his stay in town was over, the stranger asked for her hand in marriage. But the parents refused: he would take her far away from them, there was too much of an age difference between them, and they had settled on the son of a business partner. Heartbroken, the stranger left, heartbroken the daughter rocked in the parlor, occasionally doing her needlework. Then she refused nourishment, weakened, she lay in bed, and nothing her parents could do or say could console her. Finally, she died of her broken heart. After her death, her mother and father could still hear her rocking in the parlor. And we still hear her rocking, still grieving for her lost sweetheart.

Old ghosts—victims of violent deaths, star-crossed lovers, faithful wives and jealous husbands, a quiet stranger hoarding gold against the day of his wedding, a distraught mother—and old times—the Tallapoosa valley wilderness, early settlements, the War Between the States, the emergence of the new South—haunting a house still standing in 1979?

[Names of present owners, who told the story, withheld at their request.]

Uncle Bert and the Varmint

Uncle Bert Keaton and a friend were coming home from a party one night. They were in their teens and were feeling rather spry and talked loudly. Perhaps by talking so loud they could hide their fear of the wooded area they were nearing. It was a bright night with plenty of moonlight to see well on the road but shadows waited in the woods.

It wouldn't have been so bad except for the tale somebody told at the party about a large varmint "aloose," raiding chicken houses, and had even killed old Mr. Esto's new calf from his prize heifer, Little Effie. Seems that when Mr. Esto heard Little Effie lowing and bellowing the night before last, he rushed down to her pen to find that something had broken down the fence and made off with that little calf. Left three fence posts lying on the ground where they'd been broke off. It'd taken a big varmint to do that and make off with Little Effie's calf because Little Effie wasn't well known for friendliness.

That varmint made a big path straight into these very woods where the boys were about to cross.

Bert declared to himself that if he'd known about this before he went he wouldn't have gone to that party even though Mattie was there—My she did look pretty—but even that was just like all the Johnston girls. But the party was over and Bert and Will were standing still at the edge of the big woods.

They decided to walk real close to each other so they wouldn't make much noise talking and if one them saw something they could both run together. Maybe what ever the thing was wouldn't bother them if he saw two of them together.

They hadn't seen a thing and they were almost through, when all of a sudden there was something dead ahead—standing stone still, in front of them—about 15 or 20 feet away. They stopped and began to ease backwards toward some tree they thought they could climb. They were so quiet an Indian couldn't have heard them move. They eased up the tree—way up. The thing still hadn't moved. What if he'd heard them or smelled them—what if he was going to come after them? They decided to get up higher, but they couldn't see him to know what he was doing. They slipped out to a large limb that went almost right over that thing. They knew they could watch him and he couldn't get them.

About that time the limb began cracking and falling. They jumped before they hit ground and were both up and running before the limb hit ground. They didn't look back to see whether that thing was behind or in front of them. They were making tracks for the clearing out of the woods. Bert heard a crashing noise behind him but he was too afraid to look. That thing might be gaining on him. There was no time to waste looking. The boys didn't slow down at the clearing. They stopped at Bert's front door and not before.

They couldn't say a word when Bert's daddy asked them some questions. They panted a few minutes before trying but then Bert saw how his father looked like he was getting mad because the boys woke him up at such an hour.

They began and the words tumbled over each other, "big varmint, Mr. Esto's cow-fence posts, a bellowing and a lowing stomped down a big path—went off to the woods—saw something big—could have eat up them both—and everybody else too."—and how they weren't scared to go into the big woods that night and how they stood and watched it and how if they'd had a gun they'd have walked right up to him and have blown his head off and how they pulled a big tree down trying to get a limb for a club to beat him to death. They scared the animal away and had to go look for it and would've found him too but it was getting so late they had to get home. Why were they running? Oh, they were just racing to have something to do to pass the time.

The next morning Will's Pa came over to Bert's to see about the boys. Bert's Pa told him about the varmint. They considered what it might be and decided if it was a bear, it needed to be killed. The boys were to show them just where they first saw it and in which direction it ran when they chased it away.

The boys retraced their steps into the woods. Their tracks were still there. They soon came to the big tree—still standing straight—only there was an old rotten limb on the ground. By this limb—about halfway out were hand and foot prints of boys—not animals. They couldn't understand how that thing could just vanish without leaving some kind of print—there sure wasn't any animal there now—wasn't anything around but some trees and that limb lying by a big tree stump.

Marie Weed

The Three Animal Kill

Uncle Bert was the School Master at the Farmer's Academy in Coffee County, now no longer there. He was a peace-loving young man who shuddered at the thought of hunting the panthers and so forth that most other young men called sport.

Rabid fox were roaming the countryside killing small animals and infecting others. The men of the community organized a fox hunt. Bert was expected to go along. He tried to be too busy but he still had to go. His friends served another round of "courage" and they were off.

He had an old shotgun which to him was a monster. He shot it at anything that moved and was the brunt of many jokes made by the others. He was finally left with only one shot.

He saw a large animal jumping or writhing, or moving in some strange way. He decided it must be something bad so he levelled his old gun and let blast with that last shot. Down went the large animal with a thud. He was too frightened to investigate so he stood back while his friends went over to see. They shouted for him to come see what he'd done with that one shot. There lay a large panther, dead, with a Coach Whip snake wrapped around his neck, the bullet having pierced the snake's head and the panther's neck. The animal had just attacked a rabid fox and he was lying under the panther in a pool of blood.

Bert was the talk of the countryside for quite a while about his three animal kill. As for Bert? His excuse for not going the next time a hunt was organized, he had done quite a job his first time out, how could he better that? When any other man could do as well as he, he'd accompany them on their very next trip.

Marie Weed

Student Collector's Note: The Uncle Bert stories were told to me by my father.

The old Farmer's Academy was established by my great-great Grandfather Johnston who had a plantation near Victoria. Uncle Bert was hired as the School Master. He distinguished himself after this in the War Between the States. He married one of the Johnston daughters and grew to be an old and well loved gentleman by many people in this area.

Marie Weed

The Wagon Wheel

About 1907, in Coffee County, about 2 miles north of New Brockton, Mr. Drew Bailey was working in a field. His twelve-year-old daughter had left him to go down into a wooded area where a clear spring produced the coolest water around. She was leaning over the spring drinking·when she heard a strange lashing sound across the spring and up the path on the other side. She looked up to see what she thought was a large buggy wheel rolling in her direction. She quickly ran behind some bushes nearby so she could see it without its seeing her. She was not afraid of snakes and thought little about killing them in the clearing of "new ground."

As it rolled downhill, it gained speed until it got to the spring, stopped and went off into the tall grass. She rushed back to her father and told him about it. He went with her and they searched for it but it couldn't find it.

He explained to her that it was called a Hoop Snake. It moved in this manner for speed. It held its tail in the mouth and rolled toward its victim. When it got near enough, it would thrust its tail which held a thorn-like stinger which was poisonous. He said they were well known in Georgia where he had grown up and he understood there were some around this area, seen by other farmers. Evidently she had come too near the nesting area of the snake and it was merely protecting its young.

Collector's Note: Told by my mother, not prefaced with "the gospel truth," but rather, a frightening experience. She saw others after that but knew what they were.

Mrs. Selma Bailey Horn

Tall Tale Contest

The three following tales go as a group. Three men were sitting around a potbellied stove when one of them said that he could tell a bigger tale than the other two. They agreed to give a prize to which one was best. The third one won the prize.

First Tale

There was this horse that the gentleman farmer had groomed as the best mannered horse in the country. The horse would obey every command given him by his master. One day, the master hitched up his carriage to the horse and took his wife for a ride. It so happened that a bridge had collapsed over a deep gully. No one was aware of this so the horse and carriage just rode off over the ledge. However, before they started to fall, the master hollowed, "whoa," pulled back on the reins. The horse understood completely and backed up onto the ledge, turned around and trotted back home, all safe and sound.

Second Tale

There was this large, ornery mule that had wrecked two or three barns and maimed workers around him. He was so mean that the fellow who owned him couldn't sell him to anyone. However, he thought he had the mule licked when the mule came down with fever and seemed to be dying. The farmer didn't want him to die in his barn so he carried him down to the swamp and then returned later to make sure the mule had died. To his surprise, the mule was in good health, and lying in a two- or three-foot pile around the mule were millions of mosquitoes, all of them dead. They had sucked all of the bad blood out of the mule and died while doing it.

Third Tale

There was this fellow who had a craving for chewing tobacco but was too lazy to walk to the store and get it. He always got little kids around the place to go and get the tobacco. Well, one day there were no kids around so he sent his dog to the store with a note tied to his neck. The man at the store read the note, got a plug of tobacco and put it in the dog's mouth. The dog went immediately home and the fellow was happy about having the tobacco.

About two weeks later he went to the store to pay his bill and he found out that it was quite a large amount due to chewing tobacco. He knew that he had been sending the dog every day (without a note since the man at the store knew who wanted what when the dog came in) to get tobacco but the amount owed was beyond comprehension. He usually didn't chew that much tobacco in a year.

About that time the dog trotted in, the clerk gave the dog a plug of tobacco, and charged it to the friend, standing there looking crazy. He followed the dog outside and watched as the dog took a bite of the tobacco, chewed it awhile and then let out a big "ptu" and pranced off.

Grandmother (Mrs. B. R. Mann)

The Biggest Liar

Will Foley was known to be the biggest liar in Briar Creek community.

One day a group of men were working on the road when they saw Will come galloping away on his horse. He galloped up to where the men were working and stopped suddenly. One of the men yelled.

"Hey, Will, tell us the biggest un you know this morning."

Will shook his head sadly and said, "No time for lying this morning, your wife just fell out with some kind of spell and I just stopped to tell you, I'm on my way after Doc Smith now." Then Will galloped away. This man threw down his shovel and ran every step of the mile home and found his wife mopping the floor. Then he remembered telling Will to tell the biggest un he knew. Again, Will had held up his reputation of being the biggest liar in the community.

Cullen Kendrick

The Turkey Calling Champion

A few years ago, in Wilcox County, a man won the title of champion Turkey Caller. A story is told that this man was out hunting turkey one day and he was lying down behind a big log, using it for a blind. He started to call at short intervals and it wasn't long before a big gobbler started to answer. He could hear the big gobbler as he got closer and closer, but he could not see him because of the log. He knew if he raised up to look over the log the turkey would see him, so he reached through the hole and grabbed. The man couldn't pull the turkey under the log through the hole because the turkey was so big. He didn't know what to do since he knew he wouldn't have time to let loose, grab his gun and shoot the turkey, so he finally decided what to do. He let loose the gobbler, picked up his call and called the turkey around to his side of the log and killed him.

Bonnie Dean

Ironing Board

A coon hunter owned a coon dog who was such a good hunter it is almost unbelievable. When the man wanted a certain size coon he showed the dog a board on which he stretched coon hides to the dog. He always cut the board the exact size he wanted the coon skin to be.

The dog always went hunting and returned with a coon whose skin would fit the board. One day the hunter carried his wife's ironing board, and promptly the dog left the house. He has not been seen since. He is still looking for another coon whose skin can be stretched over the ironing board.

Virginia Woodham

Tale of Two Snakes Swallowing Each Other

Mr. Johnnie Shephard said that he went down in the field one time and saw two snakes going around bushes. The bunch of bushes were about as high as your head.

Each one had the other by the tail a'swallowing each other. They kept a'going around the bush and both snakes swallowed each other and disappeared.

Henry C. Scott

Fish Tale

One man said he caught a trout which weighed 47 pounds. Another man said he throwed his hook in the water and hung something he could not pull out. He kept trying and after a while he landed it. It was a lantern burning. The other man said, "You know that is not reasonable." The man replied, "We will compromise; if you will take 40 pounds off the fish, I will blow out the lantern."

J. C. Wilkinson

Homer Powell

Homer Powell was a hermit who lived on Conecuh River north of Troy. He fished and split shingles for a living.

Homer didn't come to town but once a year. People would give him clothes, a shave, and a haircut. On one of these occasions, Homer came to town without a stitch of clothes on, and his beard wasn't quite long enough to cover him.

Homer couldn't swim a lick. When he crossed the river, he merely held his nose and walked across the bottom.

Thomas Canady

Mama Berch's Hunting Tale

Once upon a time a man went hunting. He hunted nearly all day and he couldn't find anything to shoot at. He decided to sit down under a tree on the bank of the river to rest. Just about the time he sat down he heard a noise. He looked up the river and saw about eight hundred geese. He was just about ready to shoot when he heard another noise down the river, and saw eight hundred ducks. He didn't know what to do, so he decided to shoot both barrels at one time. Just about the time he got ready to shoot, he looked down and saw a rattlesnake right at his feet. So he just shot the barrels busted. One barrel went up the river and killed geese. The other barrel went down the river and killed the ducks and the ramrod went down the snake's mouth and choked him to death. The stock knocked the man in the river and he came out with both boots full of fish. They were so heavy it busted the bottom of his britches and the button flew out into the bushes and killed a rabbit. He picked up his rabbit and threw it in some bushes and killed a drove of partidges.

The man decided to go get his cart and horse and gather up his game. He loaded his cart (which had rawhide traces) with the game.

There came a big rain. When he got home he looked back and he couldn't see his cart because the rawhide traces had stretched so long. He tied his traces to a fence. One day when the sun came out he saw his cart coming up to the house.

His horse got away from him when he was tying his traces that day to the fence. His horse had a sore on his back and when he did find him, an acorn had fallen in the sore and had grown up and made a forked tree. He sawed the limbs off and made his wife a side saddle.

All who believes this stand on your head.

Mrs. George Gay

[This tale was widely circulated in nineteenth-century almanacs.]

The Coach Whip

One day a wagon was coming down the road to Sellers, Alabama. The driver saw a snake stretched completely across the road. He decided to run over it and kill it. He speeded up the horses and hit it with a bump-rattle, bump, as the wheels went over it.

Tha man looked back and to his surprise saw the snake coming after him. It put its tail in its mouth and rolled like a wheel until it caught up with him and then it ripped out like a coach whip and nearly whipped him to death.

Dutchie Sellers

A Special Gun

A man from Tennessee came to Florida, Alabama, many years ago to visit his relations. He always bragged about his gun. There were many ducks in this area at that time. One day he took his gun and went out to shoot ducks. A large drove of ducks flew over. He raised his gun and forgot to take aim and just pulled the trigger. There were duck feet and legs falling in Florida for a whole week.

Mrs. Martin

A Coon Dog

A man started to dig a well. He had dug about twenty feet when he came upon a log across where he was digging. There was coon's track on the log. The man came out and called for his old hunting dog down in the well and put him on the scent of the track. He went on about his business of making the well. He kept expecting to see his hunting dog, but he was gone for a long time. He gave up that his dog would ever return. Then one morning about daybreak a year after the dog left he returned wearing a fur coat. He had trailed the coon to the factory and back home.

Mrs. George Hagan

Big Snake

There used to be a big snake that stayed at Shot Bag Creek. Nobody ever got more than a glimpse of him, but they measured his tracks and they say he was big around as a kerosene drum; folks tried to shoot him but they couldn't kill him. He knowed when they was somebody around cause they never nobody seen more than a glimpse of him. I know that's true cause I've heared several folks say they'd saw his tracks.

Mrs. Sudie Hataway

House Keeping

There was a man in our community whose wife was a nasty house keeper. The house was so dirty that it had a bad odor. The man's brother was helping him with some odd jobs in the house and he told him that he didn't see how he could stand his wife's filth. The man replied that you could get used to anything. The brother said, "Yes, anything but a terrible odor!"

While the brother was washing up for lunch, the man took his hat out to the hen house and put some chicken manure under the band. When they went back to work the brother kept saying that he smelled chicken manure. He looked but couldn't find any. After a while he quit complaining. After the job was finished the man asked the brother if he smelled chicken manure anymore and he said, "No." So he told him that it was under his hat band and "that you could get used to anything."

Mrs. Eva Willis

The Circuit Preacher

Once each month or fourth Sunday the circuit preacher came to a small village to preach. On Saturdays he would practice his sermon in the church.

Three teenage boys were listening one Saturday and decided they would play a joke on the preacher.

The preacher was practicing his sermon about Ammon riding his ass into the city to put a curse on the people. He preached and preached on how Ammon tried to make the ass go but the ass could see the Angel of the Lord but Ammon couldn't. Finally he finished.

The boys found the word mule and slipped into the church and pasted it over the word ass in the preacher's Bible where he was going to read Sunday morning.

On Sunday morning he began to read and he read, "And Ammon hit his ———." He backed up and reread "And Ammon hit his ———." He did this three times. He looked at his audience and said, "I'll be damned if it ain't changed to a mule."

Mrs. Anne Parson

The Cat Story

I guess it was about 1908 or 1909 that the Brewton folks wanted to move the county seat to Brewton from Pollard. So they hired some men from Andalusia to come to Pollard and steal the records out of the courthouse, burn it and get the records back to Brewton. The records were kept in the house where the Garrett Flower Shop is today, next to the post office, until they built the first courthouse in Brewton.

The Pollard folks were so mad they rounded up all of the cats they could find and put them in a box car and sent them to Brewton. That's why there are so many cats in Brewton.

Achie Odom

Handkerchief   (To be played on a girl by a boy)

The boy asks the girl if she knows that you can estimate a person's intelligence by measuring his head—if she replies no, he persuades her to let him measure hers. Then he places a handkerchief or a scarf around her head so that her eyes are covered. Then he kisses her and replies: "You aren't very smart, are you?"

Prank on Schoolteacher

In olden days there was an old schoolteacher that constantly had headaches. She always carried her pills to school. One day several students slipped the medicine bottle from the desk and removed the pills and placed goat pills in the bottle. She never knew this joke was pulled on her.

Mrs. W. H. Williamson

Cane Patch

Once a farmer had a fine patch of sugar cane, but he didn't want anyone to get a stalk of his cane to chew. On Saturday night the teenage boys would try their best to slip and get some cane. (It's always better if you don't have permission.)

Five or six boys decided one cool, crisp Saturday night that the cane would be just right to chew and they planned and planned how they might get the farmer away from home. They each decided to make what we call in science a "Barking Dog." (It is made with a tin can and a resined string.) They eased in behind the farmer's mule barn and began to make their tin cans moan and howl. The mules histed their tails and began to run and snort. Louder became the wailing and faster and faster ran the mules until finally they tore the lot fence completely down.

Away ran the mules. By this time the farmer came out the door in his long underwear with a shotgun. The boys lay down in the cane patch and waited while he dressed and dashed away after his mules.

After rolling and laughing until they were exhausted the boys had a wonderful night in the cane patch while the poor farmer spent most of the night trying to locate his mules.

Hiram Kilpatrick

Buger at the Spring

A Mama and her children would gather in a circle and the Mama would send some of the children to the spring. Someone would be hiding at the spring and when the children got there, he would jump out and say "buger at the spring." This scared them and they would run back to their Mama.

Sue Peacock

Palm Reading

Picking random lines in the hand a person will ask:

Do you see this line? (answer yes) It is your life line and tells whether your life will be long or short.

This line that joins with it shows that you will get married. Each branch represents a child.

Now this line shows that your life will be happy and this one that you will gain fame and fortune.

And do you see this road here? (with "yes" answer) Then you are as crazy as I am.

Dutchie Sellers

Smut

First of all, the practical joker should tell his victim that he is going to be hypnotized and that he must follow every action of the hypnotizer. The materials needed for the joke are a clean saucer that is smutted on the bottom. The hypnotizer holds the clean saucer and rubs the bottom of it with his hand. The victim is told to imitate the leader until his hand becomes black. Then he is told to rub his face until it becomes streaked. The victim is unaware that the saucer is dirty and wonders why everyone is laughing at him.

Lurleen Messick

Snipe Hunting

A very common joke played on young boys or anybody that hasn't ever been in the woods much is snipe hunting. You take the victim out in the woods and get him to hold a sack at the end of a gully or ditch. Then you tell him that the rest of the people will scare the snipes into the sack. And then you leave the person out there in the woods. It won't take long for him to figure out what has happened.

Dumb Bull

Dumb bull is a way of joking a person that is not very common now. To make a dumb bull you take a hollow log or keg and stretch a fresh cowhide over one end of the keg (or log) then let it dry. Then you attach a long piece of leather to the center of the cowhide. Then you put resin on the leather cord. Then pull your leather cord between your fingers—creating a weird sound that will make your hair stand on end and scare off anybody anywhere around.

The Well Moving

Once three city boys came courting in a rural community. The country boys didn't like the idea of their girls courting the "city-dudes."

On every Saturday night there was a square dance in the rural community. The city boys knew how to round dance but the country boys wouldn't give them the pleasure of round dancing with the girls. All they would do was square dance, one set right after another. When they got hot everyone would go out in the yard to the well for a fresh drink of cool well-water.

The city boys just tried and tried to figure out some way they could round dance with the girls. Finally just before a set was over they eased out to get them a drink of water and came back in just before the set was over. The dancers were hot and thirsty and soon as the music stopped all the country boys headed for the well for a fresh drink of water. The city boys grabbed the girls and told the musicians to play a slow waltz.

That night they round-danced quite a while. The city boys had picked up the top well curb and set it just on the other side of the well. The well was full of country boys splashing and cussing trying to get out of the well.

Talking to the Dead

Tell a very gullible person (your best victim of this joke) that you have the power to talk to any person that has died in the victim's family. Take person to a dark room. Get two saucers. By burning a candle, put smut on the bottom of one of the saucers. Give this saucer to your victim. Then "talk" to the particular dead person. Bring the spirit into the room by doing all kinds of actions, one being that of rubbing the bottom of the saucer and putting the hands to your face.

Tell the victim to do the very same thing, thus getting the smut all over his face without his knowing that the bottom of his saucer has been smutted.

Patsy Summerford

The Rosin Strings

If boys wanted to play a trick on someone, they would try the rosin string. At night someone would put a nail between the boards of the weather stripping on a house and then would tie a string to it. The string would be pulled tight and a piece of rosin would be rubbed up and down over it. This would make a loud noise. It would sound like the boards were being ripped off the house.

Hattie Mae Willis

Seeing Stars

Ask an unsuspecting victim if he wants to see the stars, and if he says yes, make him lie down on the floor and cover him with a raincoat so that his face is covered. Tell him to close his eyes and not to open them until you tell him to. Hold the sleeve of the coat right over his eyes and tell him to look and then pour water down the sleeve into his face. The name of this game is called "Seeing the Stars" or "Seven Stars Up a Coat Sleeve."

Mrs. Priscilla Mahone Tracy

Thimble

Another joke is called "Thimble." Get a thimble full of water and write the name of a soft drink, color, or flower on a piece of paper then ask the players to name a drink, color, or flower. Whoever names the one you had written down gets the water—right in the face.

Mrs. Priscilla Mahone Tracy

Chasing Purse

My father use to take an old black purse and fill it with paper then tie a string around the handle and lay it in the middle of a road which he knew people would travel. When somebody would start to pick it up, he would jerk it out of his reach. He said that he had seen folks chase the purse trying to catch it.

Mrs. John Parks

Graveyard Ghost

Another joke my father use to play on people was that he and some other boys would get people that were scary and take them down by the graveyard. Then they would get the graveyard between them and the house so the person would have to go by the graveyard to get home. When they would pass the graveyard somebody would raise a stick with a sheet on it up through the trees. It was very effective.

Mrs. John Parks

Fortune Telling

Take two blades of grass (smut grass) and cross it in some one's mouth by telling them that you will tell their fortune this way. Tell the person that he will have to close his mouth. When he does, strip the grass through his teeth leaving the smut in his mouth.

Hattie Jordan

Uncle John's Blue Line

My Uncle John used to tell someone that he would meet them at a certain place and if he got there first he would draw a blue line and if they got there first they could rub it out.

Bobby Norris

Superstitions

Superstitions center on the fundamental experiences of all men: birth, the struggle for life, and death. Varied, strange, fanciful, often familiar, nurtured in a rural landscape, transliterated in an urban century of space travel and nuclear power, they somehow survive every attempt at eradication, persisting among the uneducated, and, though latent and often unconfessed, the educated. Actors, athletes, writers, factory workers, teachers, college students, truck drivers, farmers, circus performers, prisoners, and even a sprinkling of scientists, philosophers, medical doctors, and ministers have all admitted to some traditional folk beliefs and practices. Nearly all of us sometimes feel an uncanny truth in a superstition, a powerful, inexplicable pull to the dark beginnings of man. Once the howling of wild beasts did indeed portend death—the sounds of our modern rescue vehicles imitate those cries, and we shudder, as did our forefathers. As with the folk tale, behind every superstition stands an individual human entity who imparts to it a particular character, and, as in all folklore transmission, the specific reality of folk beliefs and practices alter as the folk alter through time. Despite these individualizing and evolutionary processes, some residual core remains: the riderless horse with stirrups reversed, an ancient mourning rite for warriors slain in battle, becomes an empty space in a jet plane formation streaming above a church where obsequies for an American astronaut are celebrated.

This collection of superstitions gathered by Troy State University students between 1958 and 1962, from predominantly white, rural and small-town, middle-class informants in central and southeastern Alabama, is part of the Anglo-European heritage of folk beliefs and practices, and the reader will find old friends as well as new on every page. Student researchers encountered the same superstitions over and over: any one item was reported by ten to one hundred informants all of whom recited several superstitions and immediately recognized others when the collector mentioned them. Many informants stated flatly that they believed certain superstitions to be true, others were dubious but open to belief, some cited evidence or proof known directly and personally or from sources that they regarded as reliable, and very few categorically denied all superstitious statements, beliefs, and practices. Most informants readily admitted to performing or abstaining from some action known to affect their

96

Ghosts and Goosebumps

"luck." The utterance of the statement came readily to their tongues, and their response to the dictates of the superstition was almost automatic. Significantly, the superstitions most widely believed and practiced had to do with the interpretation of weather omens, dreams, and death auguries, with planting crops by the signs, and with healing by means of chants, rites, exorcism, and physically endowed persons. Multifarious and omnipresent, superstitions defy classification. These from Alabama are arranged loosely according to subject or genre: Pregnancy, Birth, and Childhood, Love and Marriage, Death, Weather and the Seasons, Planting, Good Luck and Good Fortune, Making Wishes Come True, Bad Luck, and Spells, Signs, and Portents.

The superstition is a species of the genus folk beliefs and practices. These derive from primitive and ancient religious and cultural phenomena; from traditional life patterns and our early intimacy with the earth, the apprehension of natural occurrences, birth, growth, death, and resurrection, in the seasons and the landscape, in animals, plants, and man; from the interpretation and expression of those cyclical occurrences in evolving myths and intellectual systems. The designation folk beliefs and practices necessarily ranges broadly over science, natural, behavioral, and physical (folk botany, meteorology, psychology, zoology, and medicine); social, cultural, and religious rites, rituals, customs, festivals, and celebrations, especially those connected with courtship and marriage, death and birth, seasonal changes, sowing and reaping, tribal initiations and coming-of-age ceremonies; concepts and practices in magic, witchcraft, demonology, astrology, alchemy, and numerology, all of which aim at understanding and controlling events and circumstances in nature or which effect desired outcomes in individual daily life; and the verbal, musical, or oral statement of all these, song and dance, the dramatic reenactment, the tale, and the superstition. We may define a superstition as an oral statement of some folk belief and/or practice. As such, it possesses a specific linguistic, structural, and intellectual character, and it is invariably comprised of three parts: (1) the underlying concept or belief, (2) the language that conveys that belief, and (3) the commission or omission of action or practice as required or dictated by the belief and the statement. The causal relationship among these constituent parts may be summarized as Belief—Statement—Action.

Belief may be true or false; folk beliefs are almost always judged to be false. Especially since the emergence and dominance of the twentieth-century scientific method, educated laymen have regarded superstitions as irrational, unenlightened, and sinister, the entrenched enemies of our struggle to vanquish ignorance, hunger, disease, moral and intellectual prejudice, hate, and fear. Folklorists and anthropologists often have looked on them as a vast body of quaint, false, sometimes entertaining notions blown hither and thither over the earth for centuries, raggle-taggle shreds of the past, odd relics of this, that, and the other. We honor the arts, crafts, and skills of the folk, delight in their riddles, rhymes, proverbs, and speech, and are charmed by their songs, dances, and games, yet we deride their superstitions. Why? And why are so many superstitions so widely known and accepted? Why do they persist?

A folk belief is an attempt to grapple with the mysteries of human life in our universe, to answer, interpret, understand, solve, control, or come to terms with the multitudinous questions, problems, obstacles, and dilemmas that confront our instinct to survive. The aim of the folk belief and practice is the same as that of all science, of moral philosophy, myth, and religion: to define man, to perpetuate his existence and fully realize all his possibilities, to order and make use of natural phenomena, and to seek out God. In distinguishing the false belief from the true, it is well to remember that the fictive lie is also true: a black cat cannot cause evil, but black is a universal symbol of death and the cat was once worshiped as a god. Premises once dismissed as "superstitions" have now been shown to have some scientific basis—a mother may not literally "mark" her unborn child, but embryologists have made startling discoveries about *in utero* reactions to physiological, emotional, and environmental factors, and studies in biofeedback and body time show that we do indeed have "lucky" days and that certain psychological processes can alter biological functions. But the truth of a folk belief is most often the truth of the archetypal symbols of myth. These beliefs are embedded in folk life traditions, becoming a curious poetry preserved steadfastly in statement and attenuated, socialized gesture long after the extended practice or fully developed rite has ceased to exist.

Granted that superstitions are sometimes merely amusing, some beliefs are so harmful as to cause bodily injury and death—the Salem witchcraft trials are a horrible case in point. But they are much more than entertaining, anachronistic trivia. They are not nothing come from nowhere; every single one is something come from somewhere, a part of a folk continuum in which thousands upon thousands of people inherit and pass on an overwhelmingly complex body of knowledge and pseudo-knowledge. Quite simply, there are so many folk beliefs because so many of us have wrestled for so long in so many ways with the myriad questions of existence. They persist even when they are demonstrably false, because we cleave to answers, because we assimilate superstitions naturally as we do tales, songs, riddles, and games, all our folk legacy. We know that a dead snake hung over a fence cannot make rain and that we cannot walk around decapitated, but the symbolic truth drives home—we know also the desperation of drought and the fear of famine and the hope for eternal life. Hence, though reason warns us off, the longings of the spirit draw us near, and we both deride and believe. Folk belief, then, is based on experiential evidence acquired, transmitted, and confirmed through subsequent, similar observations and experiences, the continuance of traditional folk life patterns; on proof adduced from some premise already established in larger systems of thought, both premise and proof interpreted by the folk in either a true or false manner; and on analogy, those metaphors, images, and symbols drawn from human experience and natural phenomena and expressed primarily in myth.

The actions required by these Alabama folk beliefs clearly evidence their remote origins in primitive myth and religion, in magic, witchcraft, and pseudo-sciences. Universal natural symbols of birth, life, sexual fecundity, and death are everywhere in the rites prescribed for fertility and good fortune—the sun, moon, rain, wind, stars, fire, earth, water, lightning, rainbows, dews, dust, whirlwinds, smoke, fog, plants, animals, and every part of the human body, bones, nails, urine, blood, hair, teeth, tongue, ears, eyes, head, knees, elbows, fingers, arms, even moles, dimples, and wrinkles. All the major concepts of magic appear in this Alabama collection: magical transference (placing a knife under the bed to "cut" labor pains or a bridle to "hold them back"); talismanic magic (buckeye balls, cougar bones, rabbit's foot); causal magic (breaking a mirror brings seven years of bad luck); ominal magic ("Hollow moon turns west, the fish bite best"); homeopathic magic, based on similarities (swallow a fish bladder and you'll learn to swim); exorcism, the driving off or out of all evil, unlucky influences through chants, spells, and magical verbal formulas (especially relating to wishes and illnesses); foretelling or divining through dreams, auguries, and simple rites (drawing a circle and spitting in it three times); demonology (don't carry water after dark or the haints will jump in and splash the water out); and conjuring or sorcery (put the tail feather of a white rooster in a walnut and place it under the doorsteps of your enemy, or sleep with a lock of your sweetheart's hair under your pillow to make him love you more). Often, the die is already cast, one's doom is sealed, and all a poor body can do is read the omens: an approaching death is signified in the hooting of owls, the flight of crows, the midnight howling of dogs or cock-crow. Just as often disaster may be averted: don't lie to the preacher and your corn will be free of weevils and worms; don't cuss a rat, else he'll gnaw your bedstead down. Or good fortune may be procured, either as a result of the intervention of fate, nearly always expressed by omens, or through one's own efforts: two yolks in an egg bring good luck, stroke the baby's knees for nine days with a straw broom and he will grow tall. The prominence of folk beliefs about planting crops according to signs in the zodiac harks back to the medieval pseudo-science of astrology—farmers still consult the almanac for favorable signs from the heavens—but many of these agricultural practices are based on common-sense judgments. Certain cloud configurations and wind patterns do portend rain or drought or storm, plants and animals are acutely sensitive to changes in weather and seasonal cycles, and those whose bread depended solely on earth and sky had little choice but to learn to interpret those natural omens, subtle alterations in cries, breeding habits, early and late chrysalis, the peculiarities of bark, leaves, and blossoms.

Some superstitions reflect the folk perception of human character and personality: wrinkled lips signify a liar, a large mouth, a generous nature. Others are simply matter-of-fact observations: It's bad luck to hand a baby out the window. Most certainly. You may drop him. "Don't sweep out the back door after dark; 'twill bring bad luck." Anybody who lived in an isolated rural area before the days of electricity, when darkness was unrelieved for miles and miles, knows well there may be a terror in the backyard, a fox in the hen house, or a snake in the grass. And those who have lain in the same darkness and heard the wildcat and screech owl can testify to the indescribable fear those sounds evoke. Finally, it ought to be noted that the folk are not above cheating in their magical practices, well, if not cheating, manipulating to achieve a favorable outcome. Which of us has not twisted the apple stem just so, to make it pop out on the initial of a sweetheart? Or read whatever name we pleased in the tracks of a doodlebug? Not all these Alabama superstitions are in dead earnest— many of them are exercises in playful fancy we perform to while the time away, to indulge in our secret wishes, to adorn an hour of friendship or neighborliness. Whatever superstitions are, they are endless and endlessly interesting as expressions of the folk mind.

The second element of the superstition, the verbal statement, is, in many ways, the most puzzling of the three, for it exhibits marked characteristics in language and logic. First, it is brief, carrying the force and flavor of the proverb; meaning is compressed within the narrowest of linguistic limits. One wonders at the evolutionary process by which elaborate systems of thought and behavior are distilled into a sentence or two. The utterance is similar to that of the folk proverb and riddle—easy, quick, natural, as if some commandment or prohibition were being recited by rote or out of long familiarity— and these oral qualities reveal its identity as folk tradition. Often it is chanted or versified: Red sky in the morning,
Sailors take warning.

Here, rhyme and meter are mnemonic devices that facilitate learning and the transmission of both the statement and the folk practice, and the chant has much the same function as the formula in magical rites. Another striking feature of the superstition is specificity. Nothing is left for speculation—one is told precisely what to do and what not to do. Objects, substances, and personages, all quite commonplace, save for a few demons and haints, are named, circumstances, conditions, actions, and results exactly located and described. There is one notable exception—luck. In half the cases, the good or bad luck is specified—death, disease, disfigurement, marriage, riches, good health, power—but in numerous statements, favorable or unfavorable outcomes are but the abstraction luck. This specificity is conveyed through thousands of images derived from folk life, and though the poetic metaphor as such rarely appears in the verbal statement of a superstition, metaphor as logic, in particular as analogy, often underlies the statement: "To stir a teapot is to stir trouble." "If you break a mirror, leave it in running water to wash bad luck away." "When the fire spits, it means a quarrel in the family." Superstitions may appear contradictory, illogical, and sometimes senseless, but when we subject them to close study, nearly always their metaphorical intent, method, and reality become clear. The meaning of omens and the magical practices by which circumstances are altered are both rooted in association or metaphor. For example, a quick-tempered person must plant pepper if it is to be hot: here the shared quality of pepper and person is the attribute of fire, and the sower magically imbues the seed with his own personality. Metaphor and image are often expressed in the verbal statement as antithesis or balance. The first part of the statement describes conditions or circumstances or sets up a situation (often a superstition begins with *if* or *when*); the second part resolves, answers, or defines the first: "If you steal from a cemetery, the hand you steal with will wither." Note that the two divisions of the statement set up a clear cause and effect relationship. Again we are struck by the logic of the illogical and by the symbolic truth lodged deep in metaphor—the ancient curse of the Egyptian Tutankhamen, the taboo against disturbance of the dead, imaged in the withered arm that committed the offense. All these aspects of the verbal statement—rhyme and meter, image, metaphor, symbol, and oral qualities—lead us to an awareness of the superstition as a kind of poetry created over thousands of years by the folk out of their apprehension of myth and cultural phenomena, translated into their own landscape and language.

But what of the magician? Where is he? The folk tales in *Ghosts and Goosebumps* show us only now and then a witch, a conjurer, some practitioner of supernatural arts, and nowadays most communities have few resident sorcerers who lay on spells, cure warts, or concoct love philters. Remarkably, these folk beliefs and practices are thoroughly democratic. Every man reads his own omens, divines his own future, performs his own rites, as if the high calling of the magician and his arcane knowledge had been shattered into thousands of bits and any of us might lay hold of powers once invested in the shaman, high priest, or oracle. Folk beliefs and practices flow with the rhythms of daily life, arising as occasion and circumstance arise—a stubbed toe, a hard labor, a bad crop year, a colicky baby, a lingering illness, a disappointed hope, an unyielding sweetheart, a sudden death. They encompass every aspect of our existence, and perhaps their most impressive characteristic is their reflection of our human commonality. Their very stuff and substance partake of that commonness. Whatever is used for these folk magical practices is something almost everybody can lay his hand on: brooms, ladders, chairs, tables, hats, pencils, keys, pins, socks, shoes, dishes, salt, bread, butter, eggs, milk, knives, thimbles, clocks, mirrors, combs, hoes, sticks, handkerchiefs, teapots, fishing poles, matches, buttons, keys, thread, pennies. As with the preparation of medicines and foods, the building of houses, barns, pig pens, and privies, the making of garments and linens, the folk make do in their magical practices with what they have, and ordinary objects take on, through some miraculous transformation, the powers of the supernatural. Yet, this transformation is set firmly in the landscape of our own Alabama folk life: here are our foods and crops, sweet potatoes, peas, beans, onions, corn, okra, collards, watermelons, cotton, and peanuts; our trees, grasses, and fruits, sage, dogwood, apples, figs, weeping willow, cedar, pine, clover, oak, blackberries, walnuts, and chestnuts; and an incredible variety of animals and insects, mules, cows, horses, dogs, cats, turtles, possum, snakes, roosters, bees, grasshoppers, crickets, lizards, rats, raccoons, devil spitters, butterflies, spiders, frogs, hens, thousand-legged caterpillars, hawks, buzzards, robins, wrens, owls, whippoorwills, turtledoves, doodlebugs, and that defier of hell itself, the jaybird. Which all goes to show that, if you've a mind to, you can make magic anywhere, anytime, out of anything.

We speak of being "free from superstition," as if folk beliefs are a kind of bondage, but the enslavement is as much ours as it is of our fellows whom we label as "superstitious," those we sometimes despise, ridicule, and hardheadedly seek to liberate. Instead, we must rid ourselves of our own errors: armed now with the camera, tape recorder, and the tools of the anthropologist and archaeologist, folklorists must study how and why folk beliefs and practices originated and developed, examine them as related parts of a specific, evolving folk consciousness within a given folk culture, as a folk shorthand for a whole intellectual or religious system, and as expressions of the deeper truths that have always animated myth and poetry. The coherent and integrated view thus obtained undoubtedly will show the folk as possessors of both the false and the true. Then we may look upon the true "superstition" and be grateful to the folk who established and held it to be true over hundreds of years, and for the believers of the false we shall feel compassion born from our own terrible difficulties in searching out the truth.

Pregnancy, Birth, and Childhood

If someone with a young baby leaves a diaper at your house, you will become pregnant shortly.

Place a wet diaper under the bed and the woman will become pregnant.

If you find a pacifier, someone in the house will get pregnant.

If a pregnant woman touches a sage brush, it will die.

If a pregnant woman pulls okra in a garden, that garden will never produce any more okra.

If a pregnant woman handles fresh meat, it will spoil.

If a pregnant woman eats nuts from a black walnut tree, it will not bear anymore.

If a pregnant woman crawls out of bed over her husband, he will have morning sickness.

A woman loses a tooth for each child she has and her feet grow half a shoe size with each child.

After a woman has had a baby, don't sweep under her bed for it is bad luck.

When pregnant, it's bad luck to have a permanent wave.

A baby's thrash can be cured by a person who was born after the death of their father by blowing their breath in the baby's mouth.

Don't ever point the first finger of the right hand at the navel of a newborn baby. The navel, though almost well, will become inflamed and the child might die.

If a pregnant woman continually reaches up high, she will strangle her baby. A pregnant woman should never raise her arms above her head; to do so might wrap the cord around the baby's neck.

It is bad luck to have your picture made if you are pregnant.

If a child is born on Sunday, it will be gentle and kind.

If a child is born with its face toward its mother's back, it will never have any children.

It's said a seven-month baby has a better chance of living than an eight-month baby.

To determine the sex of an unborn baby, tie a bobby pin on a silk thread and hold it over the mother. If it moves in a circle, it is a girl; if it moves in a pendulum, it is a boy.

A baby carried high will be a girl, a baby carried low, a boy.

If the heart of an unborn baby beats fast the baby will be a girl, if the heart beats slow it will be a boy.

If your baby is born on a full moon, it will be a boy.

If your baby is born on a new moon, it will be a girl.

If a person plays with a cat while pregnant, her baby will look like a cat.

If a mother wants her new baby to talk plain and not stutter, she will give it water to drink from a thimble before crossing the first stream with it.

If a woman is expecting a baby and it is overdue, when the moon fulls it will be born.

If a pregnant woman cuts your hair, your baby's hair will be curly.

If a pregnant woman is badly scared, it will cause the baby to be cross-eyed.

If a child has a brown mark on its chest, it is because its mother ate too much chocolate while pregnant.

If a pregnant woman gets scared and touches some part of the body, the child will be marked in that particular spot.

If a pregnant woman looks at a deformed person, her baby will be deformed.

If you see a snake while you are expecting a baby, it will mark the baby.

A pregnant Negro woman saw a convict working; he had only one hand. Her baby was born with only one hand.

A pregnant woman killed a snake and her baby never walked but crawled like a snake.*

It's bad luck to eat fish or any other wild game before a baby is born because it will cause the baby to be wild.

A contented mother will have a good baby.

A pregnant woman should have whatever food she craves, to keep the child from being marked.

If a pregnant woman looks at a dead person, she will miscarry the baby.

A pregnant woman should not ever wear maternity clothes before she really needs them as this will surely cause a miscarriage.

A pregnant woman should never buy baby clothes during the first months as that will cause a miscarriage.

Births are said to occur as the moon changes.

The days before and after the new moon are best for bearing children.

Put a bridle on the bed after a woman has given birth to a child to help keep down pain.

If a woman is in labor, have her husband remove the left sock and place it on her chest to lessen pain.

A pregnant woman should put a butcher knife under the mattress when labor starts; this will cut the pain.

If a man throws his hat on the bed, his wife will become pregnant.

Put a pair of scissors under the bed for an easy delivery.

---

*Contributors sometimes report fantastic stories in support of superstitions.

When babies have fits, pull off their clothes and they won't have any more.

Sweep a baby's back and he will walk faster.

Brush a baby's knees with a straw broom for nine days and it will walk early.

If a child is tickled, he will become a stutterer.

To hold a baby in a standing position before he can stand alone will make it bowlegged.

Children who bite their fingernails will never grow tall and be strong.

A baby has to break out in hives to be healthy.

A sleeping baby that's smiling is listening to the angels talking and smiling at them.

A baby born on Friday the 13th will be unlucky all his life.

A child's hair will be curly if he eats burnt food.

A seventh child will always be lucky.

Hiccups mean the baby is growing.

Tea drinking will stunt the child's growth.

The seventh girl born into a family will be a fortune-teller.

Count the lines on the outside edge of your hand and that's how many children you will have.

Don't whip a child with a broom; it'll make him lazy.

If a child's first word is Mama, the next baby will be a boy; if it says Papa first, the next will be a girl.

If a baby is a boy, the father should take him out the door the first time so he'll grow up to be a gentleman.

If a baby doesn't fall off the bed by the time it's a year old, it is a sign that the baby will be unlucky.

Children that have initials that spell a word will be lucky.

Love and Marriage

As many fingernails as you have with half moons on them, that's how many boy friends you have.

When you pop your fingers, the number of times they pop represents the number of miles you reside from your sweetheart.

You can drop a spoon and the way the handle turns is the way your boy friend comes.

Put onions under the bed and they will attract a sweetheart to the house.

Burn a match and it will point to your boy friend's house.

Never give a knife as a gift to a member of the opposite sex whom you love. It will cut your love in two.

When transplanting a flower or piece of shrubbery, give it the name of your sweetheart. It will live, if the sweetheart really loves you.

One can find out a lot about their boy friend from a straw: Take a straw, go down the straw with one finger, then another, pressing the straw together, saying "he loves me, he loves me not." Next, in these indentations made by the process above, say "date, letter, phone," over and over until you reach the bottom of the straw. Next say "tall, medium, short." Next say "blonde, brunette, redhead." Next ask the day of the week that you will have the date, letter, or phone call. Start at the top of the straw with the name of the day after the present day. Then ask a friend to name each end of the straw a boy's name (of course ones you like). Then pull the straw in two. The side that is the shorter names the person all this applies to.

To sweep a spider web from the wall is a sign that you are going to find a new lover.

If you blow all the head off a thistle, then your boy friend loves you.

If you hold up a dandelion, the way the fuzz goes is the way that your girl friend lives.

If a girl goes fishing, she should name her bait before she throws it into the water. If she catches a fish the boy whom she named the bait after likes her, but if she does not catch a fish he does not like her.

If you get lipstick on your teeth, it's a sign your boy friend loves you.

If you see a red bird before dinner, you will see your boy friend before supper.

If you want a boy to love you, take some of his hair and sleep with it under your pillow.

If a young lady rises early on February 14 and looks through a keyhole and sees only one object in her first peep, she supposedly has little chance of being married that year. If she sees two or more objects in the first peep, she has a better chance of getting married that year.

If you catch a girl under mistletoe, you can kiss her.

If a boy wants to find out if a girl is smart before he marries her, he can put a broom in front of the door. If the girl picks up the broom when she comes in she is smart. If she doesn't, she is lazy.

If you step on someone's heel, if you don't shake hands with him, he will take your sweetheart.

If the bread burns, your fellow is mad at you.

If when you touch yourself you turn pink, you are jealous.

If your chin turns yellow when you put a buttercup under it, you are in love.

If your cigarette burns low on one side, the one you love is thinking of you.

If your shoes come untied, your boy friend or girl friend is standing on his head over you.

If you are lucky in playing cards, you will be lucky in love.

If you see three cars with one light in a night, it means you'll see your boy friend.

If you have a mole on the temple, you will have happiness in love.

Never step over a broom lying on the floor, if you do and are unmarried you will be an old maid.

If you have a dimple in your cheek, many hearts you will seek.

If a girl has a dimple on her chin, she is not to be trusted.

If you have a dimple in your chin, many hearts you will win.

Pluck the petals from a daisy. Say He loves me, He loves me not. The last petal will tell whatever is true.

The number of towels the girl receives at her miscellaneous shower tells the number of children she will have.

A woman will possess unusual luck if she marries two men with the same last name.

Marry on a rainy day and you won't be happy.

Where a black cat is kept, it is said that the girls will never get married.

If you are a bridesmaid over three times, you will never marry.

The one who catches the bouquet is the next to marry.

It's bad luck for any dog to go between a boy and a girl who plan to be married.

It is bad luck for the groom to see the bride on the wedding day.

After a bride has finished dressing, she shouldn't look back into the mirror until after the wedding.

Name all four corners of the bed (with a boy name) before you go to bed and the one you look at first the next morning, that one you will marry.

First male you see after cooking spaghetti, you will marry.

Put a doodlebug in the meal and he'll write the initials of the one you're going to marry.

Count stars nine times in a row and you will dream of the man you are going to marry.

Marry in blue, always be true.

A person whose eyebrows have grown together has already met his mate.

To know how soon a person will be married, get a pea pod in which are exactly nine peas. Hang it over the door, and then take notice of the next person who comes in. If the person is not of the family, not of your sex, and if he is unmarried, you will certainly be married within that year.

It's bad luck to marry exactly on the hour.

A girl should not marry a man whose last name begins with the same letter as her own.

Marry when the year is new—/ Always loving, kind and true. When February birds do mate/ You may wed, not dread the fate. If you wed when March winds blow/ Joy and sorrow both you'll know. Marry in April when you can/ Joy for maiden and for man/ Marry in the month of May/ You will surely rue the day. Marry when June roses blow/ Over the land and sea you'll go. Those who in July do wed/ Must labor always for their bread. Whoever wed in August be/ Many a change to see. Marry in September's shrine/ Your living will be rich and fine. If in October you marry/ Love will come but riches tarry. If you wed in bleak November/ Only joy will come, remember. When December's snows fall fast/ Marry and true love will last.

Put salt in your hand and then a piece of ice and run around the house three times and open your hand and there will be the initial of the person you are going to marry.

The number of ribbons you break on your wedding presents tells the number of children you will have.

If a woman loves a cat, she'll be an old maid.

If an engaged couple has a picture made together before they are married, they will separate, they will never be man and wife.

If you get married on a pretty day you will be a good wife, and if the next day is pretty your husband will be a good husband.

If you jump out of bed on your wedding morning on both feet at once, you will start your marriage on the right foot.

If you are driving across a state line with a boy, you should stand up so that you will get married.

If you drop a knife, you'll never get married.

If four people cross one another's hands when they shake hands, there will be a wedding.

If you take the last piece of bread off the plate, you will never get married.

If a girl sits on a dining table, it will be seven years before she has a chance to be married.

If you look into a well on the first day of May, you can see if you will marry, and who you will marry; if you see a coffin, you will not get married. If you do get married you will see your husband's image on the surface.

If you turn over a chair, the number you can count before you can pick it up will be the number of years before you get married.

If rain drops fall on the bride, she will have to shed tears.

If it rains on a girl's wedding day, she will shed that many tears.

If you pick up two spoons before eating, it means that there will be a wedding in the family.

When washing by hand, if you get the front of your dress wet you will marry a drunkard.

If it rains straight down, you will hear wedding bells.

If you stick your finger in a woodpecker hole, the next boy you see will be your husband.

If you have a mole on the right eye, you will have wealth and a happy marriage.

If your husband leaves you, if you will take a rag and tie up the sand from his left track as he is leaving you and put the rag under your pillow, he will come back to you.

A bride should wear something old, something new, something borrowed, and something blue.

If you are making a wedding dress and stick your finger, you will have bad luck if some of the blood gets on the dress.

Death

It is said when a person is dying, the last person's name he says will be the next to die.

Do not cut broom straw after New Year's Day. It is a sign of death.

It's bad luck for a hen to crow. It means a death in the family.

When the dog howls during the day there is a death or will be a death soon.

The family should never leave the cemetery before the grave is fixed, it means another death in the family if they do.

If a bird flies into the house, or taps at a window, it is a bad omen; it augurs death within the year to someone living in the house.

If you count the cars of a train as it passes, it will bring death to someone in the family.

If you hear someone at the door and when you go to the door, no one is really there, a death will soon come in the family.

If a dove lights in your yard with its head pointed toward your house, there will be a death in your family.

If the dust from your foot tracks gets in your mouth, you will die.

If your ears ring, it is a sign of death.

If you take a baby to a funeral, it will die before the year is out.

If you step across someone's legs while they're in bed, someone in your family will die.

If a praying mantis spits fire on you, you will die.

If a garden spider writes your name in his web, you will die.

If you plant a weeping willow tree in your yard, someone in your family will die within three years.

If Friday seems like Saturday, you can look for a death in your family connections.

If a baby doesn't crawl before he walks, he will crawl before he dies.

If someone has died in your family, and if his casket is in your home, do not keep it near the mirror. If you do, another member will die within the next year.

If a bee stings you under the nose, you will die.

If you see a thousand-legged worm, you had better close your mouth; if he counts your teeth you will die.

If you drop a comb, that is a sign that you will hear of a death.

If a picture falls from a wall, someone will die in the house before the end of the year.

When a clock that hasn't run for years suddenly strikes, a death will follow.

Bats in a house is a sign that death will come to someone in the house.

A falling star is a sign of death.

If you sew on New Year's Day, it is a sign that you will sew for a dead body before the year is out.

Do not cut out a garment for anyone who is sick, they will not live to wear it.

Rain in an open grave means another death in the family.

It is a sign of death when a dove moans.

Don't let two people comb one person's hair at the same time or one will die.

If a mockingbird tries to get into the house, someone's dying.

When someone is being buried in a family and they are all at the graveyard, the first one to the graveyard in the family will be the next one to die.

Don't move into an unfinished house. There will be a death in the family before it is finished.

The first one to go to sleep on the wedding night will be the first one to die.

Don't point at a grave. If you do you will be the next person to die.

Miss a row in planting corn and death will come to the family.

Don't count the number of cars in a funeral procession. It is a sign of death.

If a person sees a "fireball" around a house, it means a death in the family.

If you kill a butterfly, you will die.

Never call a body "angel" because it will be sure death.

If you hear death bells, someone in your family will die before the year ends.

If a screech owl hollers close to your house, someone in the family will die.

Wear a new garment to a funeral and a member of your family will be next to die.

If you catch a bird, some of your family or a close friend will die.

If the wind blows the door open and you close it, death will come to someone in the family.

If you look at the moon through a window screen and see a cross on the moon, you will die.

If a woodpecker pecks at your house, then a member of your family is going to die.

If the moon is full the first of January, more white people will die than Negroes. Vice versa.

If you plant cotton and leave a row uncovered, someone in your field gang will die.

If you hear bells ringing in your ears, some of your relatives are dying.

If you start a garment on Friday, and you can't finish the garment before the day ends, you'll die in that dress before it wears out.

If a person's teeth are ridgy, he will die with fever.

If shingles circle your body, you will die.

If you hear a wood tick in the wall, you should never count his ticks for someone you know will die within the number of days you count.

If you plant a cedar tree, when it grows big enough to shadow your grave, you will die.

Weather and the Seasons

If soot falls down the chimney, it's a sign of rain.

If bark grows heavy on trees in summer, look for a cold winter.

Folks say, "Hollow moon turns west, the fish bite best."

If it lightens in the north after the sun goes down, and it does not rain in three days, it will not rain for three weeks.

Thunder in February and it will frost on the same day in April.

If the sun should shine while it's raining, it will rain again tomorrow.

The higher the clouds, the finer the weather.

When grass is dry at morning's light, look for rain before the night.

When the dew is on the grass, rain will never come to pass.

For each time it thunders in February, it will frost on that day in May.

If the rain comes on the first of the month, then that will be a rainy month.

If January is warm, this means that bad weather is in store for the rest of the year.

If corn had extra-thick husks on its ears, this is a sign of a long, cold winter.

An extra skin on an onion means that a long, hard winter is ahead.

If it rains on Easter Sunday, it will rain four following Sundays.

If on February 2 the groundhog sees his shadow when he comes out of winter hibernation, there will be another six weeks of cold weather.

Aching corns or bunions are signs of changing weather.

If you see a lot of birds flying south, you will know that the weather will turn cold.

Smoke settling to the earth is a sign of rain.

If smoke from a chimney goes up it means dry weather, if the smoke goes down toward the ground it means rain.

Smoke coming straight from a chimney means rain.

Folks say, "Rain before seven stops before eleven."

If it thunders on February 20, it will be cold on April 20.

Lightning is not apt to strike in the same place more than once.

If an old break hurts, the weather will change.

If the raindrops are big ones, it won't rain long.

If it lightens in the north, it will rain the next day.

If in the fall the animals have real heavy fur coats, it is a sign of cold winter.

If a cat sneezes, it's a sign of rain.

When bull bats come out, it is a sign it will not rain.

Two birds flying low together is a sign of rain.

You can tell when it will rain by whether the moon is wet or dry. A quarter moon turned up is dry moon, and a wet moon is a quarter moon turned down. Wet moon, rain; dry moon, drought. When the moon is cresent shaped with the points turned up it isn't going to rain because the moon is holding water. If the points are turned down then it will rain because the moon is pouring out water.

A rainbow in the morning is a sign of bad weather. A rainbow at night is a sign of good weather.

When you wake in the morning and see big yellow thunderheads in the south, that means it will rain within two days.

When you see bay leaves turn upside down, you will have rain.

When the ash tree blooms before the oak, it means there is a drought coming.

When a cow endeavors to scratch its ear, it means a shower is very near. When it thumps it ribs with angry tail, look out for thunder, lightning, hail.

It will rain tomorrow if the sun sets behind a cloud.

A whirlwind is a sign of dry weather.

When your bones ache, it's a sign of rain.

There is always a storm after the death of an old woman.

It is a sign of rain and snow when the birds and bugs fly low.

When a mule's ears twitch a certain way, it is sure to rain that day.

"Buzzard, buzzard, when is it going to rain? Let it be known by flapping your wings." How ever many times he flaps before he is out of sight will be the number of days that will pass before it rains.

Fog in the morning and rising, it won't rain.

When you see a bad cloud, go get the ax and stick it up in the ground and leave it there; then the bad cloud will clear up.

When you hear a rooster crowing while it rains, it means it will clear up next day.

First days of January will predict the weather for the year.

Red sunset means it'll be fair weather the next day.

You can tell the weather by the loudness of the grasshopper.

If the leaves turn up, it is a sign of rain.

When a ring is around the moon, the number of stars inside the ring indicate that it will be that many days before it rains.

If it lightens in the north on Sunday it would rain on Wednesday.

When birds fly only a few yards at a time, it is sure to rain.

Blackberries bloom just before the last cold spell.

When yellow jessamine bloom, there will be no more cold weather.

When one sees ducks and geese flying north, it's a sign that cold weather is gone.

Cobwebs on the grass are a sign of fair weather.

When it thunders in the morning, it will rain before night.

If fowls roll in the sand, rain is at hand.

People say if the whirlwind goes toward a creek it will rain, but if it goes to a field it will be dry.

Cold weather never fools the blackberry bushes' bloom. When the blackberry blooms, there will not be any more cold weather.

A red sunset is a sign of clear weather and a red sunrise is a sign of rain.

If the first day of March is windy, the last day will be gentle. Vice versa.

If the robin sings in the bushes, the weather will be coarse. If the robin sings in the barn, the weather will be warm.

If you kill a black snake and hang it on a ladder, it will rain before sundown.

If it rains the first Dog Day, it will rain every day for forty days.

If you see a cat sharpening his claws, the way he is facing will be the way the wind will blow the next day.

A red sun has water in his eyes.

If red the sun begins his race, be sure the rain will fall apace.

Evening red and morning gray, help the traveler on his way;
Evening gray and morning red, bring down rain upon his head.

If the sun pale to bed, 'twill rain tomorrow, it is said.

If the morning mountains, in the evening fountains.

The wind from the northeast, neither good for man nor beast.

When the wind is in the south, the rain is in its mouth.

The wind in the west suits everyone best.

Rainbow in the morning, sailors take warning,
Rainbow at night, sailors delight.

When spider's webs in the air do fly,
The spell will soon be very dry.

Planting

Dark nights during Christmas means a good crop year.

A wet March means a bad crop year.

Dig sweet potatoes on the full moon in October.

For a good crop of beans, plant them when the moon is full.

Plant anything that bears above the ground on the decrease of the moon. Vice versa.

Garden crops planted according to calendar signs will be more prolific.

Potatoes should be planted when signs are lower to the feet.

Don't plant vegetables that grow on vines in the evening.

If you plant flowers on Flower Days, they will bloom; but if you don't they won't. Don't plant any vegetables on Flower Days because everything will turn to blooms. There are Flower Days each month. They are: January 12, 14; February 18, 20; March 7, 8; April 3, 5, 30; May 1, 2; June 24, 25; July 21, 23; August 17, 19; September 14, 15; October 11, 12; November 7, 9; December 5, 6. Don't plant a garden on these days because you will not have success with it. Don't plant on a new moon because everything will go to vines. ex: Beautiful vines—no vegetables.

If you plant on Twin Days, you will make a good crop.

Plant crops when dogwood leaves are about the size of possum ear.

Stoop over close to the ground when you plant okra and it will start bearing close to the ground.

Plant peas after whip-o-wills start singing.

Plant peanuts on the sign of twins and everywhere the vine pins down you'll make two peanuts.

To make your pepper hot, you must be angry when you plant it.

Plant beans on a full moon and you'll have a good crop.

Don't plant beans or anything that has a vine on a new moon or you get leaves and no beans.

Plant beans on twin days and there will be two beans to the limb.

Plant on the full moon and get the best result.

Plant watermelons during full moon.

Don't plant corn on growing of moon. Ears will be too high on the stalk and no good.

Plant corn after the fourth full moon in the year.

Plant snapbeans in Twin Days (when signs are in the Arms).

Kill hogs on shrinking of the moon so you can get more grease.

Plant your potatoes on February 14 and the bugs won't bother them.

If you plant crops and garden vegetables on Good Friday, you will have a good crop.

If you steal some flower cuttings, they will root if you will plant them.

If you plant beans in the morning, they will make blooms but won't make beans.

If you spit on each grain of corn you plant, the corn will grow tall and bear well.

Don't work collards during Dog Days. They will die.

If you raise peas or butterbeans, when you shell them, throw the shells in the road in front of your house and your next yield will be better than the first.

If an okra stalk is beaten before bearing time, it will bear more okra.

If a woman cuts okra while she is menstruating, it will not bear anymore.

If anyone gives you flowers to put in your garden, don't thank them or else they'll die.

If a rabbit gets in the garden, put up stakes and tie strings around them and they won't come in.

Good Luck and Good Fortune

The first person born in a family is the luckiest one.

When you dream a bad luck dream you will soon have good luck.

When the new moon is clear, then that is a sign of good luck.

Good luck charms:

A rabbit's foot (sometimes limited to the left hind foot).

A four-leaf clover.

Finding a horseshoe.

A penny found.

Animal teeth.

A buckeye ball.

A cougar bone.

A horse chestnut.

It is good luck if one finds the point of a pin toward him.

If bees hive on your house or in your yard, good luck will come.

To bring good luck from pulling a tooth, tie the tooth in a dirty handkerchief and throw it out the back door.

It's good luck to find a key.

It's good luck to kiss a newborn baby.

It's good luck to cross your fingers.

Put a dime in your shoe for good luck.

A black cat's bone in your back pocket will bring good luck.

Eat dried peas and hog jowl on New Year's Day and you'll have good health and good luck the rest of the year.

Keep fingers crossed for good luck.

Put dried peas in every pocketbook on New Year's Day and you'll be rich the rest of your life.

A picture of Saint Peter hung over the door of a house you have just moved into will bring good luck, because Saint Peter holds the key to everything and opens all doors.

When frying a fish—if the tails turn up, the person who caught them will have better luck next time.

Throwing rice over the bride and groom will bring them good luck.

When hunting, it is considered very good luck to carry the bone from the inside of a coon's penis in the pocket of your hunting coat.

If you get your head wet in the first rain in May, you'll have good luck the rest of the year.

To kill a turtle with a broken tail means good luck.

Keep the stones in a deer's stomach; it will bring you good luck.

It is good luck to rub the hand on the head of a person with red hair.

A quiver in the right eye means good luck; in the left eye bad luck.

When you pass a fire, throw in a pinch of salt for good luck.

When katydids sing, touch the tree they are in and if they quit, it is good luck.

When the moon is high and star falls, there is good luck.

Move on Sunday for good luck.

Two yolks in an egg is lucky for the one who gets it.

If a gray horse passes, you should stamp your fist in the middle of your hand and say, "Gray horse bring to me good luck."

If one sees a red bird in the morning, he will not have good luck.

If a strange cat kills the canary, you will not have good luck for two years.

If you read a whole book on Christmas Eve, you'll have good luck.

If you are given an Old Indian head penny in change for a purchase, save it and never spend it, for it brings good luck indefinitely.

If a jaybird comes down and eats with the chickens, you will have good luck.

When you make urine, spit in it for good luck.

If you find a button, put it in the bottom of your shoe and wear it there until you pull your shoe off that night. This will bring you good luck.

If you take something in first before you take something out on New Year's Day, you will be prosperous.

Making Wishes Come True

See a gray mule, make a wish, and it will come true.

Stick a pin in your left shoulder if you have picked it up from the floor and make a wish. It will come true.

When you see a car with one headlight, make a wish. Then, touch your right thumb to your tongue, rub your right thumb into your left hand palm, and then pound your right hand fist into your left palm. Your wish will come true.

If you make a wish and then blow out all the candles on your birthday cake with one breath, your wish will come true.

If you find a dead frog, draw a circle around it, spit on it, and make a wish, and it will come true.

If you see a crow flying through the air, make a wish. If the crow does not flap his wings before it is out of sight, the wish will come true.

If you see a falling star and make a wish before it gets to the ground, it will come true.

If two people make a wish and pull a wishbone, the one who pulls the larger part will have his wish.

If you let someone sweep under your feet, you'll have his wish come true.

If you hold your breath when you go over a river, make a wish and it will come true.

If you see an empty Lucky Strike cigarette pack lying on the ground, step on it and say "1, 2, 3; good luck for me," make a wish, and your wish will come true.

If you see the new moon through a tree top, make a wish and it will come true.

If the hem of your dress turns up and you kiss it, you'll get another new dress.

If you see a red bird, throw three kisses at it and you will see someone you are not expecting to see.

Make a wish on the first star you see. Say: Star light, star bright!
First star I see tonight.
I wish I may,
I wish I might,
Have the wish I wish tonight.

It's Bad Luck . . .

to carry ashes out after dark.

if you start sewing a dress on Friday.

if your first visitor on New Year's Day is a lady.

to put a man's hat on a baby's head before he is a year old.

for a cat to die on its owner's property.

if a black cat comes to your home.

to move a cat from place to place. Seven years bad luck to kill a cat.

to put your clothing on wrong-side-out. Wear it that way all day to ward off bad luck.

to go anywhere on New Year's Day: you'll be on the go all year.

if you let a locust holler in your hand.

to hang a new door and lop off one corner for a "Cat-Crack" through which the cat may go in and out.

to wear other people's new clothes before they wear them.

to wear a black dress to a wedding.

to leave Christmas trees in the house over New Year's Day.

to cut your toenails or fingernails on Sunday. It makes you unruly the next week.

to rock an empty rocking chair.

if you do not get up on the same side of the bed you went to bed on.

if the wife buys the husband a ring when they get married.

if you comb your hair on New Year's Day.

if you are handed scissors open and return them open.

if you make a baby's shoes before it is born.

if you break a teapot.

if the inside of your hand stings.

to see your image in a pool.

to shut the door when you move.

to hop on one foot downstairs.

to sit in the window.

to carry a rake in the house.

for a dead body to remain unburied over Sunday.

to leave the dead alone.

to take a baby out of the house before it is a month old.

to put the left shoe on before the right.

to let the sun go down without naming a new baby.

to take the last of anything off a dish.

to sing in bed.

to kill a red bird.

to count your teeth.

to wash on Friday before and after Christmas.

to sing a Christmas song a long time before Christmas.

for two people to sweep in the same room.

to turn a chair around one leg at a time.

to sleep under a quilt that is upside down.

to burn corncobs.

for a rooster to crow after dark.

to kill a lizard.

to see a red bird in the morning.

if a strange cat kills the canary. Two years of bad luck.

if you start on a trip and meet a woman.

to let anyone step over your body if you are lying down.

to let your fishing pole cross anybody else's.

to pay back salt that is borrowed.

to sweep dirt out of the door on New Year's Day.

to give a purse as a present without money in it. Just a penny will do.

to hand a baby out of a window.

to sing at the table.

for a strange cat to take up with you.

for a girl to cut another girl's hair.

to sit with your legs crossed on Sunday.

to take out ashes when someone is sick in the house.

to sweep your floor after dark.

to burn wood that lightning has struck.

to move a broom when you move.

to keep a live person's hair.

to pop your fingers.

to let a baby see itself in a mirror before it is one year old.

to name a baby before it is born.

to sweep the floor with two brooms at one time.

to have a two dollar bill, unless one corner has been removed.

to fall over a chair.

if you don't sit down the first time you visit a home.

to place a pair of shoes on the table.

to shake the tablecloth after sundown.

for two people to work baking a cake at the same time. The cake won't be good.

to pick up scissors that you have dropped. If someone else picks them up it is good luck.

to open an umbrella in the house.

to burn a broom.

to wash clothes, mop, or make beds on Monday.

to kill a spider in the house.

for your left eye to jump.

to seat thirteen at a dinner table.

to rake the yard after sundown.

to lie across two chairs.

to cross someone's feet if you don't cross back over them.

to prop the broom against the bed.

to sigh in bed.

to whistle in the bedroom.

to have doors and windows cut in a house after you move in.

to have another person finish the floor you started sweeping.

to play a piano with one hand.

to go out a different door from the one you came.

to sit on the table.

to pay back borrowed pepper.

to sit in bed unless you are sick.

to break bread when someone else is holding it.

to find a safety pin which has the point toward you.

to find a safety pin closed.

to break your beds.

to sleep with your shoes higher than your head.

to wear an opal when it is not your birthstone.

to bury a person with his shoes on.

to light three cigarettes with one match.

to go ahead and swallow food if you sneeze with it in your mouth.

to walk in someone's tracks.

for the groom to see the wedding dress before the wedding.

to sweep under an unmarried girl's chair.

if you step over a broom.

to take the salt shaker from somebody without first putting it down.

to burn salt.

to gather eggs after dark.

to leave a mattress out to sun after the sun has gone down.

to carry anything out of a graveyard.

to leave your house with the doors open.

to sweep under an unmarried girl's feet. She will always be an old maid.

to lose a horseshoe.

to ride or walk backwards.

to cut the fingernails of a sick person.

to sleep in a room numbered thirteen.

to kill a cricket in the house.

to walk on cracks in a sidewalk.

to watch anyone go out of sight when they are going somewhere.

to walk with one shoe off and one shoe on.

to break a window glass.

to sun beds on Friday.

to plant any seeds on the last three days of March.

to plant cedar and pine trees in your yard.

to count the stars.

to have wandering jew growing in the house. It makes the boys wander off.

to carry a dog over water when carrying off stray dogs.

to burn trash on New Year's Day.

if a rabbit crosses the road in front of you going right.

if a rooster looks at you and crows three times.

to stir buttermilk with a knife.

to sweep the bottom doorstep.

for a child to be born on Friday.

to pull off your shoes at night and turn them upside down.

if you break a chain letter.

if you become owner of a grandfather clock and sell it.

if a cow is seen on Christmas Eve with its head bowed.

if you use the eraser of a pencil before the pencil is sharpened.

to pick berries in the graveyard.

to cook onions and potatoes at the same time.

if you see the shadow of a bird and not the bird.

if you try to split a tree and it won't split.

to break a mirror (seven years).

if a baseball player changes bats after the second strike.

to take the last match from the box.

if two people wash their feet in the same basin in the same water.

to go possum hunting before sundown. (You won't catch anything.)

for a girl to try on an engagement ring that belongs to another girl.

to talk about dead folks.

for a wren to be in the house.

to wash on Friday.

to whip a child on his birthday.

to drink milk while eating fish.

to count the things you eat.

to prick yourself with a pin before starting on a journey.

to walk under a ladder.

to throw snake eyes three times in a row (a week).

to look over the left shoulder and see the new moon (until the moon changes).

Warding Off Bad Luck

If a rabbit crosses the road in front of you, curse him and you won't have bad luck.

When you yawn, snap your fingers three times. To yawn when one is not sleepy is a sign of disappointment.

It is bad luck to leave home and to go back. You should make a circle in the road, put an "x" in it and spit in it to counter the evil.

If a black cat crosses the road in front of you, you ought to turn around and go the other way or you will have bad luck.

If you see a pin and don't pick it up, all day you will have bad luck and you'll cry all day. Pick it up and you'll have good luck.

If two persons say the same thing at the same time, hook right fingers to ward off bad luck.

If a rooster crows on your top doorstep, you must walk backwards across the place he ran to ward off bad luck.

If you spill salt, you should throw some over your left shoulder to ward off bad luck.

If your hair is tangled in the morning, it means that the witches sleep with you during the night. To prevent their return, throw salt over your left shoulder into the fire before you retire.

If you break a mirror, leave it in running water to wash bad luck away.

If you cover a mirror in a storm, the lightning will not strike you.

If you stump your toes, turn around, make a circle and keep on going. If you don't things will be bad for you.

If you are walking down the road on a dark night by yourself, just look over your left shoulder and whatever you see will disappear. You have nothing to worry about—just keep on going.

Don't wish an actor good luck before he goes on stage; if you say "break a leg," good luck will overrule the bad luck.

If you were riding down the street in a car and a cat goes to your left, you turn your hat around backwards like you were going back up the street.

A pinch of salt thrown over the shoulder keeps the devil away.

When you bump your elbow, if you don't rub it on someone else or wood, you will have bad luck.

Talking about a run of good luck will only bring the bad if you don't knock on wood.

Wear a piece of garlic on a string around your neck to ward off evil spirits.

Unless you hang a horseshoe upside down, all your luck will run out.

Wrestlers wear Devil's shoe string around their waist during a match. They take 3 pieces and cross it. Put it in the back of their trunks. When this is worn they cannot be thrown.

If bad luck comes while you have on a certain dress, then don't wear it again.

If two people pass a tree and one goes on one side and one goes on the other, it's bad luck. If this happens, say together:

> Bread and butter, come to supper.
> What goes up the chimney? Smoke.
> Hope this friendship will never be broke.

If you tell a lie, throw salt over your shoulder to keep away bad luck.

> See a pin and pick it up,
> All the day you'll have good luck;
> See a pin and let it lie,
> Good luck will pass you by.

Spells, Signs, and Portents

If you sing church music at a dance, you'll have trouble in your feet.

If a pregnant sow goes through a graveyard, the pigs will have straight tails.

If the first cornsilk is red, then you will be healthy. If it is white, then you will be sick.

If you kiss your elbow, you will turn into a girl.

If you pull a horse's tail, seal it in a jar of urine and the hair will turn into a snake overnight.

If you hear a voice and there ain't no human near, then either God or the devil is trying to talk to you.

If you speak of a person he will appear.

If a man comes to your house first of the week, you'll have company all week.

If you get your hair in your mouth, you are going to kiss a fool.

If a loaf of bread is upside down on the table, it means the devil is around.

If you step over a person without stepping back, it will stop that person's growth.

If you wear two hats at one time, you'll get a spanking before the day is over.

If your right ear is burning, a man is talking about you.

If your left ear is burning, a woman is talking about you. Moisten your fingertips and put them to your ears and say, "Talk good, talk on. Talk bad, bite your tongue."

If you have a bruised spot on yourself, it is where a ghost has touched you while you were sleeping.

If you give a child a Biblical name, he will be just the opposite of that Bible person.

If water blisters are broken, new blisters will form wherever this water touches.

If you have a mole on the cheek, you will not be pleased with your fame and fortune.

If you have a mole on the chin, you will be fortunate in your choice of friends.

If you see a buzzard and don't see two, you will see somebody you're not expecting to.

If two people are hunting and their guns accidentally hit each other, these two people will meet in the exact place one year from that time.

If you suspect a person has drowned at a spot, throw a bunch of fodder in the water at the place and the corpse will rise.

If your canary sings after dark, he will not live much longer.

If two people are hoeing and strike their hoes together, it is a sign that they will hoe together tomorrow.

If you have a white scar on the back of your neck, you will live forever.

If a bird with a red breast dies in your hand, that hand will always shake.

If a yellow bee flies around you, good news is coming.

If a black bee flies around you, bad news is coming.

If a turtle bites you, he will not let you go until it thunders.

If your cow has warts on her teats, name her Filey and they will come off.

If you take food out of a bowl, and you already have that food on your plate, someone is coming.

If walking with a crowd, you stump your left toe, you are welcome, and vice versa.

If your face burns, someone is talking about you.

If a lie bump appears on your tongue, you have told a thousand lies.

If your ear itches, you are going to hear a secret.

If you sleep in moonlight, you'll go insane.

If your back itches, you are going to get a whipping.

If the first turtledove you see sings behind you, you will have a long sick spell.

If your foot itches, you'll want a date with someone.

If your right hand itches, you are going to meet a stranger.

If your right foot itches, you are going on a trip.

If your left foot itches, you are going where you are not wanted.

If a screech owl hollers at night, stick the tongs in the fire. It will burn his feet and he will go away.

If you get an old kerosene lamp and light it, then get a glass of water and set it by the lamp, look into the glass of water, and you can see your future.

If you cut your hair on a new moon, it will grow faster.

If a tooth comes out, bury it so the rest of the teeth won't rot, but if you carry a wild animal's tooth in your pocket all the time, your teeth won't rot at all.

If you throw a stick in a whirlwind and curse it, it will fly out and hit you between the eyes.

If a black cat crosses in front of you, turn around and go the other way.

If the waitress puts the piece of pie pointing toward you, you will get a letter that day.

If you make good on a test while sitting in a certain chair, sit in that chair for all tests in that class. And if you don't sit in that particular desk for every test, you'll make bad.

If you drop a dish cloth, company is coming.

If wisdom teeth are cut through before the age of twenty, it means a short life.

When you go by a graveyard, put your thumbs up and you'll go to heaven.

If you break a dish, throw salt out the window to keep from breaking more dishes.

If a little boy swallows a fish bladder, it will help him learn to swim.

If you set the hen so that the biddies hatch in May, they will sleep themselves to death.

If the weather is bad and stormy on a funeral day, the deceased will go to hell.

If you read a prayer every day, you will go to heaven.

If you feed a dog on a fork, he will become a mean yard dog.

If you count the rosebuds on a bush, the buds will all fall off.

If a bird sings before breakfast, a cat will catch him before night.

If you bite your tongue while eating, it's because you have told a fib.

If two persons reach for a piece of bread at the same time, someone is coming.

If a pupil drops his school books, he will have bad lessons the next day unless he stamps his feet on the books.

If your second toe is the largest, you will be boss in your household.

East wind is always unhealthy, everybody will be sick.

If you cuss a rat, he'll cut your bedstead down.

Intoxicated persons always tell the truth.

If a devil's horse spits in your eye, it will put it out.

If you hang your pants higher than your head, you will have a sleep-less night.

If your garment is sewed while it is on you, the person sewing it will tell as many lies about you as they make stitches.

If you hear an owl screech or hoot at night, turn your shoe upside down and it will stop.

If you burn a dead snake, don't let the smoke get in your eyes, it will blind you.

If you want a hen to have all pullets, set her in the morning.

If you cut firewood in the light of the moon, it won't spark.

If two persons yawn at the same time, one of them will be ill.

If someone is talking in his sleep, put his hand in cold water, he will tell you all about it.

When one shivers, it means a rabbit runs over his grave.

To put out a fire started by lightning use milk.

Meat cured in the light of the moon will become soft. Meat cured in the dark of the moon will be firm.

To make someone stop snoring, put his hand in water.

Spit on the bait to make the fish bite.

Put a match in your mouth while peeling onion and you won't cry.

Take a shotgun and shoot where fleas are on the ground and they will leave.

People with black eyes will have a bad future.

To drive a woman crazy, sprinkle nutmeg in her left shoe every night at midnight.

Put a lizard in a bucket and cook it. Put a person's name on it. This will cause that person to break out in a rash.

Someone who was born with a veil over his face can see "hants" and can show them to somebody else if this person will look over the gifted individual's left shoulder.

A person's taste changes every seven years.

If you want someone to leave town, go to a farmer and get a white egg from a black chicken. Take the egg home—and write the person's name on the egg as many times as possible. Take the egg out in the yard and bury it and within two weeks that person will leave town.

If you get a dog or cat and bring them home with you and if you don't want them to leave, you must cut their tails off and put them under the doorstep.

If you have company and you don't want them to come back anymore, spread black pepper on the floor and sweep it out behind them.

If a man is murdered, bury him face down and his killer will give himself up in three days.

If you eat chicken feet, you'll be pretty.

If you eat chicken livers, you'll be pretty.

If you have warts, go out and find a bone and rub it on your warts, then place it right in the same place and don't look back and your warts will go away.

Never cut a loaf of bread without forming a cross with the knife on the back of the loaf.

When passing a hearse, turn up your collar until you see a wild dog.

Always spit when a funeral passes.

Don't put a mule's hair in water or it will become a snake.

Thick black hair is a sign of good health.

White hair on a very young person is a sign of genius.

Dig a hole in the ground on the shrinking of the moon and you will not have enough dirt to fill it up again. Dig hole on the increase and you will have too much dirt.

A rattlesnake will not cross a grass rope. When camping, place a grass rope around you when sleeping and you will be protected.

Don't lie to the preacher, because if you do weevils and worms will eat your corn.

If you sweep trash out after dark, your cow will die.

When you pull a tooth and do not stick your tongue in the place, another tooth will grow.

First twelve days after Christmas are known as the "old twelve days" and each represents a month of the coming year.

Some people cannot carry water in an open bucket after dark because the hants will jump in the bucket and kick the water out.

Catch a chicken. Put a cross in front of his bill on the ground and put the chicken there. The chicken will put his bill on the cross and won't move for the world.

If a person jingles coins in his pockets, that is a sign that he really hasn't any money at all.

Don't kill hogs on the growing of the moon. If you do, you won't have much lard, and the meat will pop up when you cook it.

Don't set a hen on Friday, the eggs won't hatch.

Don't sing before rising or you'll weep before going to bed.

A crow won't touch a kernel of corn if you arrange it in a circle.

A hot wave passing by is a hant.

To speak about the Lord will scare away hants.

There is a hant around when the hair rises on the head.

If you walk down a flight of stairs and skip a step, you will skip a day in your life.

Never start anything on Friday or you'll never finish it.

If you kill a cow ant, one of your cows will die.

If you kill a frog, the cow will go dry.

Frogs cause warts.

Don't sun your beds on Monday or someone sick will lie on them before the week is out.

If you take a cup of turpentine and put it to the navel of a cow, this will make the cow give more milk.

If you kill a snake, his tail will wiggle until the sun goes down.

Some miners will not go down in the mines after a woman has been down until a miner is killed.

A red-headed person is mean.

A mole on the arm indicates a happy nature, but with something of a don't care attitude.

Don't burn scraps of cooking in a wood stove.

If you put salt on a bird's tail, he can't fly.

Do not eat oysters unless the month has an R in the spelling.

There are 40 chills in each maypop seed. Don't eat them.

When you get chilly, this means a coon is passing over where your grave is supposed to be.

When your ears get red and begin to burn, this means that someone is talking about you.

When receiving a gift of a knife or scissors, the receiver should give a piece of money in return. If you do not, it will cut your friendship in two.

A joint snake will pull itself back together after it is cut to pieces if the pieces are not buried deep and far apart.

You shouldn't walk in the mimicing ways of a cripple: you will soon have to walk that way.

If the smut on the back of the chimney burns, you are going to get fresh meat given to you.

Never talk while fishing because you'll scare the fish away.

For every gray hair pulled out of your head, two more will appear.

When you bake a cake and it gets done, don't bend your knees when you take it out of the oven. If you do, the cake will break on top.

If you walk in a person's footprints, that person will have a toothache.

If you cry on your birthday, you will cry all year.

If a left-handed person is forced to use his right hand, it will cause stuttering.

If a person bites his nails, he will not grow tall.

When it is raining and the sun is shining, it is a sure sign that the devil is beating his wife with a frying pan.

When you see butterflies, it is a sign Fall is coming.

If two hens fight, two women are coming to visit. Their colors suggest the colors of the women's clothing.

If you accidentally make a rhyme while talking, you will see your boy friend before bedtime.

If a single crow flying begins cawing near a house, it is announcing to the people who live there an approaching calamity.

If your eye itches, you will get a letter.

If you step over a dog, you will fall out of a high door.

If you go in a house and stump your toe, you are not wanted.

If you have an open fireplace and sticks of wood happen to roll off, someone is coming.

If you lay your hat on the bed, you will get disappointed.

If you drop silverware, someone is coming to visit you: a fork, a woman; a knife, a man; a spoon, a child.

If the first single crow seen in the spring is in the act of flying, it means one will take a journey.

Put cotton in the screen door to keep flies away.

When a hawk appears in the sky before sundown, follow it with your eye for it will bring you good luck.

When a child first starts talking, if it says mama first, the next child will be a boy, and vice versa.

The time to castrate a hog is when the sign of the zodiac is in his feet.

To scare a cow just before milking time will cause the milk to clabber before souring.

You can't see a jaybird on Friday because all jaybirds go to hell on Friday with a grain of sand.

To keep a corpse, put a bowl of soda on the stomach of the corpse and it will keep it from decaying.

A large mouth denotes generosity and vice versa.

A large number of wrinkles around the mouth signifies a tendency not to tell the truth.

To bite the tongue when talking means that the next remark is not true.

A little bump on the end of the tongue means that the person has told a lie.

If your sitting down place itches, you are going to ride in a new automobile.

If your shoe comes untied, your sweetheart is traveling.

Teeth apart means that one will live far from his parents; close together means he will live near his parents.

When you make a doll, don't ever put ears on it because the doll will tell a person what you said about them.

When you are walking with somebody and pass something taller than you and one walks on one side and one on the other you will have a quarrel.

Anyone who has small ears is stingy, vice versa.

When it rains, squeal to warn off evil spirits.

Snakes can't bite under water.

When a bird finds some of your hair and makes a nest of it, you will have a headache.

Don't shave hair under arms; it will take strength away.

When you burn your chicken, it means your husband is mad.

Don't eat any tomatoes because they are poisonous.

You will become sick if you eat apples and drink milk together.

When the sun is straight up in the chimney, it is twelve o'clock.

A man who has a hairy chest and arms some day will be rich.

To wear a wide leather strap around the wrist will make a man strong in his hand grip.

Cut a green forked stick, and hold it in the hand, when the stick points toward the ground you have found water.

If a dog catches a wild hog, he will not growl, and neither will the hog squeal.

Wash your hands together, friends forever; dry your hands together, enemies forever.

If you drop a pin, step on it 'cause it will mean a fight.

When you eat hot pepper, go to the chicken roost and it will cool off.

Don't set your bed crossways the world; set it east and west.

A spirit will not cross a stream.

Every stitch you sew on Sunday, you will have to root out on Judgment Day.

New-laid eggs and first (has to be first) spring onions gathered will mean meat and vegetables the rest of the year.

Be careful what you say around a jaybird because he tells the devil what you say.

A sudden clap of thunder will sour the milk.

Don't get a hog mad before you kill it. If you do, it will scent the meat.

If you dream about water, it is a sign of trouble.

Dream of muddy water; a sure sign of trouble.

Dream it is raining; you are going to shed a lot of tears.

Dream of fishing; your wife is going to have a baby—unless you are the wife, then you will have a baby.

If you dream of catching a fish, it is a sign of pregnancy.

The first dream you have in a new house will come to pass.

A Friday dream and Saturday told, Come to pass, no matter how old.

If you tell your dream before breakfast, it will come true.

To dream of death is a sign of a birth.

If you dream of birth, it is a sign of death.

Dreams are the soul of the sleeper leaving the body. You shouldn't wake a sleeper suddenly because his soul might not find its way back to the body.

Dream of head lice and you will have sickness.

If you sleep with a piece of wedding cake under your pillow, you will dream of the man you will marry.

When you dream of snakes, you will lose a friend.

If you dream of snakes, you have some enemies; if you kill them, you make friends of your enemies.

If you can put a hat over a sleeping dog's head without waking him, you will dream the same dream as the dog.

If you dream about death in the family, there will be a wedding in the family.

If you will set your shoes under the head of your bed with the toes pointing out, you won't dream bad dreams.

If you dream of crying, you are going to be sick; if you dream of fussing with someone, you are going to cry.

If you dream of eggs, it is a sign of a fuss.

To dream of going up a ladder is a sign that you will rise in life.

Go to bed singing, wake up crying.

If you have a mole on the right eye, you will have wealth and a happy marriage.

A bride should wear something old, something new, something borrowed, and something blue.

When the moon is in Leo, it is a good time to fall in love.

If you cut a watermelon crooked, it means you slept crooked.

If you see the shadow of a buzzard, somebody's coming unexpected.

If a rooster crows around the door, company's coming.

If you wash your hair in the first rain in May, you will be well all year.

If you get wet the first day of May, you won't get sick.

If you hear a turtledove early in the morning and you are standing up, you will be well.

Do not trust a person with pointed teeth.

Sit on a featherbed during lightning and it will not strike you.

Right eye itches—gonna get mad.
Left eye itches—gonna get glad.

Drop food while eating—somebody wants what you're eating.

If a boy and a girl are baptized in the same church on the same day, the girl should be sprinkled first or she will grow a beard in later life.

One's index finger is poisonous and should not be used around the head.

Good Friday is the best time to wean children.

All cattle kneel and low on Christmas Day.

Never set a hen on an even number of eggs—should have an uneven number.

A person will not drown unless he has gone under three times.

When you stump your toe, you will kill a toad.

When you have the hiccups, you are growing taller.

When a fire is burning and the smoke changes directions, it is following beauty.

When you walk backwards, you are cursing your mother.

If you throw a tooth on the ground and let a dog walk on it, you'll grow a tusk.

If you take the white tail of a rooster, stick it in a walnut and put it under the steps where someone will walk, something bad will happen to him.

If you steal from a cemetery, the hand you steal with will wither.

If you sit on a trunk, you will be disappointed.

Step over someone's pole and you will catch no fish.

Fish on Sunday and catch the devil.

Throw butterbean and pea hulls in the road and your chickens won't get the sorehead.

Poverty will come to one who sweeps the yard with a house broom.

If you plow during Holy Week, the ground will bleed.

To stir a teapot is to stir trouble.

Step on a crack and you'll fail in your lessons.

Step on a crack, break your mother's back.

Burning peanut hulls in the fireplace will cause a fuss.

If you milk a cow on the ground, she'll go dry.

When the fire spits, there'll be a quarrel in the family.

If you take another piece of bread when you already have one, somebody's coming hungry.

If you take a picture of a dog indoors, something will happen to it.

If fig leaves fall before all the fruit is gone, trouble will come next year.

Bubbles in your coffee is a sign of money.

Burn onion peels and you will have money.

If you drop a dishrag, bend over and say, "Money," somebody will come and bring you some money.

If you look up in the sky and say, "Money, money, money," and see a shooting star, you will have money.

If you're hairy, you will be a good hog raiser.

Sneeze on Monday, sneeze for a letter,
Sneeze on Tuesday, something better,
Sneeze on Wednesday, sneeze for danger,
Sneeze on Thursday, meet a stranger,
Sneeze on Friday, sneeze for sorrow,
Sneeze on Saturday, see your sweetheart tomorrow.

Whistling woman and crowing hen always come to some bad end.

ᎠᎥᏉᎤᏓᏟᎺᏛᏃᎸᎠᎾᏡᎤᏉᏈᎤᎷᏓᎠᎾᏡᎤᏓᏟᎺᏛᏃᎸᎠᎾᏡᎤᏉᎤᎷ

Alabama WPA Folklore

Ghost Stories, Superstitions, Tall Tales, and Other Folk Narratives from the Alabama WPA Folklore Collections and Slave Narratives

The establishment of the Folklore Division within the National Writers' Project of the Works Progress Administration with John Lomax as its editor in 1936 is of signal importance for it marks the only attempt in our nation's history to gather American folklore on a state-by-state basis. By 1939 thousands of manuscripts, the results of field collections all across the country, had been mailed to Washington. Although contemporary letters, memorandums, and directives clearly show that the ultimate goal was publication of these materials, a vast body remains unpublished. In Alabama, project workers collected folk tales, superstitions, and songs and interviewed hundreds of informants for two other major WPA Writers' projects, Life Histories and Slave Narratives. Most of the manuscripts are on deposit at the Library of Congress in the Rare Book Room and the Archive of Folk Song and in the Alabama State Department of Archives and History at Montgomery.

A notable exception to the failure to publish these materials is the Slave Narratives Project. Initiated by pilot studies conducted by Lawrence D. Reddick under FERA, encouraged by Sterling Brown, Editor of Negro Affairs, the program received its folklore–folk life orientation from Lomax, who devised the interview format, and his successor Benjamin Botkin, who supervised the deposit and binding of the manuscripts and prepared an anthology of excerpts, *Lay My Burden Down: A Folk History of Slavery* (Chicago: University of Chicago Press, 1945). In 1972 George P. Rawick's *The American Slave: An Autobiography* appeared (19 vols., Westport, Conn.: Greenwood Press), with sixteen volumes of reproductions of the original manuscripts, two volumes of documents gathered under FERA at Fisk University, and Rawick's introductory treatise on American slavery *From Sundown to Sunup: The Making of the Black Community*. In 1977 Rawick issued a twelve-volume supplement (Series I, No. 35, Westport, Conn.: Greenwood Press) of Slave Narrative manuscripts, which are scattered in various libraries and depositories throughout several states, and additional series are forthcoming.

In some states the folklore harvest from the Narratives was negligible or modest. In the Virginia Narratives, which were retained in the Virginia State Library and were only recently edited and published (*Weevils in the Wheat: Interviews with Virginia Ex-Slaves*, ed. by Charles L. Perdue, Jr., Thomas E. Barden, and Robert K. Phillips [Charlottesville: The University Press of Virginia, 1976]), there are far fewer folklore items and folk life profiles than in the comparable Alabama Narratives.

In Alabama it was both significant and substantial, yielding a whole view of nineteenth-century Alabama Negro folk life, interesting profiles of the informants, and excellent specimens of folklore and demonstrating the natural alliance between folk life and history. Virginia Van der Veer Hamilton has dealt admirably with the problems attendant on the uses of the Narratives as contemporary historical evidence—the bias of the interviewer, the contradictions, often within a single narrative, the informant's hesitation to speak fully and openly, the nature of human memory—in her book *Alabama: A History* (New York: W. W. Norton, 1977), and she has hit unerringly on their single most valuable aspect—the revelation of the daily life of the American slave. Although the folklorist may readily identify songs, tales, games, superstitions, remedies, he must confront some troublesome questions.

A respectable anthology of Alabama folklore could be gleaned from the Alabama Narratives, but any assessment of folk life must take into account both the persona and the WPA interviewer. Regrettably, some of the Narratives are seriously flawed by the project worker's adherence to the Old South cinematic myth, the white-pillared romance. This point of view is responsible for the chief failing of the Narratives—linguistic and human caricature, unreadable gibberish, a minstrel-show travesty of a remarkable oral folk tradition, and blatantly stereotyped "uncles," "aunts," and "pickaninnies" bobbing curtsies to "Old Massa and Missus."

Happily, such parodies are few. In the best of the Alabama Narratives, one finds numerous correctives of the myth, a vivid evocation of the individual folk personality, and, even in those tainted by an obtrusive interviewer, a fine recreation of folklife—clothing, foods, eating utensils, houses, furniture, medicines, domestic skills and crafts, occupations, farming methods and implements, accounts of baptizings, brush arbor revivals, church services, funerals and death customs, slave labor, punishments, holidays, frolics, marriage, courtship, and the family structure. Moreover, there is often an authentic impression, despite the absence of recording machines, of a Negro folk speech, a faithfulness to syntax, diction, rhythms, vocabulary, metaphor, and other rhetorical devices. Those who have called

the Narratives "voices" are right: behind every Narrative, no matter
how "improved," expanded, explained, or otherwise altered by the
project worker, is a being recounting his memories, and here the
Narratives are especially valuable, for except for the personal papers
of the literate and contemporary newspapers, we have nothing else
that speaks of and for this folk life. Once the few shoddy fakes and
misguided quackeries are sifted out, we have left a remarkable view
of one important segment of Alabama folk culture, the Negro as slave
and the Negro as folk. The Narratives gathered by such project workers as Ruby Pickens Tartt of Sumter County, Levi Shelby of Tuscum-
bia, Mary Poole and Ila Prine of Mobile, Preston Klein of Lee County,
and Rhussus L. Perry of Macon County are especially distinguished in
their revelation of folk life and folk persona, marked by editorial
detachment, fidelity to concrete details, a good ear, and an eye for
folklore genres. These profiles and sketches allow the former slave to
speak for himself on everything from games to cruel punishments,
and, although we see the informant clearly as slave, we see him also
as a fellow human, a member of the folk, even as we are, with whom
we share all the complexities of that humanness.

Several questions on the slave interview format deal with the supernatural and humorous elements of folklore—ghosts, witches, conjuring and voodoo, folk medicines and superstitions, tall tales, jokes,
anecdotes, and fairy tales. The prevailing thesis that the uneducated,
irrational, isolated Negro was particularly fertile ground for the exploration of vestigial folk beliefs long abandoned by civilized whites
is, however, not fully supported in the Narratives. Many slave informants disclaimed any belief in the supernatural, whereas others not
only readily admitted to belief but fully described their personal
experiences with apparitions, portents, and superstitious concepts
and practices. We found the same dichotomy in our investigation of
the folk supernatural in the southern and central Alabama informants of the Troy collection, nearly all of whom were white. It is
notable that similar motifs occur with almost the same frequency in
the stories told by both the black and white informants. The distinc-
tion between belief and nonbelief rests, then, on some other, deeper
and more important attribute of folk character. We believe and we do
not believe, and, as Hamlet says to Horatio, there are more things in
our philosophy than heaven or earth can ever account for.

The parallels between ghost and tall tales and the vein of humor
that often runs through the darkest tale of terror are abundantly
illustrated in Josh Horn's Sumter County narrative "Chasin' Guinea
Jim." The marvelous tall tale of the incredibly smart "nigger dog"
Brown hunting down a fugitive slave, told for the absolute truth, is
prefaced by four encounters with the supernatural: the ghost who

hitches a ride a' horseback, a sapling ghost Josh meets on the way to
revival and the headless apparition that chases his friend, the persimmon tree ghost who runs him through the woods and over the bridge
and so bewitches the possum dogs that they don't come home for
three days, and the three mysterious horsemen from whom he flees
wildly into a swamp. The ghosts chase Josh like Brown chases Guinea
Jim, and the pursuers have all the advantage; moreover, at any point
in the four ghost tales, we could easily substitute a wildcat or mythical beast, an irate wife, or a powerful enemy. In a very real sense, all
these stories are one short tall tale after another, culminating in the
extended treatment given Brown and Guinea Jim. The half-comic,
ambiguous attitude toward ghosts is illustrated also in Anthony
Abercrombie's account of another persimmon tree ghost, "a double-
jinted nigger" named Old Joe come back to pay off a debt, but Abercrombie concludes that the ghost can just as well keep his "two-bits."
West T. Jones is on his way to a lodge when he hears a ghost playing
the church organ: "I wa'n't skeered; jes' didn't keer 'bout goin' in."
George Young sees a ghost in the cotton patch and suddenly his wife
decides she "don't feel lack pickin' cotton today," and he advises us to
walk around a ghost if we see any, and if we can't see them they'll
walk around us, but if they get "too plentiful," an upside-down
horseshoe will keep them away. Ank Bishop, who meets a shaggy dog
that gets bigger and bigger, theorizes that ghosts are evil spirits des-
tined to wander over the earth until Gabriel blows the last trump.
Henry Cheatham's father, who held concourse with unnatural spirits,
killed a dog just by snapping his fingers, and Henry Barnes, born
with a "'zernin' eye" for spirits, repudiated his gift by stirring a pot of
lard renderings. Solomon Jackson had to contend with mischievous
haints who mysteriously dashed out all the spring water in his
bucket, and he is master of a rite to calm a thunderstorm, an ax to
split the whirlwind. Oliver Bell feared the eerie "Jack-Me-Lanterns"
that lure a man to lose his way in the woods and "stirs you up in yo'
min'." Eliza White met a ghost with the toothache, and Silvia With-
erspoon keeps a flour sifter by her door to ward off witches that ride
her in the night. Henry Garry sees an army of ghosts who have been
riding since the battle of Shiloh, then pulls our leg with a Steve
Renfroe anecdote.

   Although there are a number of real life stories in the Alabama
Narratives, the tall tale as such is rare; some actual comic experiences are often remembered, but the folk prank and the verbal joke
are negligible. Jake Green related two anecdotes widely circulated in
nineteenth-century Negro folklore, the malingering fiddler who
tricks his master and the tale of the mouse in the salver. Anne God-
frey gave Mrs. Tartt a fine mock oration, and Roxy Pitts knew a

version of the comic human dialogue of animals and narrated a delightful incident from her childhood. The scarcity of tall tales in the Slave Narratives certainly does not mean that storytelling traditions are not highly developed in Alabama Negro folk. To the contrary, Richard Amerson of Sumter County recorded one folk tale after another for folklore collector John Lomax on his visits to Alabama in 1936, 1937, and 1939—roarers, windies, beast fables, comic personal narratives, and tales of conjuring, conning, and sorcery—and in 1950 he was still going strong on the recordings of Alabama Negro folk song and folk tales made by Harold Courlander (*Negro Folksongs of Alabama*, 6 vols. [New York: Folk Records and Service Corp., Ethnic Folkways, 1950–1956]).

An overwhelming majority of Alabama ex-slave informants denied both the knowledge and the practice of superstitious concepts. The interview format specified voodoo and conjuring, and the structure of most narratives indicates that informants courteously and briefly answered a question they clearly believed to be irrelevant or nobody's business. There are, however, interesting exceptions. An occasional informant describes an experience with a conjurer, his own or one he has heard of, but almost always in connection with disease and healing, not witchcraft or sorcery exercised in personal matters, love, power over an enemy, success, and good luck. Folk medicine occurs more frequently in the Narratives but is only briefly mentioned, usually at the end of the interview, and represents only the most common of practical home remedies—teas and poultices made from natural substances close at hand as opposed to magical rites and spells. Alabama WPA workers conducted very few investigations of superstitions as a separate folklore category; the Library of Congress holds only eight entries in Alabama superstitions. (These include a sketch of a Montgomery Negro male conjurer, another of a female conjurer, two essays by William Edison and Bennett Marshall, evidently intended as a press release, with hundreds of general superstitions, and modest listings from project workers Mary Poole and Rhussus L. Perry.)

Ruby Pickens Tartt was the only WPA interviewer of former slaves who coherently integrated folk beliefs into the overall narrative, folk profile, and folk persona. Tom Moore's superstitions about death are subordinate to the poignant story of his son's death, not, as in some of the Alabama Narratives, ornamental, tacked on, or freakish. The narrative of Carrie Dykes, one of the finest achievements in all Alabama WPA efforts, is a superb portrait of a Negro midwife, with scores of superstitions, medicines, and practices from that folk science, all of which are communicated in her own speech. Oral folk history is now, properly, a major concern of American folklorists, and projects funded by government agencies and private sources are under way in every state. In this time of more sophisticated techniques, we do well to remember the obstacles faced by pioneers in this movement, hundreds of untrained WPA field workers struggling to convey an authentic impression of the variegated, ordinary American folk. In retrospect, their sincerity of purpose, diligence, and accomplishments—a great body of folk profiles, narratives, and histories—seem large indeed.

In 1936 and 1937, Alabama WPA project workers gathered a statewide collection of folk tales and other narratives—beast fables, ghost stories, practical jokes and anecdotes, folk tales of the supernatural, legends, and tall tales. Most of these are retellings or reconstructions of the original interview, often highly colored and romanticized by the project worker. Some evidence extensive revision by WPA editors, and in a few the project worker is so obtrusive that the original teller is lost. In the best ones, the personality of the teller, the folk life of Alabama, and the spirit of the tale emerge handsomely. Luther Clark's "Lookin' for Three Fools," an Alabama version of the Anglo-European folk tale "The Three Sillies," grafts a real folk setting onto humorous fantasy. The episodes of the four fools, drawn from our own folk life, belong to the cumulative or dependent tall tale in which one absurdity succeeds another, but here, as in folk beast fables, there is a clear didactic intent—there are fools everywhere, and who is to say which of us is the biggest one. "The 'Fraids," a comic tale about a dawdling son, his irate Papa, and a pet monkey, exhibits the worldwide motif of the scarer-gets-scared. It, too, has sources in Anglo-European tales, and there are analogues in American Negro oral folk literature, the wily slave who frightens his gullible master. The white-sheet folk prank is still pulled, and it is noteworthy that many of our folk tales center on just such practical jokes. Clark also collected three delightful, well-known folk anecdotes: "Saltin' the Puddin'," "The Three Tongue-Tied Sisters," and "The Laziest Man." Every community has a mythical prototype of some human vice or character trait—the strong man or giant, the liar, the miser, the drunkard, the dullard, the hermit—about whom numerous local legends and anecdotes accumulate, and Clark's lazy fellow is one of these. The folk comedy of errors in the pudding anecdote may well be based in reality, but the joke is on the gluttonous preacher, another character the folk love to poke fun at. The humor in "The Three Tongue-Tied Sisters" may be somewhat cruel, but it, too, has a message, one akin to the New Testament metaphor of the mote and the beam. Lillian Finnell's "The Missing Bridegroom" exemplifies what we often call the "memorable reply" or "clever retort," a species that appears everywhere in American folk humor. In Annie D.

Dean's "The Strange Demise of John Q. A. Warren," the drunkard gets his deserts, drowning in a barrel of whisky, and in "How White-Oak Tom Got His Name," a Sumter County giant is tricked by a puny slave and his crafty master, a tale with echoes from both the Old Testament story of David and Goliath and the Odysseus-Polyphemus adventure in Homer. Preston Klein's "The Witch with a Gold Ring" is one of the best known of all folk tales of the supernatural—the motifs of the severed hand and the gold ring and the migration of the human soul into an animal familiar are international in their occurrence. All these WPA tales demonstrate the vitality and diversity of Alabama's folk tale tradition, replete with sillies and lazy men, preachers and witches, brave little boys and reluctant bridegrooms, too much salt and too much whisky. Although the times and places have changed, the spirit of the folk, richly imaginative and humorous, trusting and shrewd, wry and poignant, fearful and courageous, is unaltered.

The selections from the Alabama Slave Narratives printed here are from manuscripts on deposit at the Alabama Archives. The manuscripts of "Lookin' for Three Fools," "The 'Fraids," "Saltin' the Puddin'," "The Laziest Man," and "The Witch with the Gold Ring" are deposited in the Library of Congress under Alabama Folk Tales; "The Strange Demise of John Q. A. Warren" exists in two manuscripts filed at the Alabama Archives with the Slave Narratives collection and was sent to Washington originally as a Slave Narrative and deposited with several other Alabama Narratives in the Archive of Folk Song. "The Three Tongue-Tied Sisters" is deposited at the Alabama Archives with WPA folklore materials from Sumter County. "How White-Oak Tom Got His Name" is on deposit at the Alabama Archives under the Sumter County WPA folklore classification.

Luther Clark
Birmingham, Alabama
1937–37
W15

Lookin' for Three Fools

That gal, Tildy Moore, had done had her cap sot fer John Spencer fer nearbout a year. She had been drappin' hints an' sideise looks all along, but John was young an' skittish an' didn't ketch on fast. Howsomever, one bright May day in church, when he finely seen her kinda cuttin' her eye tward him, he reared back an' tuck notice.

After church, when ever'body was bunchin' around askin' the reverend to dinner an' braggin' to each other 'bout their crops an' just generally bein' sociable, John he sashayed over to where Tildy was prancin' around her maw an' a passel of other women-folks.

"Might I have the pleasure of seein' you home, Miss Tildy?" he sat her, tippin' his hat as clever as you please.

"Why, John," Tildy sorty giggled, "you'll have to ast Maw; but I wouldn't mind."

Ole Miz Moore was hard put to keep a straight face, she was that pleased, but she put on her solidest look an' said, "Well, I reckon you can walk home with John but don't you all dast meander an' dally on the way fur I'll be a needin' you to help about dinner."

Well, the two on 'em they strolled down the road to her house— 'tw'nt more'n two mile—an' John he pulled up a cheer on the piazzer clost to whur old man Moore was a-settin' an' they talked about this an' that while the wimmen was a-scarin' up dinner.

Whilst she was a-settin' the table the old lady seen the syrup pitcher was near bout dry, so she said, "Tildy, you run to the smoke-house an' fetch some mo'lasses."

Tildy tuck the pitcher and went out tuh the smokehouse, and she stayed, an' she stayed, an' she stayed.

'Twa'nt so very long 'till her maw got right oneasy and so she called and she called but Tildy didn't answer. So her maw throwed a cloth over the table to keep the flies offen the vittles and she tuck 'n went to the smokehouse to see what the matter was.

Well, there sot Tildy by the syrup kag with her knees drawed up an' her chin on her hands, and the syrup just a-runnin out over the edge of the pitcher and makin' a puddle on the dirt.

"Well, my goodness, Tildy, whatever in the world's got possission of ye?" she yelled at the gal.

Tildy lifted up her head and looked at her maw with sorty bland, starin' eyes, "Why Maw, I'm jest a-thinkin' and a-thinkin' about whatever shall we name our fu'st child when me an John git mar'ied."

"Well, now, Tildy, I declare that is to be thought about," the old lady said, an' she sot down in the puddle of syrup beside Tildy an' put her hands on her knees an' her chin on her hands and started a-helpin' her think.

Now they is hardly a patienter man to be found that that old man Moore are sometimes, but mealtimes when he was hungry was not one of them times. Him an' John got to talkin' less and less and he commenced fidgetin' worser and worser. Finely he couldn't stand it no longer so he tuck his feet off the bannister and went stompin' into the kitchen a-walkin' his mad walk. There was the table all kivered up, but no wife and no Tildy.

He yelled out, "Maw, whur ye at?" When he didn't git no anser he was mad enough to chaw up sawdust an' spit out scantlin's. Then he looked out the back door an' seen the smokehouse door open an' got awful oneasy, thinkin' maybe they had both went out an' got snake bit.

He tore out down them back steps and went abustin' out to that smokehouse like the devil beatin' tanbark and poked his head in the door. His eyes near bugged out. There sot Tildy and her maw with their hands on their knees an' their chins on their hands, a-thinkin', an' the syrup was apourin' out and amakin' a reg'lar lake.

"Old woman, what on earth air ye a-doin'?" he hollered.

Old Miz Moore raised them blank eyes ov hern an' told him, "We air just a-tryin' to think up a name fer the fu'st child when John and Tildy get mar'ied," she said.

That tuck the old man up short. He said, "Well, now that is somp'n to be thought about," he said and down he sot in the syrup an' begun a-helpin' 'em think.

Well, John like to wore out that rawhide cheer bottom a-fidgitin'. He didn't know should he go home or should he stay. Finely he sot jest as still as he could an' strained his ear a-listenin' for them people. He didn't hear nothin'. Well, it got to where he jes' couldn't hold himself in no longer. He had to know what the matter was, manners or no manners. So he up an' went to see if he could find 'em. He even hollered for the ole man a time or two, but it bein' Sunday he wouldn't holler too loud. Finely he seen the smokehouse door open an' he went a'sailin' out there as hard as he could tear an' looked inside.

There was the whole kit an bilin' of the Moores, a-settin' half-leg deep in syrup with their hands on their knees an' their chins on their hands lookin' into space.

John, he scratched his head an' kicked his foot an' said, "Excuse me, y'all, but did you git bad news?"

The old man didn't so much as raise his head, an' he told him, "We're a-thinkin' up a name for the fust chile when you an Tildy git mah'ied!"

Well that fair tuck John's breath away for a minute an' then he said, "Well, I never! If that don't beat anything I ever see. I bet I kin go on up thisyere road as fur's it goes an' I won't never find three more as big fools as y'all. If I do, I'll come right back an' marry the gal!" He didn't say no more, but he stuck his hat on his head an' went off down the road. It was a powerful thin-settled country up around there an' he had to walk a right smart piece before he come to another house. This was an old house an' the boards on the kiver had this here green moss-stuff a-growin' out thick all over 'em. Well, right out in the front yard he seen a man a'tryin' to drive a old skinny cow up the ladder that was a leanin' up against the house.

John stopped dead an' for a spell he just gaped at the man. Finely he made so bold as to ast him, "Mister, I'm a stranger in these here parts but I shore would like to know what you're tryin' to do?"

The man, he worked his chaw of tabacco over to one side of his mouth an' spit at a horsefly an' near'bout hit it, an' then he said, "Why, I'm a tryin' to git this here consarned creetur to go up thar 'n eat that there moss offen them shingles but, dang her contrary hide, looks like she'd ruther starve plum to death then to climb that there ladder."

John ast him, "Well then, why don't you scrape the dad-burn stuff off and let her eat it down here? Looks like if them rafters ain't strong enough to hold up her weight. She shore will ruin the top o' your house!"

The ol' man, he reached down an' got that cow by the tail, but afore he twisted her, he turned around to John an' he says, "Well, son, I been a-pasturin' my stock since your grandpa wa'n't no bigger than a groundpuppy an' I reckon I can still pasture my cow withouten no advice from any of you soft-headed Spencers."

An' with that he twisted that critter's tail so hard that she run up nine rungs of the ladder an' stood there swayin'. Now John thought he might step up an' fetch the ol' man a slap an' then he thought he mightn't, for he was a-lookin' for fools an' not fights. So he went on with his hands in his pockets a-cussin' an' a-hawkin' an' a-spittin', lowin' he'd done found one fool.

Along late in the evenin' he come to the next house. It was after night an' the moon was a-shinin' when he seen it. An' he seen somp'm else which surprised him a heap. A woman was a-tearin' round an' round the house a-pushin' a wheelba'r, an' ever' time she made the third trip around she'd shove the wheelba'r up inside the house an' dump it. Then she'd skeedaddle back out and run around agin, an' there wa'n't anything in that ba'rr. Well, John he watched and he watched an' he figgured an' he figgured an' he couldn't make it out. Finely he busted out as polite as he knew how, "Please, ma'am, mought I ast what you're a-doin'?"

She was a little woman an' swift. "Son, I ain't got no time to answer no foolish questions. Here I've been a-scourin' floors all afternoon an' tain't but three hours 'til moonset with me still havin' to haul in enough moonshine to dry the parlor floor."

An' she kept right on a-goin'.

John didn't have nothin' a-tall to say to that. He just scratched his head as he went on off and said to hisse'f, "Well, that shore makes two."

He was so wore out and hungry he didn't go but jus' a few mile fu'ther on till he laid down under a tree with his coat fer a piller an' slep' till big daylight. Then he got up an' went on.

Jest about sun'up he come around a bend in the road an' there sot a house. They wa'nt nobody stirrin' an' no smoke comin' outen the chimbly but it looked like somebody must stay there so he went to the door an' knocked. He didn't git no answer so he knocked again. 'Bout that time he heard a funny bumpin' noise to'rd the back side of the house, an' bein' brash an' young, he went around to see what that noise mought be.

Well, they was a man under a peach tree in the back yard an' he didn't have on a thing but his shirt and drawers. His pants was a-hangin' on a limb of the peach tree an' that air man would jump up as high as he could an' kick at the top of the breeches with both feet an' fall back an' bump hisself on the ground. That was what was makin' the bumpin' noise. He'd git right back up an' dust off where he had bumped hisself and jump 'n kick at the breeches again.

John was too weak tuh talk loud but he spoke up as stout as he could an' said, "Mister, mought a pore stranger ast ye what ye're a-doin'?"

"I'm a-tryin' to put my britches on, smart aleck, what does hit look like I'm a-doin'?"

That made John sorter mad so he said, "Well, why in the dickens don't ye take 'em down from there, then, and step into 'em one foot at the time?"

The man turned around and looked at John like he could go plum through him, and then he reared up his head and said, "Boy, this here is how my paw and his paw afore him put on their britches, and what was good enough fer them is shore-Gawd good enough fer me!" Then he give a pertic'ler hard jump and got one foot in the breeches and fell kerbip, a-sprawlin'. "Most made hit that time," he said. But ol' John Spencer never heard him for he was half way back to Tildy's house by that time, 'cause he had sure enough found him three bigger fools than Tildy and her maw and paw.

The 'Fraids

Luther Clark
June 7, 1939

The old man John Smith had a nice bunch of milk cows, and every evening late he would send his boy, young John, down to the swamp paster to drive them cows home for milkin. Well, this boy was a triflin' dawdler, and every day he would piddle and play around till plumb dark before he got them cows home.

The old man told him and told him about doin' that way, because he was anxious to git them cows home and git 'em milked by dark. He tried whippin' and that didn't do no good; he tried arguin' and that didn't mend matters one bit. Finely he tried scarin' the boy.

"Don't you know sumpen's gonna ketch you in them woods some night?" he ast little John. "Nearbout everybody is afraid in them woods."

Little John didn't pay much tenshun to his daddy; he thought the old man was tellin him about a varmint named Fraid. He said, "Huh, ain't no 'Fraid gonna ketch me!"

So he just went on bein' later and later gittin' the cows home, and the old man kept gittin' worrieder and worrider about it.

Well, one night he just couldn't stand it no longer. Here it was black dark and no cows even in bell-hearin' distance. He decided he would scare that boy within a inch of his life. So he went into his bedroom and got a sheet and wrapped it all around hisself good, and went down the cowpath towards the branch where the cows had to ford it. The footlog was over in the bushes kinda-like, and he walked part way across it and hunkered down to wait for the boy.

Now the old man Smith had a pet monkey that done everything it seen its master do. When the monkey seen the old man wrop up in the bedsheet and go out, why it run and got a pillow case and pulled over its head and went a-trottin' after him. The pore little monkey had a terrible time a-tryin' to keep up, and finely it got 'way behind. But old man John didn't git out of its sight, and in a minit or two after he squatted down on the footlog, why it clim up on the footlog and got up purty close to its master and hunkered down just like John had done.

Well, the old man he looked around and seen the monkey settin' there and it like to of scared him to death. Course it was all covered up in the sheet or he'd a knowed right off what it was. It was good dusky dark by then, and that thick woods around the branch was a awful scary place anyway.

Old man John sot there for a minit or two more, scared half to death but hopin' the monkey would say sompem or go away and let him alone, but it just sot there. Just as little John come in sight he couldn't stand it no longer. The monkey was on the log between him and home, so he just give a wild jump out in the middle of the branch and went a-bustin' through that cold water back towards the house.

When the monkey saw its master tear out thataway, why it jumped offa the log and went a-splashin' and a-scramblin' right after him. When the old man looked back he seen the white thing was right behind him, and he run faster than ever.

Little John was a-comin' pokin' along, lettin' the cows mosey and take their time, when he happened to look up and seen the two white things goin' tearin' out through the woods.

He laughed to hisself and said, "Dog my cats! I bet that is some of them 'Fraids Paw was tellin' me about. They shore do look funny." Then he throwed back his head and hollered: "Run big 'Fraid; don't little 'Fraid'll ketch you!"

By the time he got to the house the old man was slap out of breath. He didn't see the monkey, so he jumped up and set down on the end of the porch. Before he could take three long breaths, here come the monkey and jumped up side of him again. He took one look and lit out again.

He was runnin' across the field that time, and when he come to a hedgerow and tried to jump it the sheet caught on a bush and jerked off. He didn't stop for it but just kept right on a-goin!

When the monkey got to the hedgerow he seen the sheet there and thought his master had throwed it down a-purpose, so he took off his pillowcase and throwed it down there too. Then he lit out after old man John again.

After he had run a piece further, the old man cut his eye around again, and didn't see nothin' but the monkey after him so he stopped. It didn't take him long to figger out what had happened but after he went back and got that sheet and pillowcase, it took him nearly two hours to git his breath back, and it was close to midnight fore he got the cows milked. He never tried to scare that boy no more.

[Clark attributed this tale to a man named Tribble of Birmingham.]

Luther Clark
Nov. 30, 1936
W26

Saltin' the Puddin'

I never will fergit one time old lady Simpson was goin' to have a wood-sawin' an' thought she'd show off some by havin' puddin' fer the crowd. Course she was agwine to have a candy pullin' and a goober poppin' same as usual. The puddin' was extry.

Well, that day ever'thing was a hustle and a bustle over at Simpson's and the upshot of it all was, here 'twas comin' on night an' no puddin' cooked. Well, the old lady had done made her brags all around and she just had to have that puddin'. All the gals—they was five of them Simpson gals—was as busy as a bee in a tar bar'l; washin' and ironin' and primpin' and cleanin' up the house like they was lookin' fer the evangelist durin' big meetin'. So the ol' lady she tore out to the kitchen and started chunkin' things together to make that puddin'.

Now, she was give up to be the best puddin' maker in the hull settlement. But she was so flabberbasted and aggrevated that evenin' she plum fergot to salt the puddin'. Now rale good puddin' don't take but just a TEE-NINCY pinch o' salt, but if it ain't got that it just ain't puddin'.

She got the fire goin' just right in the stove and slammed the puddin' in thar, then she flurried out to the settin' room to dustin' the cheers an' the organ.

'Bout that time she remembered the salt. Her hands was that dirty she knowed she couldn't salt the puddin' without washin' 'em. So she just went ahead a-dustin' and a-scurryin' around and thought she'd call on one of the gals to 'tend to it fer her.

"Sue, will you go salt the puddin'? I done got my hands dirty."

"Kain't maw. I'm greasin' my shoes."

"Sairy, how 'bout you?"

"Maw, you know I'm a-tryin' to get this dress done."

"Berthy, kin you salt the puddin'?"

"No."

"Jenny, go salt the puddin'."

"Let Lil do it, maw. I'm starchin' and ornin' to beat the band."

"All right. Lil, run salt the puddin' now, honey."

"Shan't. I'm a-lookin' high and low for my hair ribbin and I hain't a-gonna do nothin' else 'til I find it."

The old lady drawed a long sigh and throwed her dustin' rag across a cheer back and went and washed her hands and salted the puddin'.

Jest about the time she got back to her dustin', Lil got to thinkin' 'bout how she'd orta mind her maw, so she sorter eased into the kitchen and salted the puddin'.

She hadn't more 'n got back s'archin' fer her hair ribbin when Jenny got to feelin' oneasy 'bout bein' so sassy and here she come and salted the puddin'.

Well, so help me, she had sca'cely set back down on the back piazzer and picked up the slipper she was a-greasin' when here went Sairy and salted the puddin'.

Berthy always was the lady of the family. She didn't do nothin' much none of the time. She was propped in her room a-readin' a novelty when all this was a-happenin'. But if they wuz one thing that gal liked better 'n readin' a novelty it wuz eatin' puddin'. She got to thinkin' 'bout that puddin' and got into a twidget. Finely she got up and tiptoed to the kitchen and got there right after Sairy left. So they all salted the puddin'.

That puddin' shore baked purty and when old lady Simpson come a-mincin' out with it that night you could hear ever body sorter bend back and smack their lips.

The preacher had come over to sorter look over the goin's on and natcherlly he got the fust helpin'. With his face shinin' he said somp'n 'bout "Neckter and Ambrosy" and then took a whoppin' big moufful.

When he bit down to sorter let the flavor soak in, his face looked like somebody had kivered up the sun wi a blanket.

"Upthem!" he said and grabbed fer the warter gourd.

Ever'body there wuz plum flabbergasted. Old lady Simpson warn't slow to ketch on that somp'n wuz wrong so she took a taste herself. Then she knowed.

"Which of you gals put salt in this puddin'?" she wanted to know.

" "I did" all five uv 'em said together.

"And I did too," the old lady said. "Hit shore looks like too many cooks sp'iled the puddin'.

And they warn't nobody could deny it.

G. L. Clark
Birmingham, Alabama
6-16-38
10127

The Laziest Man

Nick Weldon was an awfully lazy man. He would not work at anything. All he did was eat and lie back with his feet cocked in the air, while he looked until he fell asleep. His parents fed him till he was a man grown but they finally worked themselves to death and left Nick to shinny for himself. The neighbors, as is the custom of good neighbors, brought over a lot of good things to eat after his mother died and he ate them all. After that he was hungry.

Everybody in the community knew he was too lazy to live but they were sorry for him and finally got into the habit of sending a child around once in a while with a plate of victuals for him to eat. Several families kept this up for a month or two and in this way Nick kept alive. But he was getting lanky on the uncertain food, and still he made no effort to do a thing for himself. Finally, the good neighbors got tired of being put upon in such a manner and got together to talk the matter over.

It was a hopeless case, they decided, and Nick must be disposed of once and for all. They could not continue to waste the time and supplies to care for him, and so he must die. Of course they could just refuse to send him any more food and he would soon die of starvation. But that, they felt sure, was too cruel a death for even Nick. So they decided to haul him out to the boneyard and knock him in the head.

Early the next morning two of them took a cart and drove over to get Nick. When they told him why they were there he offered no protest so they lifted him into the cart and started down the road.

It was a long drive to the boneyard and after they had gone a long way they were stopped by a man who wanted to know where they were going. He had not heard of Nick, so they told him the whole story.

"Why," he offered generously when he had heard the tale, "I can spare a bushel of corn. I'll give him that and he can live a while longer. It is a bad thing to kill a man and I don't want to see it done."

At that Nick slowly turned his head in the cart so he could see the man. "Is it shelled?" he asked in a whiny drawl.

The charitable man answered, "Why, no, but the four of us can shell it in just a little while."

"Ne'mind," whined Nick, "jes' drive on to the boneyard, boys!"

Reference: Mrs. Leonidas Cockrell, Route 2, Livingston, Ala. Age 65

The Three Tougue-Tied Sisters

G. L. Clark
Oct 21, 1936

There was once a young man who, having decided to get married, found his choice limited to three sisters. They were all able, energetic girls and about equally goodlooking. And they suffered from a common handicap: They were all tongue-tied.

As he plowed the cotton and hoed the corn the young fellow gave long earnest thought to the matter but could not decide which would make him the more desirable wife. Finally, however, he hit upon a plan. He would propose to the one who was least tongue-tied.

That night he put on his best clothes and hied himself to the home of the candidates. The entire family gathered with him in the parlor and a general conversation started. Meantime the young man was watching each of the girls as closely as possible and listening with both ears.

Suddenly one of the girls rose and walked out on the porch. A minute or two later she came back in remarking, "I fink it's goinne yain tonight."

One of her sisters giggled and said, "You can't spleak splain."

The other piped up, "En-nu nain't nunner!"

Reference: Mrs. Leonidas Cockrell, Route 2, Livingston, Ala.

How White-Oak Tom
Got His Name

Ruby Pickens Tartt
Sumter County, Alabama

I heer'd Pappy say one time way back yonder durin' de war he seed his ole Massa make two hundred dollars 'fo' de roosters quit crowin' fer day-break.

He sed Ole Massa bought er nigger en give a hundred dollars fer him en hit jes' near 'bout broke him, so dere wuz er white man whut owned de 'jinin' plantation en he wuz a gamberlin' man en rich ez cream, too, en mighty braggin' lac. So Pappy say Ole Massa tole dis here man dat he 'lowed he had er nigger on his place w'at could out-whoop air nigger he had on his whole plantation anytime, day er night. En ef he didn't whoop him, he'd jes' natchully nigh 'bout skeer him ter death, or elser he'd give him er hundred dollars. (You sees Ole Massa wuz er bettin' bofe ways: ef he got skeered en wouldn't fight his nigger, or ef he did n' got whooped, but shoo, Ole Massa knowd he had dat rich man right whar de mink had de goslin'.)

So Pappy sed dat rich man had one ov de bigges', blackes', blue-gummes' niggers he ever seed. He sed his nappy head wuz big ez er beer-bar'l, so widout no rigmarole or 'sputin', de rich man'greed. En so he tole Ole Massa hit wuz a trade but he said furthermore he'd give Massa *two* hundred dollars ef enny nigger Massa had could whoop his'n er either skeer him mighty nigh ter death.

So dey sets de day fer de fight to be early nex' mawnin' 'bout sun-up, en dat night Pappy said Ole Massa tuck him, en er whole passel ov niggers down in de swamp, en dey digs up de bigges' size white-oak tree they kin git, en dey fetches hit up de hill 'roun' back uv de black-smif shop, en dey digs a hole in de groun', en dey sots de tree out en stomps de grass back jes' lac hit's been a-growin' dere all uv hit's life. Den he say Ole Massa put a ring in de tree en he tied de bigges' nigger he had to hit, en den Ole Massa jes' sot down on a stump en waited. Pretty soon here dey comes, de rich man a-bringin' dat big fightin' nigger.

En Pappy say he say to hisse'f he ain't never seed no nigger look so spindlin' en puny ez dat po' nigger whut Massa done tied ter dat tree. He said he 'low'd twuz gonna be jes' lac rastlin' wid his own shadow fer ter whoop him. But den Ole Massa knowd all along his nigger wa'n't no fighter, but all he wuz atter wuz t' make him 'peer lac he wuz mighty near lac dat trumpet whut brought down Jerusalem's walls en jes' natchully *skeer* dat rich man's nigger to death.

So Ole Massa jes' tuck his time, en he crope up 'hind de nigger whut wuz tied to de white-oak tree lac he wuz fixin' to untie him, but ef dat rich man wuz 'spectin' dat nigger to fight, he wuz sho knockin' at de wrong do', fer bless goodness when he got sight uv dat big nigger 'vancin' on him, fo'e Ole Massa ever commence to say nuthin' to him, he pulled dat white-oak tree outer dat groun' lac hit wuz a saplin' en tuck off down th'oo de goober-patch, tree en all.

But Pappy said dat wa'n't nothin' to whut dat rich man's nigger done. He said when he seed dat nigger pull up dat tree 'thout even so much ez layin' er hand on it, he jes' turned his heels in t'other direction jes' lac he been shot outen er muskit, en Pappy sed fur ez he knos dey ain't nobody never seed dat nigger since.

Dat's how come ter dis day dem folks roun' dere talks er bout Massa's ole nigger en calls him "White-Oak Tom" . . . Yasser, dat's whut he go by—"White-Oak Tom!"

The Strange Demise of
John Q. A. Warren

Annie Dee Dean
Evergreen, Alabama

Mr. John Q. A. Warren wuz a leetle shawt pusson, jes' erbout dis high. But he muster weighed nigh on ter 200 pounds er mo'. Now, he's de one whut died in de whiskey. Jes' lack I tole yer. Beens he wuz so low and so fat an' luv his whiskey too, he kep' two niggers dat did'n do er Gawd's thing but foller roun' atter him, an him a continu'lly go'in all de time. Wheresumever Mister John went, dar you'd see dem two niggers, follerin' him er roun'. An' all in Gawd's name dey done wuz ter put him on his hawse, an take him offen de hawse an set him down on de groun'. He mos'n generul set dar, cawse his laigs wuz too onsteady ter hole'm up.

It look lack atter a'while, Mister John Q. jes' could'n get satchified no ways in de wurl. He gits so desspit he sont way off down yonder ter Mobile an bought hissef' two treemendjuss barruls fuller whiskey. De very bess dat wuz down dere. An bless Gawd if he did'n shuck off his close an make dem niggers drap him in one uv dem barruls er licker! Yes Lawd, an ef he did'n make'm po'm slam fuller whiskey whut cum frum outen 'tother barrul. Jes' as long as his goozle could run up en down, he kep' on a swoller'n an a swoller'n whilst dem niggers po'd it down'm, twell bye'n bye he jes' up an lopped over daid! Yes Lawd! He died rite dar in de whiskey.

Lillian Finnell
Tuscaloosa, Alabama
6–24–38

The Missing Bridegroom

The marriage of a young backwoods couple had been announced to take place on a certain night. When the night came a hard rain had been falling all the afternoon. Those who had been invited to the marriage, however, assembled at the bride's home at the time appointed for the wedding.

The groom had not arrived and the ceremony was thus delayed. Time passed and still he did not appear. After sufficient time had passed to account for his delay because of bad roads, two of the male guests volunteered to go and learn what was keeping him. They set out walking along the rain soaked path through the woods, picking their way across gullys, lighted by the flickering gleams of pine wood torches. They expected momentarily to meet the belated groom, but reached his home without seeing anything of him. Worried inquiry at his home elicited the fact that he was there, but that he had gone to bed. Demanding admittance to his bedroom they asked him, why in the world he had not come to "get married." Had he forgotten this was the night?

"No," he replied, "I didn't forget it, but it was raining so hard, I didn't think anybody else would be there, so I didn't go either."

The Witch with a Gold Ring

Preston Klein
Lee County
12–21–38

Once upon a time Mr. Dave, a wealthy man, owned a large mill. At this mill he kept an overseer for day and one for night, as the mill ran twenty-four hours daily.

He and his wife lived alone in a large house upon a hill overlooking this mill, and friends were always welcome. His wife was a woman who did not care for finery, but just wore a plain gold ring. She was regarded as peculiar because she always wore an odd smile, unlike that of other people.

As it happened this land owner had hired a great number of night foremen at the mill. Repeatedly these foremen were killed in the night. Thus he began to have a hard time getting a man to stay on that account.

One night the local preacher came to spend the night and was met in friendly fashion by the man of the house and was given a welcome by the good wife, but she greeted him with that peculiar knowing smile of hers. During the general conversation Mr. Dave explained the difficult time he was having in getting someone to run the mill at night as the watchmen were being killed as fast as he hired them.

This preacher said, "I'll stay down there for you tonight. I'm not afraid." "O, no, I can't think of letting you take a chance of being killed," was the answer but he was finally overpersuaded and the preacher said, "All I want is my Bible and this dagger of mine." But the good wife begged him not to go. After supper the parson got his Bible and proceeded down to the mill office, lighted his lamp, made up a good fire and prepared to read his Bible. Before he sat down, in looking the room over he noticed the door had a cat-hole cut in the bottom, but thinking nothing of it, he made hisself comfortable with his dagger in his hand and began to read his Bible. In the night, when all was quiet but the spit-spit of the mill, he noticed a black cat creeping through the hole in the door. The preacher didn't say a word but kept one eye on the cat and one eye on his Bible and his hand on his blade. The cat stole in a little closer, intently watching the man. A little nearer and a little nearer he crept, the parson still with one eye on his Bible, blade in hand and the other eye on the cat but still pretending not to be noticing. Suddenly the cat gave a great "Yeow," and pounced on the preacher, but the parson as quick as the cat, gave a slash and cut off one of its front paws.

The paw fell at the parson's feet, but when he looked for the cat it had disappeared. Then turning to kick the cat's foot away, lo and behold, he was thunderstruck, for instead of the cat's foot, a woman's hand bearing the gold band of his host's wife was there. He rolled it in a piece of paper and tied it up.

The next morning when he went to the house for breakfast, the landlord was plainly surprised to see him alive, but asked what kind of a night he had spent. He replied that he had passed a perfectly quiet night with the exception of a wild cat trying to scratch him but that he had his blade and cut off one of its front paws.

"But I wrapped its claw up and brought it along to show," he said, and added, "By the way where is your wife this morning?" "She hasn't gotten up this morning," answered his host. "She is not feeling well."

The preacher unwrapped his little package to show, laying it on the table, without a word. The husband fell back in astonishment and said, "My fathers, that is my wife's hand and gold ring!" "You go up and ask her where I got it," answered the preacher. "She can tell you better than I can."

As they both entered her room, she shrank down under the covers, but her husband made her show her arm and the hand was missing. Then he asked her what it all meant. She was so cowed and ashamed she could not talk but she finally admitted that she was a witch but that her spell had been broken. The old mill ran from that time forward without any further deaths.

TALES FROM EX-SLAVE NARRATIVES

The following tales are excerpted from complete narratives found in the WPA collection of Alabama Slave Narratives. Only those parts of the narratives that deal with ghosts, or "haints," and other matters of the supernatural and superstitious are presented here. The original manuscripts of the Alabama narratives are housed in the Alabama Archives at Montgomery and at the Archive of Folk Song and the Rare Book Room, Library of Congress, Washington, D.C.

From: Josh Horn, "Chasing Guinea Jim"

Collected by
Ruby Pickens Tartt,
Sumter County

(Josh Horn tells several ghost stories and one tall tale. Alice is Josh's wife. Guinea Jim is a runaway; Mr. Beesley is the hunter; and the remarkable Brown is the lead dog.)

"Yassum," said Josh, "if you wants to hear ghost tales, I kin sho tell 'em, ca'se I seed dis here wid my own eyes. Tain't no made-up nothing needer; jes' somepin' I *seed* jes' lak I tells you.

"Green Hale and Isham Mathews b'longed to *New Hope* church, and de Reverend Bird Hall pastored dere. Dey axed me down to hear him preach one night, and us three, me and Green and Isham, was riding along side and side. I's riding a mule, but it was a fast mule, and Green couldn't keep up, en Isham said: 'Somebody been hunting.' I looked up and 'twas a sapling right 'cross de road. He said, 'Fellow oughten leave nothing lak dat. When de moon git low, it hit him in de face.' De moon was straight up and down den, and I said: 'Dat's right,' and I's telling you de troof, dat sapling jes' riz up, turned aroun' in de air, en de bresh part tickled my mule and Isham's hoss in de face. If you ever seed 'em buck and rare and jump up, dey sho did. Den dey took off down de road, and we didn't hold 'em back, and here come Green. We lef' him behind, 'cause his mule couldn't keep up. If you ever heard a man pray more earnester dan old Green, I ain't! He come down de road a-yelling: 'Lord, us live togedder, let us die togedder.' He meant for us to wait on him, but I couldn't hold dat mule, and I wan't trying to hold him! I was gitting away from dar!

"When us come togedder, us was a mile from whar us done been, den us had to decide what to do. Isham said for us to go wid him, and

Green said no, us nearer to his house; but us wan't *near* to nobody and I was so scared, hadn't been for Alice, I'd a jes' stayed right whar us was 'tell sun-up. I said, 'No, every man better take keer his own self,' en us did. When I got home, I didn't take nothing off dat mule but myself. I jes' left him standing at de do' wid de saddle on. What skeered Green so, was a man, he said, what was ridin' right 'side him en didn't have no head! 'Twas a good thing he didn't tell me dat den, I'd jes' nacherly drap dead!

"No'm, I don't 'zackly believes in ghosties, but I heared Mr. Marshall Lee say he was riding on home one night and a woman stepped out in de road and say: 'Marshall, let me ride.' He say: 'My hoss won't tote double.' She say: 'Yes it will,' and she jump up behind him, and dat hoss bucked and jumped nigh 'bout from under him, but when he got home, she wan't dere. He say, his sister had jes' died and it mout been her.

" 'Nother time, one Friday night, Alice say us better git a 'possum for Sunday. She say she didn't want none caught atter midnight on Sadday. I went down whar I knowed dey was 'simmon tree; dem dogs never treed nothing; dey jes' run 'round dat 'simmon tree lak dey gone crazy. I'm telling you do troof, sompin' jump outer dat tree, had a head back'erds en for'erds and look lak a flame shooting out it eyes! 'Twan't lak no possum I ever seed, 'twan't lak nothing. Dem dogs, Liz and Roger en Cuba, made a bluge at me. Cotton was waist high, and I run down de cotton row and cross de road and dey trail me. I say: 'What ail you, dogs?' And dey jes' come on a-barkin', and dey run me to de bridge over Konkabyer. So I clumb on de banisters. I seed dey had my trail and dey gonna ketch me, so I turn 'round and tore out for de slough. Dey lost my trail dere and when I got home, 'bout daylight, de thorns and de briars and all done tore my clothes plum off me. 'Twas t'ree days 'fore, I ever seed dem dogs ag'in.

"And I kin tell you somepin' else. It's jes' lak I say, I's always been a hunter, en one night I went down in de post oak woods hunting by myself. Dis is a fact; 'tain't no lie. It's what I done. I had a mighty good dog, and I jes' kept walking and walking, and I got mighty nigh to Mr. Redhead Jim Lee's place, and I walked on and atter while I seed I'd lost my dog. I couldn't see him nowhar and I couldn't hear him nowhar, and den somepin' say to me, jes' lak dis: 'Josh, blow your horn!' Jes' lak dat, lak somebody talking to me. Well I give three loud, long blows and set dere awhile longer but dat dog didn't come. Co'se I knowed he'd come sometime, and so I jes' set dere on dat log and I jes' turned a fool, I reckon, but 'twas jes' lak somebody talking to me, lak it 'peared to me was whispering: 'Josh, you out here in dese woods by yo'self. You blowed dat horn and your enemy heard you. You's a fool, you is.' And I whispered back: 'Dat's a fact.' I couldn't hear what it was a-whispering to me, but us jes' talk back to one 'nuther, and 'bout dat time I look up and here come three men ridin' on new saddles wid shiny buckles gwine, 'squeechy, squeechy', jes' lak dat. I hear de hosses feet jes' as nachel as could be. I thought sho I seed 'em, and it 'pears to look clean outer reason, but dem men come riding right on up to me, and I jump over dat log and lay down flat on de other side, and it look lak I could see right through dat log and heared 'em say: 'Dar he, is dar he is,' and I seed 'em p'inting dey finger right whar I was. I knowed dem hosses gwineter step over de log on top me, and I's telling you de troof, I jump up from 'hind dat log and run 'bout two miles, and if it hadn't been for dat slough, I don't know whar I'd a went. I come to myself in de middle of dat water, up to hyar, waist high, and dar was my dog, old Cuba, done treed a 'possum.

[Here begins the tale of chasing Guinea Jim.]

"And bimeby Mr. Beesley, what live not fur from Marse Ike, he rode up and had five dogs, five nigger dogs, what dey call 'em, and soon as he come, Marse Ike's hoss was saddled up and Marse Ike and him rode off down de road and de dogs wid 'em, 'head of us. Us followed 'long behind 'em, stay close as dey 'low us, to see what dey was up to. When dey got close to de ginhouse, ginhouse right 'side de road, dey stop us and Mr. Beesley told old Brown to go ahead. Old Brown was de lead dog and had a bell on him and dey was fasten togedder wid a rod, jes' lak steers. He turn 'em loose, and den he popped de whip and hollered at old Brown and told him 'nigger.' Old Brown hollered lak he hit. He want to go. And dey was a fence on bofe sides made it a lane, so he put Old Brown over de fence on de ginhouse side, and told Brown to 'go ahead.' He went ahead and run aroun' de ginhouse and dey let him in de gin-room and he grabbled in de cottonseed in a hole.

"Den somebody holler 'Guinea Jim,'

"I looks and I didn't see him. Didn't nobody see him, but dey know dat's whar he been hiding. Mr. Beesley told old Brown he jes' fooling him, and Old Brown holler ag'in, lak he killing him, and Mr. Beesley say! 'Go git dat nigger' and old Brown started 'way from dar lak he hadn't been hunting nothing, but he went aroun' and aroun' dat gin and Mr. Beesley told him he hatter do better dan dat or he'd kill him, 'cause he hadn't come dar for nothing.

"Brown made a circle aroun' dat gin 'way down to de fence dat time, and he was so fat he couldn't git through de fence. You know what sort of fence, a rail fence it was. Den he stop and bark for help. Now I seed dis wid my own eyes. Dey put Brown on top de fence and he jump way out in de road, didn't stay on de fence. He jump and run up and down in de road, and couldn't find no scent of Jim. You knows how dey used to make dem rail fences?

"Well, Brown come back dar, and dis is de trufe, so help me Gawd.

He bark, look lak, for dem to lift him back up on de fence, and bless God, if dat dog didn't walk dat rail fence lak he walking a log, as fur as from here to dat gate yonder, and track Jim jes' lak he was on de groun'. He fell off once, and dey had to put him back, and he run his track right on to whar Jim jumped off de fence way out in de road. Old Brown run right cross de road to de other fence and treed ag'in on t'other side de road toward Konkabia. Old Brown walk de fence on dat side de road a good piece, jes' lak he done on de other side, and dem other dogs, he hadn't never turned dem loose.

"When Brown he jump off dat fence, he jump jes' as fur as he kin on de fiel' side, lak he gwine ketch Jim lak a gnat or somepin' and he never stop barking no more, jes' lak he jumping a rabbit. Den, Mr. Beesley turn dem other dogs loose dat he hadn't never turned loose, 'ca'se he say old Brown done got de thing straight. And he had it straight. Dem dogs run dat track right on down to Konkabia and crossed it to de Blacksher side. Dey was a big old straw field dar den and dey cross it and come on through dat field, all dem dogs barkin' jes' lak dey looking at Jim. 'Reckley, dey come up on Jim running wid a pine bresh tied behind him to drag his scent away, but it didn't bother old Brown.

"When dem dogs 'gin to push him, Jim drap de bresh and runned back toward Konkabia. Now on Konkabia dere used to be beavers worse den on Sucarnatchee now. Dey was a big beaver dam 'twixt de bridge and de Hale place, and Jim run to dat beaver dam. You know when beavers build dey dam, dey cut down trees and let 'em fall in de creek, and pull in trash en bresh same as folks, to dam de water up dar tell its knee-deep. De dogs seen him, old Brown looking at him, jes' 'fore he jump in 'bove de dam right 'mongst de trash and things dey'd drug in dar. Brown seed him and he jump in right behind him. Jim jes' dive down under de raff, en let he nose stick outer de water. Every once in a while Jim he put he head down under, he holding to a pole down dar, and once Mr. Beesley seed him, he jes' let him stay dar.

"Brown would swim 'bout 'mongst de bresh, backerds and for'erds, and terreckly Mr. Beesley tole old Brown, 'Go git him.' Den all de men got poles and dug 'bout in de raff hunting him. Dey knowed he was dar, en Marse Ike had a pole giggen aroun' trying to find him too. Den he told Mr. Beesley to give him de hatchet and let him fix he pole. He sharpen de pole right sharp, den Marse Ike start to dig aroun' wid de pole, and he kinder laugh to hisself, 'ca'se he knowed he done found Jim. 'Bout dat time Jim poke he head up and say: 'Dis here me,' and everybody holler. Den he ax 'em please, for God's sake, don't let dem dogs git him. Dey told him come on out.

"You see, Jim belonged to Miss Mary Lee, Mr. John Lee's Ma, and his Pa was kilt in de war, so Mr. Beesley was looking out for her. Well, dey took Jim outer dar, and Mr. Beesley whipped him a little and told him: 'Jim, you put up a pretty good fight and I's gwine to give you a start for a run wid de dogs.'

"Jim took out towards Miss Mary's, and Mr. Beesley helt old Brown as long as he could. Dey caught Jim and bit him right smart. You see dey had to let em bite him a little to satisfy de dogs, Jim could have made it, 'cept he was all hot and wore out."

From: Oliver Bell, "De Bes' Friend a Nigger Ever Had"

collected by
Ruby Pickens Tartt
Sumter County

Speakin' 'bout graveyard, I was passin' dere one night, ridin' on 'bout midnight, as' sumpin' come draggin' a chain by me lak a dog. I got down off'n my horse, but couldn't see nothin' wid no chain, so I got back on de horse an' dere raght in front of me was a Jack-Me-Lantern wid de brightes' light you ever seed. It was tryin' to lead me off, an' ev'y time I'd git back in de road it would led me off ag'in. You sho' will git los' if you follow a Jack-Me-Lantern.

One of dem led a man down to de creek by dem double bridges; said he foun' he was travelin' in de wrong direction, gittin' frum home stidder clo'ster, so he jes' sit down under a tree an waited 'till daylight. I ain't skeered of nothin' but dem Jack-Me-Lanterns, but dey stirs you up in yo' min' 'till you can't tell whar you's at; an' dey's so bright dey nigh 'bout puts yo eyes out. Dey is plenty of 'em over by de graveyard raght over yonder whar all my white folks is buried, an' mammy an' pappy, too.

From: Dellie Lewis, "Dellie Lewis Knows Cures and Conjer"

collected by
Mary Poole, Mobile;
J. M. Smith, editor

My grandmammy was a midwife an' she useta gibe women cloves

an' whiskey to ease de pain. She also gib 'em dried watermelon seeds
to git rid of de grabel in de kidneys. For night sweats Grandmammy
would put an axe under de bed of de sick pusson wid de blade a-sittin'
straight up. An' iffen yo' is sick an' wants to keep de visitors away,
jus' put a fresh laid aig in front of de do' an' dey won't come in. If you
is anxious fo' yo' sweetheart to come back f'um a trip put a pin in de
groun' wid de point up an' den put a aig on de point. When all de
insides runs outen de aig yo' sweetheart will return.

From: Ank Bishop
"Gabr'el, Blow Sof"!,
Gabr'el, Blow Loud"

collected by
Ruby Pickens Tartt
Sumter County, Alabama

Dis is de evil sper't what de Bible tells about when hit say a person
has got two sper'ts, a good one an' a evil one. De good sper't goes to a
place of happiness an' rest, an' you doan' see hit no mo', but de evil
sper't ain't got no place to go. Hit's dwellin' place done tore down
when de body died, an' hit's jes' a wand'rin' an a waitin' for Gabr'el
to blow his trump, den de worl' gwineter come to an en'. But when
God say, 'Take down de silver mouf trump an' blow, Gabr'el, an'
Gabr'el say, "Lord, how loud shell I blow?" Den de Lord say, "Blow
easy, Gabr'el, en ca'm, not to 'larm my lilies." De secon' time Gabr'el
say, "How loud mus' I blow, Lord?" Den de Lord say, "Blow hit as
loud as seben claps of thunder all added into one echo, so as to wake
up dem damnable sper'ts sleepin' in de grave-ya'ds what ain't never
made no peace wid dey God, jes' alayin' dere in dey sins."

But de Christen Army, hit gits up wid de fus' trump, an' dem what
is deef is de evil ones what anybody kin see anytime. I ain't skeered of
'em, though. I passes 'em an' goes right on plowin', but iffen you
wants 'em to git outten your way, all you gotter do is jes' turn your
head least bit an' look back. Dey gone jes' lack dat! When my fus' wife
died 'bout thirty years ago, I was goin' up to Gaston to see Sara
Drayden, old Scot Drayden's wife, an' I tuck out through Kennedy
bottom 'bout sundown right after a rain. I seed sompin acomin' down
de road 'bout dat high, 'bout size a little black shaggy dog, an' I says,
"What's dat I sees comin' down de road? Ain't nobody 'roun' here got
no black shaggy dog?" Hit kep' acomin' an' kep' agittin' bigger an'
bigger an' closer an' closer, an' time hit got right to me 'twuz as big as
a ha'f growed yearlin', black as a crow. It had four feet an' drop years,
jes' lack a dog, but 'twa'n't no dog, I knows dat. Den he shy out in de

bushes, an' he come right back in de road, an' hit went on de way I was comin' from, so I went on de way hit was comin' from. I ain't never seed dat thing no mo'. But I'ze gotter pretty good notion 'bout who hit 'twuz.

From: Henry Cheatham
"I Heard Lincoln Set Us Free"

collected by
Ila Prine, Mobile

I knows dere is gostes, 'caze when I was a little boy my mammy come in from de fiel' an' laid across de bed an' I was sittin' in front of de fireplace an' a big somp'n lak a cow widout no haid come in de do' an' I commence to beat on it wid my fists. Den my mammy say: "What matter wid you, nigger?" Den dat critter he walk right out de do.' I looked outen de window an' dere it was a-goin' in Aunt Marfa's cabin. I neber did see it no mo'. Den anudder time a white man died an' my mammy was a stayin' wid his sister an' dis spirit lak an angel come to my mammy an' tol' her to tell de white lady to read de Bible backards three times, 'caze dere was one talent 'tween her an' Jesus. After dat she were comforted. Anudder time, my pappy, Sam Cheatam, who was a wicked man, was a-sittin' in front of de fire an' a big brindle dog come to de do' an' started barkin'. My pappy say: "What in de Hell am dat?" an' snapped his fingers at de dog. De dog he den dropped daid. Some folks say dat dere ain't no sich things as gostes, but I know dere is, 'caze dere is good spirits an' bad spirits.

From: "Ex-Slave Liza White"

collected by
Preston Klein, Lee County

I seed a haint one time, I knowed it wus, one old man had been having the toothache so I wus going to see him and he used to keep his jaw tied up all the time; well fore I got there I saw him coming, and nearer I got to him he turned to a man on a mule or horseback, wearing a big hat an 'fore I got to the house he wus clear gone, and I know it was a haint.

From: Henry Barnes
"He Misses Dem Set-Down Hawgs"

collected by
Ila Prine, Mobile

Lady, you ax me iffen us knowed anyt'ng 'bout hoodoo? Yes, ma'am dere sho' was folkses what could put spells on you. I sho' was skeered o' dem kin' too. Atter I was nearly growed, dere was a gal name Penny what been down sick a long time an' dere was a cunjer doctor wukkin' on her tryin' cyure her, but her wan't 'greeable, so he let her die. Den a boy, name Ed, he had a mis'ry in he foot, an' hit went up he leg an' he cripple. Dere was a hoodoo doctor in de forks o' 'Bigbee Ribber come tend on him, an' he tol' ebber'body git outten de house 'cep'n' him an' Ed an' de Debil. He cyured Ed smack well.

My mammy said I was borned wid a 'zernin' eye to see sperits, an' I seed sump'n lak a cow wid no haid. So mammy made me stir de fresh lard when dey was rendin' hit, 'caze dat cyures you of seein' de sperits. Atter I stirred de lard, I didn't see 'em no mo'.

One time I was splittin' rails wid a nigger what could do anythin', but he was a bad man an' I was 'feered of him. I tol' him, iffen I had a pain or anything hurt me, I sho' would kill him wid my ax. I wudda split dat nigger wide open, jes' lak I split dem rails, iffen he try dat hoodoo on me.

From: George Young
"Peter Had No Keys Cep'in His"

collected by
Ruby Pickens Tartt
Sumter County

No'm, I dunno nuthin' 'bout no spirits, either, but Christ 'peered to de 'postles, didn't He, atter he been dead? An' I'se seed folks done been dead jes' as na'chel in de day as you is now. One day me an' my wife was pickin' cotton right out yonder on Mr. White's place, an' I looked up an' seed a man all dressed in black, wid a white shirt bosom, his hat a-sittin' on one side, ridin' a black hoss.

I stoop down to pick some cotton, den look up an' he was gone. I said to my wife, I call her Glover but she go by two names, I said, "Glover, wonder whar dat man went what was ridin' long yonder on dat pacin' hoss?" She say, "What pacin' hoss an' what man?" I said, "He was comin' down dat bank by dat ditch. Dey ain't no bridge dere, an' no hoss could jump hit." Glover said, "Well, I'm gwine in de house 'caze I don't feel lack pickin' cotton today." But I ain't skeered of 'em. I gets out de patch plenty times to let 'em by, an' iffen you kin see 'em, walk 'roun' 'em. Iffen you can't see 'em, den dey'll walk 'roun' you. Iffen dey gets too plentiful, I jes' hangs a hoss shoe upside down over de do' and don' have no mo' trouble.

From: "Wade Owens Heard Lincoln Speak"

collected by
Preston Klein, Lee County

Dey would tell us chillun all kinds of ghos' stories 'bout witches gittin' outter dey skins. . . . One night I was at Notasulga an' I heered some singing. I stopped an' hit was right at my feet an' would go further off. I took out wid hit an' hit kept stopping an' startin' off ag'in 'twell hit giv' out entirely. I looked to see where I was an' I was at de cemetery an' nothin' didn't bother me neither. I eased out an' shut de gate an' never foun' whut carried me dere.

From the narrative of West T. Jones

collected by
Ruby Pickens Tartt
Sumter County

I got a brother Ed ten years youngern me to the day. You ought to talk wid him 'bout things. He knows a man that deals in witchcraft en says he kin make a snake run a man out of the field en things like that. I doan know how, but he swears hit's so. I know I was comin' down de road there by Mr. Leitch's goin' on to my lodge, en I passed by the church ther where the roads cross, en I heard the organ jes' soundin' different notes plain es day. Some of 'em say, "Well, I wouldn't be hearing hit long!" but I didn't run a step, jus' walked on slow listenin' to hit. 'Bout den, the bell to de lodge rung en drowned hit out, but I wa'n't skeered; jes' didn't keer 'bout goin' in. I tole Miss Marie Claire—I knowed her all her life—I said, "I heared de organ playin'," en she said, "Oh go way frum me, Wes', you ain't heered nothin'." But I said, "I ain't tell you no story! I heered it jes' about sundown, an de doors wuz shut en wa'n't nobody in there." Then she said "Must a been a rat." En I said, "I didn't go in, but I ain't never heered a rat play de organ, is you?"

From: "Solomon and the Thirsty Haints"

collected by
Annie Dee Dean
Evergreen, Alabama

Dey is one thing I sho' kin' see an' dat is "spaits," I calls 'em ha'nts, an when I sees dem things I sho' kin' move!

On a moonshiny night hit sho is easy ter see'm movin' mongst the lightnin' bugs an' the fox fire, but you don't see so much of it now lack you did in de ole days. Too much new groun' been cleared off.

Back yonder at Miss Marg'ret's, look lack ever' time I had to go to de spring fer water atter th' moon done riz, dem ha'nts wanter ter git out an' play. Sometimes day looked natchel lack folks, an' sometimes they wuz white as a sheet, wid long arms an' fingers that retched out at you. They made a curious fuss lack somebody draggin' somethin', an' when you stopped, dey stopped. Yes ma'am! Sometimes now, dey gits atter me when I tries to walk aroun' at night. Den is when I fergits I is gittin' ole an' blind.

No'me dem ha'nts ain't done nothin' to me yit, but a heap er times I got up to de big house frum de spring wid th' water—hit wouldn' be no more'n a cup full in de bucket, an' lawd knows I hadn't spilled nary drap. Dem ghosties done away wid it somehow. Sometimes I got so scairt an' run so fas', hit look lack my shadder wuz go'ner overtake me. Hits de Gawd's trufe! Dem ha'nts kep' right up wid me, no matter how fas' I run. . . .

You wants ter know 'bout cunjerin'? Well I ain't never b'lieve in none er dat, but I was alluz heard 'bout it, an' once't I seed a woman dat drapped a brass ring in a glass fullo' water an' hit kicked ever' drap o' water plum outer de glass, jes' lack a bird playin' in it. Dat's de Gawd's trufe!

Now dere is one thing I knows for a fact. I has done it all o' my life. When it goes to thunderin' an' lightnin' an' de wind is a blowin', I goes in de yard an' gits a ax an' walks right out terwards the wind, an' when hits comin' right terwards my face, I jes' raises my axe lack dis an' comes down ter de grown' an' cuts right in the dirt. I leaves her standin' dar an' she splits de wind. Yessum, an' hit can't harm nobody. I follows dat right now ever' time de wind blows. Dey ain't no mistake in doin' dat. No ma'am! De fust thin I does when I sees a dark cloud comin' up is to git my axe!

From: Silvia Witherspoon
"Foots Get Tired
From Choppin' Cotton"

collected by
Susie O'Brien, Uniontown

Does I believe in ghosties? Sho I does. I don't suppose you was bawn wid a veil on yo' face lak I was, 'ca'se I can see dem ghosties as plain as dey was here raght now. I'll tell you 'bout one dat comes out de white folks chu'ch yard. On dark rainy nights, I sees him, tall wid long white robes drappin f'um him. He carries a big light so bright dat you can't see his face, but he looks jus' lak a man. It don't bother me none, 'ca'se I don't bother it.

I keeps a flour sifter an' a fork by my bed to keep de witches f'um ridin' me. How come I knows dey rides me? Honey, I bees so tired in de mawnin' I kin scarcely git outten by bed, an' its all on account of dem witches ridin' me, so I putt de sifter dere to cotch 'em. Sometimes I wears dis dime wid de hole in it aroun' my ankle to keep off de conjure, but since Monroe King tuk an' died us ain't had much conjerin' 'roun' here.

"Carrie Dykes—Midwife"

collected by
Ruby Pickens Tartt
Belmont, Alabama

I hear 'em say de doctor kin tell whether hits gonna be a boy or a girl, I couldn't never do that wid folks, but I kin wid *beasties*. If you gonna breed a mare en you turns her head to de East, the colt'll be lack the mare. If you turns her head to de West de colt'll be a horse. My pappy tole me dat, en tole me always breed a mare nine days atter de last colt come, en I ain't know'd hit to fail. There's a colt in de pastor now what'll prove whut I say. Do fust baby I brought in full by myse'f was Lithenia Spence's en she call him "Fo'day" cause he come zackly fo' day break. Us wuz livin' down at Double Creek den en somehow Lithenia loss her notchin' stick, dat's whut de call keepin' up wid de month, but she knowed hit wuz on de change uv de moon, an' so want no doctor dere nor nobody. . . . Well, dey sarnt atter me. . . . I didn't use no ginger tea nor nothin' ter steamerlate her. You see on de change uv de moon water come mo' freely, an dat's whut make hit easy.

Dey say way they go by de moon hit work wid de person's blood. On a young woman dey say you'd have a better time on de change of the moon 'stead of on a full moon. On de full moon, if the baby born then, wouldn't be as free. But I cut de navel string en all, by myse'f, an' greased hit. . . . You see, I had done kilt my hogs en boiled de feet widout no salt real done, den I pours dat water off. Now you gonna eat dem hogs feet, so you kin go put salt in 'em en fix 'em jes' lack you wants 'em, but doan put no salt in no hogs feet oil for dat navel. Now you dreens dat water off uv dat grease what's riz to de top, en skims hit an' strains hit en pours hit in de bottle en hang hit up where can't nobody bother hit en you is all ready fer de navel. But you has to take a skillet en put hit on de fire en put a light-'ood knot under hit en put some ole linen cloth in hit, what de white folks gives us outer old table cloth, en let hit brown, en take some cotton from de gin house en you take de ban' off en you lay hit wid de navel on de bed, den jes' gwiner put hit in de skillet jes' er minute, en wheel hit right over 'til hit git brown 'fore you knows hit, den put some uv dat grease out de bottle on dat cotton an' put hit on de baby's navel. Then put de belly ban' on top dat en pin hit on roun' him, en ain't no baby never had no trouble wid no navel. Dat ban' stay on dat baby three days en dat navel comin' right off, dat is, if you keeps de baby warm, and hit won't never fail you. I takes dat back. Miss Monie Bates say hers had to stay on nine days but den I didn't nuss her so I doan know. Now when dat navel come off you got to take hit en put hit direct in the fire, en don't let hit touch de floor. Now jes' lack you dressin' de baby, en you take de ban' off en you lay hit wid de navel on de bed, den jes' lack I tell you dat baby gwiner wet de bed, from then on. I is seed folks lay hit down en I said to myse'f "unk-unk, don't you lay dat down nowhere. Jes' throw hit direct in de fire."

Now I didn't tell you 'bout de atter birth 'cause dem chillun wuz listenin' but you takes hit en sprinkle salt on hit but don't let no salt git roun' de bed. En you puts hit in de fire-place den burn hit up en dats one reason don't want no ashes took up in de fire-place, 'cause they's needed; then hits bad luck too, jes' lack salt roun' de bed when a baby born. I heard my Mammy say two women wuz fretted wid one nother, en one of 'em foun' a baby en de tother one hung a sack uv salt over her head in de cracks up under de rafters en a ole man come one day en say she was mighty sick, "Somethin' 'roun' dis bed cast a spell on her," En he look en sho' 'nough dere was de bag uv salt 'tween dem boards en he took hit down en she got well. . . .

I don't b'lieve in no conjurin' but I does b'lieve in dem old home-grown remedies like puttin' a ole ax or a ole sweep under de center of de bed for after pains when de baby comes—jes' so hits rusty. I do dat right now and hit sho works. I doan sweep under dat bed neither nor take no ashes outer dat room. Hit sho' bad luck, Sweep de room all over, but don't bother under dat bed. Seems funny but dey didn't have no trouble dem days when I wuz nussin' lack they do now; folks want so hard headed.

Now atter dat baby is a month old, take up dem ashes, sweep up de room, take ev'y thing offen dat bed en scrub up, clean ev'ything she been usin' en leave dat room jes' lack hit wuz when she went in, but fus' yu takes meal bran' en put hit on de hearth, en put hot embers over 'em en make a smoke. Den atter you done wash her clothes en dry 'em press 'em, hang 'em on a chair over dat smoke, den get her up an' wash her good en put her on dem clothes, en give her catnip tea or 'sippin' bark tea. Bile de water in a clean coffee pot en bresh hit wid a little sugar, en they calls hit sweatin' de fever. Give hit ev'y mornin' en evenin'. Then you takes her outer dere en she got to go 'round de house, en go to de spring en git her a drink uv spring water. Carry a thimble wid her; hits good fer de baby in teethin' time. Take de gourd off de nail en fill up dat thimble wid dat water en drink dat *fust*. Then you kin drink all de water you want outer dat gourd, but you better drink outer dat thimble fust, or your baby sho have trouble teethin', en dats right ter this here day.

There's a heap to midwifin'—'bout de baby die if de diaper tech de flo' en all dat. An' cose you know while de woman is "keepin' house," she can't cross no stream. En she can't set in no room but hers 'til de babys a month ole, but she kin git up on de nine-day period lack some uv 'em does now. Some folks calls dem ole timey remedies foolish, en dats how come I doan practice no mo'. . . .

One night I seed a sumpin' switch de willow branches right in front er me, en I stop en say, "Whut dat!" Den hit switch de willow branches agin. I jes' stopped still en commence ter holler. Needn't worry 'bout what I'm gonna do when *I'm* skeered, 'cause I jes' stan' still en holler til somebody come git me! Den my husban' he come up to see what ail me, en weren't nuthin' but a little steer yearlin' wid horns switchin' down branches.

But one time when I wuz little I wuz out wid my mother en hit wuz a moonlight night. We wuz goin' home cross de lot, en there wuz a mule name Mary, jes' standin' dere wid her years bucked lack she wuz lookin' at sumpin'. An' in a minute she snort "Urrunh!" An' Mammy grabbed me an' run. She say de mule seed sumpin' ter make her snort lack dat, an' dat mule wuz lookin' right toward dat hill en' they says dey is sperits up dar. But I always do say ain't nothin' ever skeered me but come ter find out hit wuz sompin' I knowed.

My husban' believed in sperits though, en I used to tease him en make him so mad! He say one night he wuz out huntin' wid some men en he had a ole dog name Boo-tee en' he saw a sperit walkin' longside er Boo-tee wid a switch in its han'. Didn't none uv de others see de sperit, but he swore hit wuz a sumpin' tall en white. 'Bout time he wuz fixing ter call ole Boo-tee de sperit hit him side de head, en you know dat dog carried his head ter one side till he died. My husban' always said twuz on account uv de lick de sperits give him, but I useter laugh at him en say "How come you think hit wuz a sperit? That old dog jes' got sumpin' in his year ter make him cock his haid dataway!" en he get so mad! But whutever twuz dat dog sho carried his haid ter one side frum den on!

No, Ma'am, I doan believe in conju'. I wouldn't give a nickel to have nobody workin' on me! All I know about conju' is whut Aunt Susan tole me. She useter tell me lots about hit, but she so ole now she doan like to mention it.

She say one night she dream she walkin' along de road en she thought she step on a needle en hit hurt her severe. She got hit out. She chewed hit up. Whut she represented was the needle wuz planted dere fer her. En she got hit. De next mornin' atter she dreamed this, she went down de road, personally, en got it, whutever it was, en de day atter dat, she couldn't walk!

I had conju' woman workin' me once. God knows I don't believe in hit, but I had sumpin' in my ankle en I doan keer whur I walked when I came back home I'd be lame fer two days. So I went to de conju' woman's house. She warn't dere, so I waited in de yard en pretty soon she come a-skippin' along. She had straight hair lack a witch er de pictures in de funny books. She come thu de gate en say, "Hmmm, somebody been here today, drawed my coffin!" En sho nuff, dere wuz de marks on de side uv de house! Cose, she could 'er fixed dat up fo' I got dere, I doan know about dat. Den she went in de house en fixed up sumpin', I didn't see whut she got, but she rubbed off de marks.

I told her about my ankle how hit would hurt me when I walked any piece on hit, en she say "Hmmm, somebody throwed at you. Grudge whut you got." But she say sho could uphand anything brought befo' her so I asked her to work on me. She took de house en got three things, I doan know whut they wuz, but they wuz three things she put on my ankle en rubbed hit. En dat wuz jes' ez well ez de other one, en hit ain't bothered me a bit since!

From: "Tom Moore and His Death Money" (on the death of his son)

collected by
Ruby Pickens Tartt
Coatopa, Sumter County

Safrony dare is mos' los' her reason she's so troubled; says she seen ghosts wid polka dot dresses on en when she go ter shake hands ain't nothin' dere but smoke. She say she seed one jes' lack a woman, jes' lack folks—close ez from me to you walkin' by dat rail fence en she walk in every crook in de fence en Safrony say she jes' stayed in de road and when she got to de gap she jes lef' her standin' dere jes lack a woman then she passed away jes lack I'm looking at you en takes my eye offen you then you is gone;—must be de air.

Den she say she seed one en hit flew down jes lack a big white hen en hit de ground en bounce up; den hit growed tall as de eves on dis here house en don't keer how much fuss the chillun make hit won't leave til all us turn de corner uv de house. I ain' seed none yit, but Safrony do all de time en dey keeps her so bothered in her mind. I says hit might be Jerry comin' back trying to say something, but he wouldn't wear no polka dot dress!

Hit could be some of dem home remedies she taken cause us ain't got no money to go to no doctor, been had so many debts ter pay for de funeral. But Safrony says hit could be bad luck on account of when dey brought Jerry in a corpse dey had to take him out over some of de same road to de graveyard and you nacherley can't pass over de same ground twice or hit show will bring dem whuts lef' bad luck. Hit could be dat; den hit all happen so sudden lack didn't nobody think 'bout stoppin' de clock or turning dat lookin' glass to de wall so hit kin be a whole parcel uv things Miss, till I doan know which one but a spell is sho' on Safrony. Hit all happened one Saturday en us had ter hurry en get de grave dug en bury Jerry fore dust on Sunday caze we knowed hit nacherley won't do to carry him over in de house on Sunday or some of de res' would be gone fore dis year is up—an I'd done had enough bad luck th'out having no more 'ceasting goin' on. I ought ter been spectin' hit case I'd dreamed 'bout white hosses, but I jes said ter my se'f, "Shucks tain't nothin' to dat," but hit bothered me mightily an I tole Jerry dat same Satday, "be keerful wid dem mules," en Malindy wuz wid him en she say he wuz, en dey wuz on they side uv de road, en when he hit em she say she know'd Jerry was dead, en de man from Texas stop en she said, "Please Sir, I can't move but drag Jerry over here. I know he's dead but lay him out in de grass side de road where can't nobody run over him no mo": en a man come by from Tommsuby goin' ter Selma en de man from Texas say, "Take deze niggers to de horsepital en I'll pay de bills:" en he tuck em en' dat same white man from Toomsuby didn't know me, ain't never seed me, but he took dem chillum to de horsepital en he come back dat night en come right here ter dis here house en tole me 'bout whut done happen. He sho wuz a good white man. But you know Miss dat Texas man ain't never been heared uv since, en I had all dem bills ter pay. Miss, can't you get somebody to help dis po' ole nigger git his pay? I needs dat death money mighty bad.

From: Anthony Abercrombie
"Old Joe Can Keep His Two Bits"

collected by
Susie O'Brien
Uniontown

Marse Jim had 'bout three hundred slaves, and he had one mighty bad overseer. But he got killed down on de bank of de creek one night. Dey never did find out who killed him, but Marse Jim always b'lieved de field han's done it. 'Fore dat us niggers useta go down to de creek to wash ourselves, but atter de overseer got killed down dar, us jes' leave off dat washin', 'cause some of 'em seed de overseer's hant down dar floatin' over de creek.

Dar was another hant on de plantation, too. Marse Jim had some trouble wid a big double-jinted nigger named Joe. One day he turn on Marse Jim wid a fence rail, and Marse Jim had to pull his gun an' kill him. Well, dat happen in a skirt of woods whar I get my lightwood what I use to start a fire. One day I went to dem same woods to get some 'simmons. Another nigger went wid me, and he clumb de tree to shake de 'simmons down whilst I be pickin' 'em up. 'Fore long I heared another tree shakin' every time us shake our tree, dat other tree shake too, and down come de 'simmons from it. I say to myself, "Dats Joe, 'cause he likes 'simmons too." Den I grab my basket and holler to de boy in de tree, "Nigger turn loose and drap down from dar, and ketch up wid me if you can, I's leavin' here right now, 'cause Old Joe is over dar gettin' 'simmons too."

Den another time I was in de woods choppin' lightwood. It was 'bout sundown, an' every time my ax go "whack" on de lightwood knot, I hear another whack 'sides mine. I stops and lis'ens and don't hear nothin'. Den I starts choppin' ag'in, and ag'in I hears de yuther whacks. By dat time my old houn' dog was crouchin' at my feets, wid de hair standin' up on his back and I couldn't make him git up nor budge.

Dis time I din' stop for nothin'. I jes' drap my ax right dar, an' me and dat houn' dog tore out for home lickety split. When us got dar Marse Jim was settin' on de porch, an' he say: "Nigger, you been up to somep'n you got no business. You is all outer breath. Who you runnin' from?" Den I say, "Marse Jim, somebody 'sides me is choppin' in yo' woods, an' I can't see him." And Marse Jim, he say, "Ah, dat ain't nobody but Old Joe. Did he owe you anythin?" And I say, "Yassah, he own me two-bits for helpin' him shuck corn." "Well," Marse Jim say, "don't pay him no mind, it jes' Old Joe come back to pay you."

Anyhow, I didn' go back to dem woods no mo'. Old Joe can jes' have de two-bits what he owe me, 'cause I don't want him follerin' 'round atter me. When he do I ca's't keep my mind on my bizness.

From: Henry Garry
"Mr. Renfroe Hung from a
Chinyberry Tree"

collected by
W. F. Jordan
Birmingham

I was a mighty little shaver, but I 'members one night atter supper, my daddy and mammy an' us chilluns was settin' under a big tree by our cabin in de quarters when all at wunst, lickety split, heah come gallopin' down de road what look lak a whole army of ghos'es. Mus' hab been 'bout a hundert an' dey was men ridin' hosses wid de men and hosses bofe robed in white.

Cap'n, dem mens look lak dey ten feet high an' dey hosses big as elephan's. Dey didn't bobber nobody at de qua'ters, but de leader of de crowd ride right in de front gate an' up to de big dug well back of our cabin an' holler to my daddy. "Come heah nigguh!" Ho-oh!, 'cose we skeered. Yassuh, look lak our time done come.

My daddy went ober to whar he settin' on his hoss at de well. Den he say, "Nigguh git a bucket an' draw me some cool water." Daddy got a bucket fill it up an' han' it to him. Cap'n, would you b'lieve it? Dat man jes' lif' dat bucket to his mouf' an' neber stop twell it empty. Did he hab 'nough? He jes' smack his mouf an' call for mo'. Jes' lak dat, he didn't stop twell he drunk three buckets full. Den he jes' wipe his mouf an' say, "Lawdy, dat sho' was good. Hit was de fust drink of water I'se had sense I was killed at de battle of Shiloh".....

One night a gang took him outten de Livingston jail an' go 'bout a mile outten town an' han'd him (Steve Renfroe) to a chinyberry tree. I'se heard iffen you go to dat tree today an' kinda tap on hit an say, "Renfroe, Renfroe; what did you do?" De tree say right back to you, "Nothin'."

Nawsuh, foks down 'roun' Gainesville didn' pay much min' to signs an' conju' an' all dat stuff. My mammy wouldn't let us tote a axe on our shoulder th'ough de house, an' she wouldn't 'low a umbrella to be opened in de house, say hit bring bad luck. She neber fail to hab cown-fiel' peas an hawg-jowl for dinner on New Yeah's Day. She say hit a sign you hab plenty to eat balance ob de yeah. She put a ball of azzifittity on a string an' make all us chillun wear it 'roun' our neck to keep off sickness. If a owl begin to hoot ober in Tombigbee bottom too close to de house, she put de shovel in de fire to make him stop.

collected by
Ruby Pickens Tartt
Sumter County

From Jake Green

Mr. Whitehead owned Dirtin Ferry down to Belmont, en dey had er darkie dere named Dick what claim sick all de time. So de Massta man said, "Dick, dam it, go to de house. I can't get no work out ov you." So Dick went on, en he was a fiddler so day jes' tuck his vittuls to him for seven years. Den one day, Old Massa say to de overseer man, "Let's slip up dere en see whut Dick doin'," "so dey did, en dere sot Dick, fat as he could be a-playin' de fiddle and a-singin',

> Fool my Massa seben years
> Gwiner fool him seben mo'
> He diddle de diddle de diddle de do'.

He had one [slave] do', call him John, an' hit come a traveler an stayed all night, en Ole Massa p'inted out John, an said, "He ain't never tole me a lie in his life." De traveler bet Massa a hundred dollars 'ginst fo' bits he'd ketch John in a lie 'fo' he lef'. Next mawnin' at de table de mice was pretty bad, so de traveler co't one by de tail an put him inside er kiver-lid dish whut was settin' dere on de table, as he tole Ole Marsa tell John he could eat sumpin' out of ev'y dish atter dey got th'oo but dat kiver-lid one an not to take de kiver offen hit. En John said, "Nossuh, I won't." But John jes' nachully had to see what was in dat dish, so he raise de lid, en out hopped de mouse. Den hyar come Ole Marsa en axed John iffen he done whut he tole him not to do, en John 'nied hit. Den de traveler look in de dish an de mouse wa'n't dere, an' he said, "See dere, John been lyin' to you all de time, you jes' ain't knowed hit." An I reckon he right 'case us had.

collected by
Preston Klein
Lee County

From: "Ex-Slave Roxy Pitts"

Member bout de wah? Sho, I members bout de wah; but us didn't hab no wah whar us was. Old Marster got kilt in Virginny, dey said, en he didn't nebber come back home, en dem what did come back was all crippled up en hurt. Us didn't see no Yankees twel day come erlong after de wah was gone, en day tuck Old Mistis' good hosses en lef some po ole mules, en dey tuk all us's co'n en didn't lef' us nuddin to eat in de smokehouse. Dey runned off all de chickens dey cudden ketch, en jes' fo' dey lef', de old rooster flewed up on de fence hine de orchard en crow: *"IS-DE-YANKEES-G-O-N-E-E-E?"* En de guinea settin on de lot fence, say: *"Not Yit, Not Yit"* en de ole drake what was hid under de house, he say: *"Hush-h-h, Hush-h-h, Hush!"*

Us chilluns sho wus mischus. One time, atter a big rain, us foun two hens swimmin eroun' in de tater house, en us tuk en helt em under de water twel deys done drownded dead, en we tuk em to Mammy en she cooked em in er pot en shot de kitchen do'. When dem chickens got done, us went under de flo' en riz up er plank en got in de kitchen en stole one ob dem chickens outen de pot en et it smack up. Den Mammy foun' dat chicken gone, she tuk er brush broom an wo' us plum out. But us didn't keer; de brush broom didn't hurt nigh lak de chickens taste good.

collected by
Ruby Pickens Tartt
Sumter County

From: Anne Godfrey

I 'members Marse David myself but can't say zackly how ole I is. Ain't never been ter no school, but I kin talk Greek en I kin present politics. My reason for stammer, I ain't studied grammer. I come from a part uv de country where dey use coarse gravel sand fer hominy, an' fine gravel sand for salt, eel skin fer shoe leather, ma' leuse hids fer bakin', mosquito wings fer umbrellas. If you can't interprat dat come back tomorrow afternoon, bring a silver spoon an' a fat racoon. May God be with you amen. . . .

Taint much ter laugh at dese days, but folks used ter come ter hear me ax funny riddles, en they kep' up such a uproar couldn't nobody get in a word edgeways. But times is diffe'nt, you can't be funny when you is worried, can't even see nothin' funny when you hongry, so crippled can't git ter church, never hear no singin' an' shoutin', jest sittin' tryin' make hit 'til de truck come again.

Notes for Further Study

A general overview of American folklore collection and scholarship may be found in the editors' *Cracklin Bread and Asfidity* (University, Ala.: The University of Alabama Press, 1979). Useful comments and examples of folk beliefs and folk tales may be found in *Standard Dictionary of Folklore, Mythology, and Legend*, two volumes, edited by Maria Leach (New York: Funk and Wagnalls, 1949–1950); Kenneth and Mary Clark, *Introducing Folklore* (New York: Holt, Rinehart, and Winston, 1963); and Jan Harold Brunvand, *The Study of American Folklore: An Introduction* (New York: W. W. Norton, 1966). *Our Living Traditions: An Introduction to American Folklore*, edited by Tristram Coffin (New York: Basic Books, 1978), contains twenty-five essays by America's foremost folklore scholars. Duncan Emrich, *Folklore on the American Land* (Boston: Little, Brown, 1972) is a fine anthology of tales, songs, superstitions, folk beliefs, folk medicine, names, rhymes, riddles, proverbs, and epitaphs for the general reader. *Folklore in America* (Garden City: Doubleday, 1966, rep. Anchor Books, 1970) contains a potpourri of folklore–folk life selected from the *Journal of American Folklore* by Tristram P. Coffin and Hennig Cohen, and their companion volume, *Folklore from the Working Folk of America* (Garden City: Doubleday-Anchor, 1973), also gleaned from folklore journals, offers substantial urban and contemporary lore. Richard Dorson's *American Folklore* (Chicago: University of Chicago Press, 1959) is an authoritative survey of regional folk cultures, colonial, Negro, and immigrant folklore, and American folk heroes. The bibliographical issues of *Southern Folklore* and Tristram Coffin's *An Analytical Index to the Journal of American Folklore* (Washington, D.C.: Publications of the American Folklore Society, Bibliographical and Special Series, vol. 7, 1958) will further aid the reader in locating specific studies and collections.

Bookstores are a veritable witches' caldron of works on every conceivable, and inconceivable, aspect of the supernatural: flying saucers and astronaut-gods, the Bermuda Triangle, ESP, palmistry, astrology, I Ching, numerology, witchcraft, magic, reincarnation, and legions of ghosts, vampires, werewolves, and demons. J. R. R. Tolkien's Ring stories inspired a whirlwind of fantasies and elaborate, personal folklore, much of which draws on ancient European myths and folk tales. Archetypal symbols and motifs appear in new form; old stories are laid in new settings in far-off galaxies of the future or in worlds unbounded by dimensions of earth time and space. Myths and folk tales that used to be the kingdom of old women and children in the chimney corner are now being taken seriously—histories and encyclopedias of gnomes and fairies, compendiums of apparitions, reissues of famous editions of fairy and folk tales, and volumes of critical explication. As is true of all literary movements and fashions, some of these works are charming and beautifully crafted, some are mediocre, and a little will endure.

General reading in mythology will serve as a background for the study of folk beliefs, superstitions, and the folk tale. Edith Hamilton's *Mythology* (Boston: Little, Brown, 1940, rep. New York: New American Library, 1969) is a lucid, beautifully written account of the Greek gods and of the tales in Ovid and Homer. Robert Graves retells the myths more elaborately in two volumes, *The Greek Myths* (Baltimore: Penguin Books, 1955, 1966); Graves has also written the introduction to the famous *Larousse Encyclopedia of Mythology* (New York: Paul Hamlyn, new edition, 1968). The foundation for studies in comparative mythology was laid by Sir James Frazer, whose *The Golden Bough* first appeared in 1810. His findings on magic, religion, and folk customs fill twelve volumes, and though some of his scholarship has been discredited, the student of folklore will want to take account of his work, reissued in a one-volume abridgment by Theodore H. Gastor (New York: Criterion Books, 1959). The concern of twentieth-century literary criticism with the importance of myth in modern fiction, from Melville and Hawthorne to Joyce, Faulkner, and such contemporary writers as John Barth and John Gardner, is largely a result of the burgeoning science of psychology, especially in the writings of Freud and Jung. In Joseph Campbell's brilliant four-volume *The Masks of God* (New York: Viking, 1971, first published in 1959), modern intellectual thought in anthropology, archaeology, literature and the arts, psychology, sociology, philosophy, and religion is brought to bear on an exploration of world mythology, primitive, occidental, oriental, and modern. In the Prologue to the first volume Campbell defends the necessity of myth and proposes "the fundamental unity of the spiritual history of mankind" (p. 5). The chief value of his work for the folklorist is its emphasis on worldwide, universal motifs that are observable "everywhere in new combinations while remaining, like the elements of a kaleidoscope, only a few and always the same."

The folk supernatural, whether expressed in beliefs, superstitions, customs, rites, and festivals or in oral literature, is dominated by witchcraft, a species of magic. Bronislaw Malinowski's *Magic, Science, and Religion* (New York: Doubleday, 1954) was one of the first attempts to study the interrelationships among those three domains and to define their limits from the anthropological point of view. There are numerous popular encyclopedias and studies of witchcraft; a three-volume work first published in 1903 has recently been reissued, *Encyclopedia of Superstitions, Folklore, and the Occult Sciences* (Detroit: Gale Research Co., 1971), and George Lyman Kittredge's *Witchcraft in Old and New England* (3 vols., Cambridge: Harvard University Press, 1929) is still one of the finest studies of the subject. Among the most fascinating contemporary treatments of witchcraft are four remarkable volumes by Carlos Castaneda, *The Teachings of Don Juan* (Berkeley: University of California Press, 1968, New York: Pocket Books, Inc., 1974), *A Separate Reality* (New York: Simon & Schuster, 1971, New York: Pocket Books, Inc., 1976), *Journey to Ixtlan* (New York: Simon & Schuster, 1972, New York: Pocket Books, Inc., 1976), and *Tales of Power* (New York: Simon & Schuster, 1974), all of which present complex principles of magic and supernatural power in the manner of a Platonic dialogue.

Although scholarly publishing in folklore does not match in volume the popular literature of the supernatural, there are abundant critical materials and a fair number of published authentic collections, despite some disagreement over approach, methodology, and terminology. With the aid of motion pictures, tape recorders, and still cameras, the folklorist can now present a comprehensive view of a given folk culture. Francis E. Abernethy has created such a folk life–folklore profile in his *Tales from the Big Thicket* (Austin: The University of Texas Press, 1966), which brings together the history, customs, folk beliefs, tales, anecdotes, songs, and reminiscences of an area in Texas especially rich in folklore. The *Foxfire* volumes produced by high school students at Rabun Gap, Georgia, under B. Elliot Wigginton (Garden City: Doubleday-Anchor, 1972, 1973, 1975, 1977), and *I wish I could give my son a wild raccoon* (Garden City: Doubleday, 1976) depend extensively on in-depth interviews and monologues as well as photographs and drawings in their evocation of southern Appalachian folk life and lore. The catalog approach is still valuable, especially as a source of analytical study, although there are some problems in classification and definition. The American scholar preeminent in the collection and study of American folk beliefs is Wayland Hand, who edited *Popular Beliefs and Superstitions from North Carolina* (volumes 6 and 7 of *The Frank C. Brown Collection of North Carolina Folklore* [Durham: Duke University Press, 1952–1964]). He devised a system of classification with fourteen categories that has become standard in folklore research, and his work in the compilation of a dictionary of over two hundred thousand superstitions and folk beliefs continues at the University of California at Los Angeles. Hand's essay in Tristram Coffin's *Our Living Traditions* ("The Fear of the Gods: Superstition and Popular Belief," pp. 215–27) is both a summary of his lifelong findings and a statement of theories concerning the origins and nature of Anglo-European folk beliefs: arising out of "fear of the gods," they represent man's efforts "to order his own world of thought and action." Closely following Frazer, Hand points out that superstitions constitute "a rudimentary science" in which associative thought processes lead to the development of magical practices (ominal, causal, and sympathetic, both homeopathic, or that of similarities, and contagious, operative in witchcraft, sorcery, and folk medicine) and that such beliefs permeate folk legends and are given physical expression in various "customs, practices, and rituals." In distinguishing the superstition from the folk belief, he avers that "compliance with the dictates of superstition invariably leads to error and eventual harm," but folk beliefs, on the other hand, are "harmless ideas that rest on mistaken judgment or error" that "arouse awe and wonder on the one hand or simply evoke idle amusement and delight on the other." Duncan Emrich's approach is somewhat more pragmatic: in *Folklore on the American Land* he brings together for the general reader hundreds of folk beliefs and practices in the areas of medicine, weather lore, birth, marriage, and death. He demonstrates that much of our folk meteorology is soundly based in accurate observation of natural phenomena and holds that folk cures and remedies "cannot be lightly dismissed: some are as effective as any medicine for psychosomatic or psychological reasons; others, with some research, may well have value for the medical profession" (p. 613). Emrich's primary concern is with the human significance of folk beliefs: "Above all, they have meaning for the folk: they mean the difference between hope and despair, often between life and death."

Many of the superstitions Emrich cites are drawn from Harry M. Hyatt's collection of over sixteen thousand superstitions from midwestern America, *Folklore from Adams County, Illinois* (Memoirs of the Alma Egan Hyatt Foundation, New York: Stechert, 1935, rev. ed. 1965). An early excellent guide to and sampling of American beliefs is Vance Randolph's *Ozark Superstitions* ([New York: Columbia University Press, 1947], reprinted by Dover as *Ozark Magic and Folklore*, 1964). Carl Carmer's *Stars Fell on Alabama* (New York: Farrar & Rinehart, 1934), an investigation of Alabama folklore and folk life touches on the supernatural in folk tales, folk medicine, and superstitions. Small collections and studies of superstitions often appear in folklore journals; see, for example, Michael Owen Jones, "Towards an Understanding of Folk Medical Beliefs in North Carolina" (*North Carolina Folklore* 15 [May 1967]: 23–27), and his article "Folk Beliefs: Knowledge and Action" (*Southern Folklore Quarterly* 30 [December 1967]: 304–9). Ray B. Browne published superstitions and remedies in *Popular Beliefs and Practices from Alabama* (Berkeley and Los Angeles: University of California Press, 1958, Folklore Studies 9). The results of a field investigation made in the summer of 1954 (Sheffield, Northport, Millport, Sulligent, Vernon, Huntsville, McKenzie, Fort Payne, Roanoke, Montgomery, Fernbank, Thomasville, Daphne, Attalla, Florence, Eclectic, Tuscaloosa, Prattville, Cullman, Moundville, Camden, Newtonville, Oneonta), these are 4,340 items arranged according to Hand's fourteen categories; also included are customs, the lore and skills of farming, fishing, hunting, domestic crafts, and some short tales.

Stith Thompson, *The Folktale* (New York: Dryden Press, 1946) is an excellent discussion of the genre of folk narratives, and *The Types of the Folktale: A Classification and Bibliography*, edited and translated by Thompson and Antti Aarne, Folklore Fellows Communications, No. 184 (Helsinki: Soumalainen Tiedeakatemia, 1961, 2nd edition), is the definitive work for comparative study of Indo-European tales. Ernest W. Baughman's *Type and Motif Index of the Folktales of England and North America* (The Hague: Mouton, 1966) is useful for the identification of motifs. *American Folk Legend: A Symposium*, edited by Wayland Hand (Berkeley: University of California Press, 1971), presents current scholarly views of our folk tale storehouse. As with superstitions, folklore scholars have a difficult time sorting out, identifying, and defining the various kinds of folk tales. Richard Dorson, who coined the word "fakelore" as a designation for pseudo-folklore manufactured for profitable mass consumption, gives extended treatment to several American heroes of folk tales, including Paul Bunyan, Davy Crockett, Johnny Appleseed, and Jesse James, in his *American Folklore* and analyzes their folk, popular, and literary history. The Walt Disney Johnny Appleseed, he finds, is totally transformed from the ragamuffin original; Paul Bunyan, with only the shadow of folk origins, was created largely in newspapers and books for children; Davy Crockett exhibits the pattern of oral folk to "subliterary almanac," newspapers, and books to a final version as hero in a children's movie and in a 1950s popular song; Gib Morgan, an oil driller whose lies and yarns were collected by the Texas folklorist Mody Boatright, emerges as an authentic hero and teller of American tall tales. Dorson summarizes his views in his essay "Legends and Tall Tales" (Coffin, *Our Living Traditions*, pp. 154–69). He defines legend as a species of oral folk literature "known to a number of people united by their area of residence or occupation or nationality of faith," which, although it claims to be historically accurate, contains some elements of the supernatural. He gives examples of the three major types—heroic, saintly, and anecdotal—the last subdivided into numerous exemplats of American character traits, laziness, rascality, stinginess, and eccentricity, and contrasts the popular-literary folk hero with the genuine folk item. Coffin's collection of essays also includes Roger D. Abraham's analysis of international tales of the trickster, especially Brer Rabbit in America ("Trickster, the Outrageous Hero," pp. 170–78), and Leonard Roberts's "Magic Folktales in America" (pp. 142–53) with particular reference to Appalachian reworkings of European *Maärchen*. Daniel Hoffman's *Paul Bunyan: Last of the Frontier Demigods* (Philadelphia: Temple University Press, 1952) is the definitive assessment of that American folk hero. Dorson's *Davy Crockett: American Comic Legend* (New York: Arno Press, 1977) brings together the folk-literary-popular elements and reprints selections from Crockett almanacs. Robert Price examines both the historical and the mythical hero in *Johnny Appleseed: Man and Myth* (Bloomington: Indiana University Press, 1954). Tales of Mike Fink, who receives literary treatment in Eudora Welty's *The Robber Bridegroom* (New York: Atheneum, 1963) are narrated in *Mike Fink: King of Mississippi Keelboatmen* by Walter Blair and Franklin J. Meine (New York, 1933). The hero of Negro folk song and ballad John Henry has been studied by Guy B. Johnson, *John Henry: Tracking Down a Negro Legend* (Chapel Hill: University of North Carolina Press, 1929), and Louis W. Chappell, *John Henry: A Folk-Lore Study* (Jena: W. Biedermann, 1933).

Nearly every state and region can boast a collection of folk tales. Richard Chase published two Appalachian anthologies: *The Grandfather Tales* (New York: Houghton Mifflin, 1948) and *The Jack Tales* (New York: Houghton Mifflin, 1943), the latter a collection of the adventures of the English Jack-the-giant-killer transmogrified into an audacious hill country boy who consorts with dragons and Satan in an American mountain setting. Chase's *American Folk Tales and Songs* (New York: New American Library of World Literature, 1962) offers a general introduction to American folklore. Ozark tales have been gathered by Vance Randolph in several volumes: *Who Blowed up the Church House* (New York: Columbia University Press, 1952), *The Devil's Pretty Daughter*, (New York: Columbia University Press, 1955), *The Talking Turtle* (New York: Columbia University Press, 1957), *We Always Lie to Strangers: Tall Tales from the Ozarks* (New York: Columbia University Press, 1951), and *Sticks in the Knapsack* (New York: Columbia University Press, 1958). Richard Dorson has gathered tales from Michigan in *Bloodstoppers and Bearwalkers: Folk Traditions of the Upper Peninsula* (Cambridge: Harvard University Press, 1952) and from New England in *Jonathan Draws the Long Bow: New England Popular Tales and Legends* (Cambridge: Harvard University Press, 1946), and his *American Negro Folktales* (Greenwich, Conn.: Fawcett, 1967) is a superb collection from informants in Arkansas and Mississippi and from southern Negroes who migrated to Michigan. Kentucky folk tales have been collected and edited by Leonard Roberts in two volumes, *South from Hell-fer-sartin* (Lexington: University of Kentucky Press, 1955, reissued in paperback, 1964) and *Up Cutshin and Down Greasy* (Lexington; University of Kentucky Press, 1959). West Virginia tales of the supernatural appear in Ruth Ann Mesick's *The Telltale Lilac Bush and Other West Virginia Ghost Tales* (Lexington: University of Kentucky Press, 1965), and Nancy and Bruce Roberts have edited fourteen ghost tales from North Carolina, West Virginia, and Mississippi, *This Haunted Land* (Charlotte, N.C.: McNally and Loftin, 1970). The best edition of Joel Chandler Harris is *The Complete Tales of Uncle Remus*, compiled by Richard Chase (New York: Houghton Mifflin, 1955), with original illustrations by A. B. Frost, J. M. Condé, F. S. Church, E. W. Kemble, and W. H. Beard. Stella Brewer Brooke's *Joel Chandler Harris: Folklorist* (Athens: University of Georgia Press, 1950) will complement the reading of the adventures of Brer Rabbit and his animal friends and foes.

Alabama is represented by Kathryn Tucker Windham's Jeffrey series: *13 Alabama Ghosts and Jeffrey* (with Margaret Gillis Figh, Huntsville: Strode Publishers, 1969) and *One Big Front Porch* (Huntsville: Strode Publishers, 1975). Of particular interest in the former are the universal folk tale motifs, the inexplicable ball of fire, the trench that can never be filled in the Bill Skeeto legend, and the ineradicable image in the tale of Henry Wells and the burning of the courthouse at Carrollton, Pickens County, Alabama. See also Windham's *13 Georgia Ghosts and Jeffrey* (Huntsville: Strode Publishers, 1969), *13 Mississippi Ghosts* (Huntsville: Strode Publishers, 1973), *13 Tennessee Ghosts*, (Huntsville: Strode Publishers, 1977) and *Jeffrey Introduces 13 More Southern Ghosts* (Huntsville: Strode Publishers, 1971). Carl Carmer's *Stars Fell on Alabama* contains some Brer Rabbit beast fables as well as retellings of several legends of the Black Belt and of the tales of Railroad Bill, Rube Burrows, and Steve Renfroe, Alabama's folk outlaw-heroes. Marion Brunson's *Pea River Reflections* (Tuscaloosa: Portals Press, 1975) touches on the ghost of Grancer ("Grand-Sir") Harrison and Rube Burrows and provides interesting details of nineteenth-century Alabama folk life. Alabama's Cajun folklore and tales are collected and studied in Julian Rayford's *Whistlin' Woman and Crowin' Hen* (Mobile: Rankin Press, 1956).

Similarities exist between the folk tales in *Ghosts and Goosebumps* and those collected by Ray B. Browne in northern Alabama, including Fayette, Clarke, Lamar, Randolph, Winston, and Cullman counties. In the summers of 1952, 1953, and 1954, Browne traveled throughout Alabama collecting folklore. The results of his field studies appear in numerous articles in folklore periodicals, the previously cited monograph on folk beliefs, a wide-ranging collection of folk songs primarily from Randolph and Lamar counties, and a book of 250 folk tales, *"A Night with the Hants" and Other Alabama Folk Experiences* (Bowling Green, Ohio: Center for the Study of Popular Culture, The Bowling Green University Popular Press, 1978), to which Carlos Drake has appended useful notes, an Index of Motifs, and a List of Tales with Distinguishable Motifs. Most significant in the Browne collection is the authentic transcription of an all-night story-telling session that occurred in August 1954 at Crane Hill in Cullman County, where the prime tale teller was Weaver Sinyard, whose stories and anecdotes elicited varying responses from his listeners, congenial friends, and neighbors who had known each other all their lives. Browne calls it "the most extended, most realistic story-telling session yet presented by collectors." A single printed tale may, by reason of its language, structure, and psychological power, leap off the page into life, as indeed the shorter tales in the Browne collection do, but the communication of the total folk experience of tale-telling in *"Hants"* is innovative and wonderfully satisfying. Like the ones in this volume, many of the tales are short, yet their brevity is an advantage—one feels as though in the room with the speaker. The "Additional Tales" exhibit all the motifs discoverable in this present south and central Alabama collection: mysterious lights, balls of fire, headless apparitions, reviving corpses, floating chains, savage bears, panthers, and alligators, hundreds of sinister cats, tales of ghosts that turn out to be cows, lunatic wanderers, rabbit tobacco, geese, or goats, trickster preachers and coward preachers, thieving Baptists and witty Methodists, a whole world of supernatural and real folk characters. One of the Browne tales is a variant of "One Little Pear," and some of them have also been reported by Alabama WPA field workers, notably the anecdote of the tongue-tied sisters, the tale of a pet monkey mistaken for a ghost, and the terrifying myth of a little girl who daily feeds a serpent.

All folk tales should be heard, and ideally one should be in the presence of the storyteller. Katheryn Tucker Windham often tells her ghost stories to delighted audiences, and, with her encouragement, in October 1979, the Selma Public Library and the Tourism Council of the Selma–Dallas County Chamber of Commerce initiated the Tale-tellin' Festival as a part of the annual River Front Market Day sponsored by the Selma–Dallas County Historic Preservation Society. There is a national festival of tale-telling at Jonesboro, Tennessee; and performers at the Appalachian folklore center, Appalshop, in Whitesburg, Kentucky, have done much with their traveling story theater to restore the telling of folk tales to its rightful position as entertainment and as a folk art to be cherished, nurtured, and passed on to future generations. Their recordings of folk tales may be ordered from June Appal Recordings, Box 743, Whitesburg, Kentucky 41858. The Library of Congress also offers recordings of folk tales; bibliographies are available upon request.

The history of WPA folklore and Slave Narratives projects is documented in William F. McDonald's *Federal Relief and the Arts* (Columbus: Ohio University Press, 1969) and Jerry Mangione's *The Dream and the Deal: The Federal Writers' Project, 1935–1943* (New York: Avon, 1974, hardcover, Miami: Banyan Books, 1972). Joseph C. Hickerson has compiled a Library of Congress checklist, *Folklore and the W.P.A.: A Preliminary Bibliography*, which shows that published WPA folklore in folk tales, songs, and treasuries comes primarily from only seventeen states; these include collections of folk tales from North Carolina, Indiana, and Louisiana, general anthologies from Idaho and Nebraska, and collections of folk songs from Kentucky, West Virginia, and Illinois. In addition to Botkin's publication of Slave Narrative excerpts and Rawick's thirty-one volumes there are three other selected editions of narratives: *To Be a Slave* by Julius Lester (New York: Dial Press, 1968), *Voices from Slavery* by John Harris (New York: Tower Publications, 1971), and Norman Yetman's one hundred narratives entitled *Voices from Slavery* (New York: Holt, Rinehart, and Winston, 1971). The Library of Congress has issued three bibliographies of Alabama WPA folklore materials: the Bibliography of Reproduced or Original Items lists one newspaper, *The Eufala Express*, January 19, 1860, and twenty-one reproductions and/ or photographs; the Documents Bibliography lists 142 separate documents including contemporary newspaper articles on slavery, Alabama legislative acts regarding slavery prior to 1861, baptismal records, wills, and miscellaneous papers; the Slave Narratives Bibliography indexes 149 separate interviews.

No bibliographies of the remainder of the Alabama WPA materials have been issued, but the Library of Congress holds a modest collection of Alabama folk songs, principally from Mobile, Montgomery, Roanoke, Lee County, Selma, Randolph County, Montgomery, Birmingham, and Tuscaloosa, a collection of folk tales gathered throughout the state, and eight entries under Beliefs and Customs: W38, 10–19–36, William Edison, "Alabama Superstitions," essay with hundreds of general superstitions; W3399, 6–24–38, William Edison and Bennett Marshall, shorter version of the above; W3400, 6–24–38, Mary A. Poole, "Crabs are Fatter . . ." two pages; W3402, 6–24–38, G. L. Clark, "It's Good Luck to See . . .," two pages; W3488, 12–6–36, Rhussus L. Perry, "Signs of the Moon," fifty-four miscellaneous superstitions; W3398, 2–20–38, W. B. Strickland, "Conjuring Estelle," sketch of a woman who loses her husband to a conjurer; W3530, 1938–39, Adelaide Rogers, "Gab'ul, Chune dat Harp," portrait of a Negro conjure man from Montgomery; W12, 1936–37, "Superstition in the Deep South," sketch of the superstitions and haints of the Dickerson and Scuffert families.

Except for a few in the Alabama Archives, the Alabama Life Histories are on deposit at the Wilson Library, the Southern Historical Collection, the University of North Carolina at Chapel Hill, presumably because W. T. Conch was working there on the Southern Life History Project; sixty-six separate histories are listed on the inventory. On deposit at the Alabama Archives are numerous directives, model folklore projects, and interviews from the Washington office and letters to Myrtle Miles, the Alabama WPA director; several folders dealing with the history, notable persons and events, and architecture of various counties; duplicates or fragments of the essays and collections of superstitions filed in the Library of Congress; an extensive collection of Negro folk songs made by Ruby Pickens Tartt in Sumter County; a collection of folk songs from other parts of Alabama made by various project workers, a few of which are duplicates of manuscripts held by the Library of Congress; and a major collection of Slave Narratives manuscripts, which includes several items intended for both the Life Histories and Documents projects. The Slave Narratives manuscripts present several difficulties. Rawick's volume 6, Series I, reproduced 127 Alabama Narratives derived from manuscripts in the Rare Book Room of the Library of Congress; his volume 1 of the Series I Supplement contains manuscripts from the Archive of Folk Song, the Library of Congress, the Alabama Archives, and a microfilm loaned by Virginia Hamilton, University of Alabama at Birmingham, all of which are purported to be "new" and to "more than double" the size of the Alabama collection. A comparison of the Rawick volumes with a microfilm of the Alabama Archives Slave Narratives manuscripts, prepared by Sarah Ann Warren for the Benjamin Russell Library of Alexander City Junior College in 1975, shows, however, that only fifty-eight narratives in the 1977 volume 1 Supplement are "new," that is, previously unpublished, while forty-eight are earlier, later, or different versions of those published in the 1972 volume 6 of Series I. Many of Rawick's supplementary narratives were originally intended for other projects and may not be classified properly as Slave Narratives, and fourteen of the Alabama Archives manuscripts do not appear in either Rawick's volume 6 or volume 1 Supplement. At least half of the Alabama Archives manuscripts exist in duplicate or multiple copies, some rewritten by editors, others with numerous penciled corrections, revisions, and additions. Many of the same informants appear in both the Rawick volumes; the actual increase in "new" informants who appear in the Volume 1 Supplement is less than one-half.

Because of these manuscript problems, the present editors have prepared an annotated Index of Slave Narratives in the Alabama Archives that cites the location of all known manuscripts in the Library of Congress, the Alabama Archives, and Rawick's volumes 6 and 1; the index is filed with the Archives and available for use. Only thirteen of the Alabama Narratives listed in the Library of Congress bibliography do not appear on the Alexander City State Junior College microfilm; these include two that exist only as recordings. The problem of multiple manuscripts and different versions of the same interview points inevitably to more serious questions concerning methodology, authenticity, and deliberate suppressions of inflammatory passages. Rawick considers the aspect of suppression at some length in the General Introduction to the Series I Supplement, arguing that although evidence points strongly to deliberate suppression in some states, in Alabama, "There are relatively few examples of deliberately tampering with the ones that were sent [to Washington]"; rather, the Narratives either came in too late or were judged as not in compliance with the Washington interview format. Our own reading of the Archives manuscripts and related documents and comparison with Rawick's editions suggests that Alabama WPA workers made every effort to follow the national guidelines, some to the extent that a narrative may read like answers to the interview questions, that different manuscript versions and duplicates were retained in the interest of historical preservation, and that there were no attempts to suppress materials on any social or political basis. To the contrary, those many passages that explicitly describe or refer to every sort of brutality on the part of slave masters are right beside the happy plantation memoirs. Only two narratives touch on the suppression problem, that of Hattie Ann Nettles, Lee County, and Hannah Irwin, Barbour County; both involve Ku Klux Klan violence, both were revised to include details of the occurrence, and in both cases the editorially revised manuscript was mailed to Washington. The methodology of WPA research, however, leaves a bit to be desired. Doubtless responding to warnings from the Washington office about distorted phonetic transcriptions of dialect, many WPA workers often submitted a two- or three-page narrative or report summary, and WPA editors often supplied dialogue and details, expanding one page into four. It is highly unlikely that an editor left his desk in Birmingham and drove to Mobile or Evergreen or Eufaula to reinterview the informant, and there is no evidence that project worker and editor actively collaborated. Editorial rewrites were not always done. Interviews already full-fleshed were barely touched, notably those of Ruby Pickens Tartt, F. L. Diard, Ila Prine, Levi Shelby, Mary Poole, and Annie D. Dean. Differences in manuscripts are usually stylistic—an overall structure may be reversed, point of view shifted (usually to the first person), details added or deleted, dialogue expanded, introductory material omitted or revised—but, although the substance remains the same, these differences bear on considerations of authenticity. Even so, we are all the richer in having the Alabama Slave Narratives, for, taken in their entirety and at their best, they present not only the lore and daily life of an entire folk culture in a perplexing period of our history but the spirit of a people who suffered the tragic paradox of freedom and slavery.

And, finally, congratulations to the Alabama Folklife Association, founded April 13, 1980, at The University of Alabama, with Henry Willet, Montgomery, Alabama, as its first president.

ᏩᏲᏣᏍᎩᏅᎾᏛᎣᏍᎦᏯᏩᏲᏣᏍᏅᏯᏩᏲᏣᏍᎩᏅᎾᏛᎣᏍᎦᏯᏩᏲᏣᏍᏅ

Alabama Folk Tales in the Library of Congress

W3414 1–25–39; "Wolf Brand," Woodrow Hand, Birmingham. A descriptive sketch of a potent Shelby County moonshine.

W3410 6–23–38; "The Good Father," no field worker or editorial writer listed, Montgomery. Legend of a Catholic priest at Cusseta, a Promethean giver of good gifts to an Indian tribe.

W3411 6–25–38; "Legend of Oneta," Maude Driesbach, Jefferson County. An Alabama Indian Romeo-and-Juliet.

W3412 11–16–38; "The Man with the Red Feather," Jack Kytle, editorial department. A romantic account of Red Bird, legendary founder of the Cajuns.

W4 1937; "Ghost Story," Annie D. Dean, Conecuh County. A folk comedy of ghostly error in a cemetery.

W24 12–9–36; "Pleas and the Snake," Lillian Finnell, Tuscaloosa. You-can-get-used-to-anything anecdote.

W3413 1–19–39; "I Hear Old Reuben Moanin'," Woodrow Hand, Birmingham. An anecdote about a road worker who always had to hold somebody in his lap when he rode to work.

W3495 11–18–39; "Pirates of Lost Bay," Lawerance F. Evans, Fairhope. A lumber company manager encounters a nest of pirates at Perdido Bay.

W3519 12–21–38; "Joe's Tall Story," Woodrow Hand, Birmingham. A coal miner's "miraculous" escape from a mine explosion.

W3509 6–23–38; "The Mysterious Husband," Clarke County. An innkeeper's daughter marries a stranger who turns out to be a member of a band of outlaws.

W3516 6–24–38; "Pegue's Ghost," Mabel Farrior, Montgomery. The mysterious ball of light that appears at Old Cahaba, gleaned from Anna M. Gayle Fry's *Memories of Old Cahaba.*

W3515 6–24–38; "The Pot of Gold Mystery," Florence Dennis, Montgomery. Apparition directs a young girl to a pot of gold.

W3507 6–28–38; "Carrollton's Ghost," Jack Kytle, Jefferson County. A short version of the widely known Alabama tale of the ghostly face emblazoned in a window pane of the courthouse in Pickens County.

W6 11–30–36; "They Were Good to Chinnabee," Blanch Fleetwood, Talladega. Talladega Chief Chinnabee makes a peace treaty with President Jackson.

W3463 10–19–38; "A Witch Story" and "Weavly Wheat," Jennie Sue Williams, Bridgeport. A woman transforms her son-in-law into a horse, with four stanzas of the play party song "Weavly Wheat."

W3497 6–15–38; "A Country Grace," Maggie Boswell, Montgomery. Anecdote about table grace in Elmore County.

W3436 12–21–38; "Mary was Borned in de Middle er de Road," Lee County. A Tuskegee slaveowner earns a bonus from his slave trade.

W3500 6–15–38; "Jim and the Ghost," Lillian Finell, Tuscaloosa. A released prisoner boasts of not being afraid of ghosts and "sets up" with a corpse.

W3531 6–13–39; "Greeny Gibbons," Shelby Southward, Birmingham. Prefaced with a letter to Benjamin Botkin from Myrtle Miles, State director of Federal Writers' Project. A fat pole lineman runs for coroner of Limestone County.

W3506 6–24–38; "Hoodoo Murder," Jack Kytle, editorial department. F. L. Diard, Mobile. Man digging for gold in a cemetery uses voodoo to frighten other would-be treasure seekers.

W3401 6–24–38; "The Burned Wedding Dress," Ila B. Prine, Mobile. An expanded superstition about the consequences of marrying in spite of evil omens.

W17   11–30–36; "Aunt Jemima and the Beavers," Hester Pratt, Carrollton. A washwoman believes that the sounds of the beavers are the devils washing their clothes.

W30   8–8–36; "Legend of the Old Theophilus L. Toulmin Home," Ila B. Prine, Mobile. Part history, part romantic ghost tale of the Old South, the Yankee invasion, and buried treasure centered on the prominent legislator Theophilus L. Toulmin who compiled the important *Alabama Digest of Laws*, 1823.

W25   1936–1937; "The Law of the Hills," Sue Russell. A north Alabama tale about a woman unjustly condemned by the community.

W14   1936–1937; "Hiss Folks Remember," Annie D. Dean and Pettersen Marzoni, Evergreen. Character sketch of a Negro named Buck, beloved by whites of Evergreen, Alabama, also filed at the Alabama Archives with the Slave Narratives Collection.

W5   5–1–37; "Twelve Miles from Montgomery," Jo Hanna Skinner. One-page ghost tale about the Elmore County Maul house.

W3505 6–2–38; "A Ghost Was Seen," Lilliam Finell, Tuscaloosa. First-person account of a horseman stalked by a ghost from a nearby cemetery.

W3511 6–23–38; "The Laughing Voice," Montgomery. A woman in white appears to two Negro teachers in rural Elmore County.

W3513 6–24–38; "Murdered Girl's Spirit Lives," Maggie Boswell, Lowndes County. The spirit of a girl murdered by slaves appears and plays the piano.

W3409 1–25–39; "You Got To B'lieve in Hants fur to See 'Em," Adelaide Rogers, Montgomery. Two ghost stories from Montgomery, one about a "mannish" female spectre in the old Rice home, the other of a door that opens mysteriously.

W3518 6–23–38; "The Ghost in the Masonic Home," Lillian Finell, Tuscaloosa. A first-person account of a Confederate soldier's ghost who haunted the Masonic home in Tuscaloosa.

W3494 12–13–38; "The Legend of the 'Red Cardinal,'" Francois L. Diard, Mobile. A carriage driver mistakes famous actor Charles Couldock for the "Cardinal" ghost.

W3493 12–14–38; "Calling on Miss Lucy," Woodrow Hand. The country boys in Shelby County pull a prank on city fellows.

W29   1936–1937; "He Wanted to Ask a Question," Lillian Finnell, Tuscaloosa. A shaggy dog tale about a World War I Negro soldier, as remembered by his commanding officer.

W3510 6–23–38; "The Frog Case," Mabel Ford-Leake, Birmingham. A doctor tricks a patient into believing he has removed a frog from her stomach.

W3498 6–15–38; "Jaybirds," Lillian Finnell, Tuscaloosa. Why the jaybird always goes to hell on Friday.

W0240 7–6–37; "I'se Suein for De Whole Total Loss," William B. Strickland, John Morgan Smith. Widely known anecdote of the rooster theft.

W3525 1938–1939; "Lookin at de Poor Wid de Eye of Pity," R. L. Perry, Macon County. A Negro couple, Mother and Father Baker, remember slavery, their masters, overseers, and the "paderole."

W3524 1938–1939; "Thank God I Done Seed Roosevelt," R. L. Perry, Macon County. Father Baker finally gets to see his beloved President Roosevelt at Tuskegee Institute.

W3434 11–5–38; "A Figgerin' Po Dog," R. L. Perry, Macon County. A dog named Bruno steals whole hams from his master.

W3508 6–23–38; "The Legend of the Exploded Well," G. L. Clark, Birmingham. A tale of gold that vanishes without a trace and a bottomless well in Sumter County near Livingston.

W7   1936–1937; "Solomon and the Thirsty Ha'nts," Annie D. Dean, Evergreen. A first-person narrative by Solomon Jackson, a Negro informant from Conecuh County who remembers the stakes where "patterollers" tied runaways and recounts how "ha'nts" steal his bucket of spring water.

W3499 6–15–38; "Negro Humor," Mitchell Dombrow, Montgomery. Essay with numerous examples of jingles and songs, erroneously classified by the Washington office as "Tales"; also on deposit at the Alabama Archives.

W3408 12–21–38; "A Funeral in the Country," Birmingham. An account of an Alabama funeral that takes a long time to get under way.

W16   11–30–36; "Why the Deer Don't Like the Terrapin," Mary Warren, Mobile. The Brer Rabbit–Terrapin race tale with the Deer substituting for Brer Rabbit.

W3466 10–14–38; "Ebenezer Remembers," Luther Clark, Birmingham. A wily slave with incredible powers of memory aids his lawyer-master in confounding all his courtroom opponents, outlives him, takes over the practice, and outwits the devil. A shorter version, credited to Mabel Farrior, Montgomery, 12–3–36, is filed at the Alabama Archives with the manuscripts of the Alabama Slave Narratives.

W3   1936–1937; "Homespun Clues," Annie D. Dean, Evergreen, edited by Pettersen Marzoni. How they found out who done it; a tale based on the murder of Allen Page, which actually occurred in Conecuh County, featuring the motif of the trench that never can be filled. Another version exists in two duplicate manuscripts filed at the State Department of Archives and History, one of which is dated 7–28–37; this version also appears in the Library of Congress Archive of Folk Song collection of Alabama Slave Narratives and is listed in the Alabama LC Documents Bibliography as LC10069.

W3417 1938–1939; "Great Fair Fields of Eden," Rhussus L. Perry, Macon County. Father Baker preaches at Mt. Sharron Primitive Baptist Church, near Tuskegee. A fine example of a Negro folk sermon.

———— 8–14–39; "Luke Warn," R. V. Waldrop, Franklin County. Sketch of an Alabama farmer, intended for Life Histories series; also filed at Wilson Library, Carolina at Chapel Hill.

———— 6–24–39; "Candy Town," R. V. Waldrop, Hodges School, Franklin County. Fairy tale with Hansel and Gretel antecedents.

———— 8–15–39; "Henry Williams and Bradley Jones," R. V. Waldrop, Franklin County. Portrait of two shine boys, intended for Life Histories series.

———— 7–9–37; "Sic Semper Sycamore," Demps Oden, Jefferson County. A black straw boss, the giant Sycamore Ransom, grows tyrannical and arthritic but outruns everybody after he is frightened during a possum hunt. Three manuscripts are filed at the Alabama State Department of Archives and History; evidently sent in as a Slave Narrative but placed by Botkin in the Rare Book Room, Library of Congress.